SWORD ARt ONlINE PROGRE≶≶IVE

003

REKI KAWAHARA
ILLUSTRATION BY abec
DESIGN BY bee-pee

"Aaah, this feels so great! Let's just head straight out of town!"

Asuna

A player trapped inside *Sword Art Online*. Without a care for her life, she throws herself into battle against monsters.

"Aye-aye, sir."

Kirito

A swordsman aiming to beat the top floor of Aincrad. He adventures as a solo player but temporaily teams up with Asuna.

"So you wear these 'swemsoots' in the bath. Humankind certainly has some strange customs."

Kizmel

A Dark Elf NPC from the third floor's campaign quest. She was scripted to die in the beta version of the game, but now...

"Uh, I guess."

"This bath is quite wonderful itself."

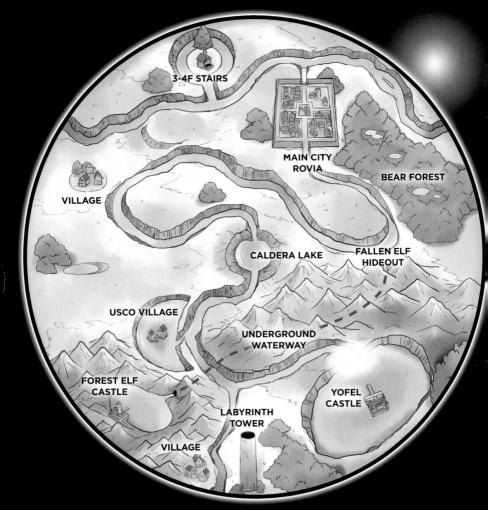

Map labels (clockwise):

3-4F STAIRS

MAIN CITY ROVIA

BEAR FOREST

VILLAGE

FALLEN ELF HIDEOUT

CALDERA LAKE

USCO VILLAGE

UNDERGROUND WATERWAY

FOREST ELF CASTLE

YOFEL CASTLE

LABYRINTH TOWER

VILLAGE

FLOATING CASTLE AINCRAD FLOOR DATA   AINCRAD

FOURTH FLOOR

The design theme of this floor during the beta test was a parched canyon zone, with dried, narrow valleys crisscrossing like spiderwebs. But when Kirito reached the fourth floor in the retail game, he was shocked to see how significantly it had been changed. The layout of the land is the same, but simple hills became islands, and blasted, dry dirt was transformed into lush green cover. All the narrow, detailed canyons are now full of water, turning the fourth floor's design theme into "waterways."

The main city is known as Rovia, with a large forest to the southeast of the settlement. By following the main river south, one eventually reaches a caldera lake, about three hundred yards across. Even further south along the waterway is the labyrinth tower that houses the floor boss.

The boss of the fourth floor is Wythege the Hippocampus, a monster with the body of a horse for its front half and the fins of a fish for its back half. As with the major shift in the floor design, it is highly likely that this boss's normal and special attacks will be greatly different from the beta test.

Map Illustration: Tatsuya Kurusu

SWORD ART ONLINE PROGRESSIVE

VOLUME 3

Reki Kawahara

abec

bee-pee

YEN ON

NEW YORK

SWORD ART ONLINE PROGRESSIVE Volume 3
© REKI KAWAHARA

Translation by Stephen Paul

SWORD ART ONLINE PROGRESSIVE
© REKI KAWAHARA 2014
All rights reserved. ,
Edited by ASCII MEDIA WORKS
First published in Japan in 2014 by KADOKAWA CORPORATION, Tokyo.
English translation rights arranged with KADOKAWA CORPORATION, Tokyo, through Tuttle-Mori Agency, Inc., Tokyo.

English translation © 2015 by Yen Press, LLC

Yen On
1290 Avenue of the Americas
New York, NY 10104
www.yenpress.com

Yen On is an imprint of Yen Press, LLC.
The Yen On name and logo are trademarks of Yen Press, LLC.

The publisher is not responsible for websites (or their content) that are not owned by the publisher.

First Yen On Edition: October 2015

ISBN: 978-0-316-34883-6

10 9 8 7 6

LSC-C

Printed in the United States of America

"THIS MIGHT BE A GAME, BUT IT'S NOT SOMETHING YOU PLAY."

—Akihiko Kayaba, *Sword Art Online* programmer

SWORD ART ONLINE
PROGRESSIVE

BARCAROLLE OF FROTH

FOURTH FLOOR OF AINCRAD, DECEMBER 2022

I STARED SILENTLY AT THE BLUE-TINGED STONE DOOR.

It was the end point of the spiral staircase that connected the fourth floor of Aincrad to the lair of the third-floor boss monster. Through this door was the virgin territory of the fourth floor. As a front-runner among the game's population, being the first to venture into new, unspoiled lands was *supposed* to be one of my greatest joys.

But just three steps from the final landing, I stopped still. After a few dozen seconds, my brown-haired fencer companion grew tired of waiting on the next step up.

"So how long are you going to just stand there? You've spent enough time examining the carved relief on the door. Or are you afraid because it's the fourth floor?"

Just before that question could pass straight from my right ear through to the left, my brain latched onto it, and I turned to look at her.

"...What do you mean, because it's the fourth floor?"

The fencer looked down at me with half-irritation and half-mischief in her eyes.

"You know how some people are. They don't want a room on the thirteenth floor of the hotel or the fourth because it's associated with death. Are you one of them?"

I finally understood what she was saying and quickly shook

my head. "N-no way. Look at this all-black outfit. Would I really wear this color if I believed in omens and stuff like that?"

"Well, why are you just standing there, then?"

"Um, because…" I mumbled, looking to the massive door again.

The ten-foot-tall double door was carved with detailed reliefs. The designs were different for each and every floor and typically made some reference to the theme or story of the floor to which they led. For example, there was a bull's-head relief on the door before the second floor, which was commonly known as the "Cow Floor." The door to the "Forest and Elf Floor" depicted two knights dueling beneath a massive tree.

In the center of the massive door before me now was a carving of a traveler rowing a small boat that looked like a gondola.

"Is there something about that picture? Didn't you see this in the beta test?" she asked, her irritation rising to 60 percent now. I slowly shook my head.

"No…not this. I saw the door, all right…but not this relief."

"Huh? What do you mean?"

"The *picture's* different. In the beta, it was a traveler wandering through a desert canyon. But in this one, he's on a boat…"

She tilted her head in confusion. Her long hair shook, scattering pale light in the dim stairway hall.

"What was the fourth floor like in the beta?"

"Um…the entire floor was a crisscrossing web of canyons that were sandy at the bottom, and you had no choice but to travel through those canyons, only the sand made it really hard to walk."

"Hmm…Sounds appropriate for the picture of the man in the desert canyon. So if the picture's been changed, then…"

She continued up to the top of the stairs and put her hand on the gondola relief at the center of the door, then pushed.

With a heavy *thunk*, the two halves of the massive stone door began to part to the sides. I quickly raced up the stairs to draw even with the fencer.

As the doors opened ever so slowly, brilliant afternoon light flooded out, blinding me with pure white. I squinted to shut out the glare, but I heard the sound before my vision returned.

It sounded like a low, deep roiling and a high-pitched leaping intertwined.

Water.

When my eyes had finished adjusting to the level of light, I found not the dried-out canyons I remembered, but a fierce, rushing mountain stream.

A hand clapped me on the shoulder.

"Well, that's that," said the fencer, sounding proud for some reason.

1

1:32 PM ON WEDNESDAY, DECEMBER 21, 2022.

After a few minutes lost in discussion before passing through the door, I—Kirito the level-16 swordsman—and my temporary partner, Asuna the level-15 fencer, were the first in the entire game to set foot on the fourth floor of the floating castle Aincrad.

If the fourth floor of the game at the point of the beta test had a theme, it would be "desert canyons." As I'd explained to Asuna, the entire map of the floor was a spiderweb of narrow intersecting canyons that were impossible to scale, meaning that all travel had to go through those canyons, which were slow and tedious to traverse, not to mention easy to get lost within.

But what I saw couldn't have been more different from what I remembered.

The pavilion into which the staircase exited was at the top of a steep hill. The terrain itself looked the same as what it had been before, but the gravelly, reddish-brown land was now covered in lush greenery. I looked in all directions around the wall-less pavilion and saw only a single tree growing behind us and no monsters or NPCs in sight.

The hill, about ninety feet across, was surrounded by cliffs that loomed over the nearby area, but two slender paths heading to the southeast and southwest led to separate canyons. Water rushed vigorously from the southwest canyon and circled around the hill until it eventually left via the southeast canyon. In other words, what had once been a simple hill was now effectively an island.

We were already painfully aware that the retail version of *Sword Art Online*, which its creator Akihiko Kayaba had turned into a deadly, inescapable trap, was different from the beta test in many ways. But nothing had changed the look of the terrain in such a dramatic way before. It was not the desert canyon floor anymore.

In fact, the canyons were the only means of getting out of this area during the beta. If they were now filled with rushing white-water rapids, that meant—

"So how long are you going to stand there?" Asuna asked, jabbing me with an elbow. I recovered from the mental stun effect and apologized to my partner.

"Er...my bad. I was spacing out."

"I wasn't asking for an apology, but there are plenty of people waiting for us to reach the main city and activate the teleporter."

"Oh, right. Well...first, we should inform Argo that we defeated the boss."

Nerius the Evil Treant, the tree-shaped boss of the third floor, had been dispatched without a single casualty just twenty minutes before, but there was no way to send an instant message from within a dungeon, so no one aside from the members of the raid party knew that the boss was dead. As we were the first to reach the next floor and exit the dungeon, we needed to inform Argo the Rat, the game's preeminent information agent, that the boss was dead, so the rest of the population could be informed.

I raised my hand to open my game window, but Asuna caught it.

"I already contacted her while you were off in la-la land."

"Ah, th-thanks. Very considerate of you..."

"Now let's get going to that main city. Whether there's water in the canyons or not, the route is still the same as before, right?"

"Um, well...I think so..."

"Then lead the way!"

She slapped me on the back, and I had no choice but to proceed.

We left the stone pavilion and headed down the damp, mossy south face of the hill. I stopped at the edge of the water and watched it race by.

The stream itself was very clear, which meant I could see all the way down to the white sand at the bottom of the waterway, but it was quite deep. By eye, I judged it to be at least six feet, if not more. There was no way for us to walk through it.

Asuna stopped next to me and looked into the river as well, then seemed to understand my consternation at last.

"Wait…why is it so deep? We can't cross to the other side like this."

"That's right…In fact, I don't think there *is* an other side."

"…What do you mean?"

"Exactly what I said. In the beta, these canyons were the only way to get to the towns and dungeons on the floor. I bet they're all deep rivers at this point—the entire floor."

The fencer's brow furrowed deeper.

"Meaning…there's no path at all now?"

"Indeed."

"…"

When I realized this fact at the top of the hill, I took a good three minutes to think over the challenge ahead of us, but Asuna required only five seconds to get her head in gear again. She glanced around.

"What's it like on top of those cliffs?"

I followed her gaze to the sheer walls that surrounded the circular hill. The gleaming wet rock proceeded vertically upward for at least ninety feet, the top of the cliff shrouded in white mist.

"I don't know. Nobody was able to climb it in the beta."

"So it's basically a system-designated barrier?"

"Not explicitly, but the rock was too fragile—everyone fell down partway, including me. And once you fell from above the halfway point, pretty much every landing was fatal."

"…That sounds too dangerous to test out, even if the landing below is in water now," Asuna murmured. I nodded silently. No one was going to risk their lives for a trial-and-error attempt at scaling those cliffs.

Next, she looked down into the water again.

"Then I suppose our only option is to swim the river."

I couldn't immediately agree. I glanced at her equipment of dark red hooded cape over breastplate and leather skirt.

"Um…have you ever swum here in *SAO*, Asuna?"

"…"

She covered her body with her left arm for some odd reason and shook her head.

"N-no."

"I see. Then let me just explain that the way you use your body to swim in *SAO* is completely different from real life. It takes a lot of practice to be able to swim properly, and even practice doesn't prevent the danger of drowning."

"What happens…if you drown?" she asked, her face tense. My answer was simple.

"When your body is submerged in water above the head, your HP begin dropping. So if you don't emerge from the surface of the water, you die."

Even after that, Asuna did nothing more than bite her lip. She glanced at the blue water again and summoned her courage.

"How much practice are we talking about?"

"Well…it depends on the person, but it took me over an hour. And that was in the shallows, just three feet deep. It's too dangerous to practice in a deep, rushing river like this."

"I see…In that case, we should go back to an earlier floor and find a safe place to practice, I suppose," she muttered, looking down. I was still searching for the right answer when she nodded and continued.

"Let's do this, then. You swim from here for the main town. I'll take the stairs back down to the third floor. I recall the perfect lake on the north side of the floor that I can use to practice. Once I'm ready, I'll use the teleport gate to the fourth floor. That means the party breaks up for a bit," she chattered, faster than her usual speed, and raised her hand for the menu screen.

This time it was my turn to grab her arm.

"..."

Her hazel-colored eyes stared right back at me. The reflection of the light off the surface of the river danced against her pupils, hiding the emotion within them.

Even a complete idiot like me, when it came to personal communication, could see that Asuna would refuse an offer to go back together and help her practice. The proud fencer would refuse to accept the idea of the teleport gate being late to open on her account. It would probably be useless to point out that if we didn't do it, Lind or Kibaou would activate the teleporter or that it would automatically turn on two hours after the third-floor boss's defeat.

Instead, I finally put the feeling of wrongness I'd been grappling with since seeing the fourth floor's dramatic change into words.

"Umm...I don't think I like that."

"...What about it?" she asked quietly. I looked away toward the flowing river.

"Like I said earlier, swimming in *SAO* is quite dangerous. And now that dying is permanent, it's insane to imagine that they would just toss us into a map that requires you to swim to advance. We must have missed something. Maybe there's not another path, but some kind of insurance, a backup method somewhere on this island..."

By the end I was more talking to myself than anything. I looked up at the island behind us. The circular hill, barely ninety feet across, had no other monsters or NPCs on it. The only objects of any interest were the pavilion that housed the staircase and the deciduous tree at the north end beyond it...

"...Hmm?"

My eyes shot back about six feet in the previous direction. I squinted and glared at the spot that caught my attention.

"What is it?" Asuna asked, looking curious. I took a step up the hill, then another, still holding on to her hand. As soon as I was certain of what I saw, I took off running at full speed.

"Whobful!"

I dragged her straight up the side of the hill, as she blurted out what was probably supposed to be "*Whoa, be careful!*" I rounded the pavilion and stood at the root of the large tree, looking up at the branches far above.

"See that?"

I removed my grip on her hand to point up above. She pointedly took her time to straighten her skirt before indulging my request, and her grumpy expression got about 20 percent brighter.

"Oh, it's growing fruit. And they look so cute!"

As she noted, near the top of the broadleaf tree hung a number of small fruit in a variety of colors. Most striking of all was their shape, which was circular with a hole in the middle—essentially, donuts. Even in the beta test, I had never seen a fruit shaped like that.

But the pale smile on Asuna's lips disappeared just as quickly as it formed.

"They look tasty...but this isn't time to be enjoying a snack. Lind's group will be done divvying up their items soon. If we need to practice our swimming to get to the main city, we ought to go and let them know before they come all the way up here..."

"Let's try knocking down some of the fruit first," I said, reaching up with both hands to grab a branch that was a good foot and a half around. I lowered my waist and tensed my legs, using all of my strength in an attempt to shake the branch. The tree didn't budge an inch, and needless to say, none of the fruit fell.

The bark of the tree was smooth and sleek, and without the Acrobatics skill, there was no way for me to climb it. I thought about tossing a pebble, but without the Throwing Knives skill, I wouldn't be able to hit it.

"Argh, if only I had three...no, five more skill slots!"

It was a desire that every player in *SAO* felt. I smacked the branch with my balled-up fist in frustration. Somehow, the basic martial arts technique Flash Blow activated, and my fist glowed red as it struck the branch. The resulting shock wave set the entire massive tree rattling.

"...Ah."

Asuna grunted and two of the donut-like fruit fell without a sound. I caught one in each hand and smiled confidently, trying to hide the fact that it was nothing more than a lucky coincidence.

She sighed exasperatedly and shrugged.

"Okay, fine, it turned out all right, but what if you'd broken the tree in half? We're still technically part of the Dark Elf team, so we have to respect nature."

"Of course. Sorry..."

I thought of the Dark Elf knight Kizmel, who was somewhere out there on this floor. Was she stuck like us now that the canyons were rivers? Or was she using her elven magic to walk on the surface of the water?

Asuna was quiet for a time just like me, thinking about Kizmel, but she came back to her senses quicker.

"So what's the plan with the donut fruit? If we're eating them, I'd prefer the yellow one."

One of the fruits in my hands was a brilliant cobalt blue, while the other was a pale lemon yellow. The blue one did not pique my hunger in the least, but fortunately, eating them wasn't the plan.

"I don't think these are meant to be shaped like donuts."

"...What are they shaped like, then?"

Rather than answering her, I brought the blue one up to my mouth. Asuna made a face like, *I knew you were eating it*, but I shot her a look of warning and popped the fruit's stem, a small protuberance half an inch long, into my mouth.

I sucked in a deep breath through my nose and blew as hard as I could into the tube stem. There was a powerful resistance at first, but then, as though a valve had opened, the air flooded into the fruit.

Bomp! The blue fruit instantly erupted into a much larger size.

The three-inch-wide fruit suddenly measured a good three feet. It was no longer a donut.

"Y-you mean…it's an…inner tube?" Asuna marveled. I grinned and handed her the yellow fruit.

"Try it out, Asuna."

"Um…okay," she replied, and popped the stem into her pursed lips. She sucked in a deep, arching breath and closed her eyes to blow.

There was another high-pitched pop, and an inner tube appeared. Her surprise at how light it was for its size caused her to bobble it, and she jogged along, batting it up into the air like a volleyball before she could grab it tight with both hands.

"Good grief…I do not know what's going on here," she sighed.

"You *donut* know," I replied on instinct before I could stop myself. A gaze well below the freezing point pierced the spot between my eyebrows.

"You were the one who said they weren't donuts," she snapped. "If you want to stand around cracking jokes, feel free to go do some stand-up at the teleport gate plaza."

"Wait…you mean you'll be my comedy partner?"

"Of course not!! Why not team up with Kibaou?!"

"…"

For an instant, I imagined myself onstage with Kibaou, who cut into me with a fierce "*Whaddaya mean?!*" I quickly shook my head to clear the thought.

"Uh…no, thanks."

I brought up my menu to check the time. Fifteen minutes had already passed since we emerged on the fourth floor, thirty-five since the boss was killed.

After producing a blank scroll of parchment, I began writing a quick message. Inside, I mentioned using an impact-type skill to drop the fruit and the way to inflate them. A quick tap on the scroll made it automatically roll up, and I placed it on the ground next to the pavilion.

Left on the ground like that, its durability would eventually dwindle and cause the item to vanish, but it would last at least until Lind and Kibaou made it up the stairs.

"Well, now that we've got our floaty tubes, that changes our plan of action, doesn't it?" I noted. Asuna looked down doubtfully at the massive tube in her hands.

"...You mean that even a beginner can swim with one of these?"

"I'll try it first, of course, but I'm pretty sure we'll be fine. As long as your head doesn't go underwater, you won't lose HP while swimming. We'll make it to the main town by going through the canyon just to the south and then east. The only thing is..."

"...Is what?"

"We should probably remove our heavy equipment, just in case."

"How heavy are we talking?"

I looked her over from head to toe several times, doing some quick weight calculations before answering.

"Let's see...You should probably take off the hooded cape. The rapier and the breastplate as well, obviously, and the boots and gloves, too. Probably the vest, too...And that leather skirt's a lot heavier than you'd think. As for the tunic, well..."

"...If I take all of them off, I won't be wearing any equipment at all!"

Asuna threw the inner tube smack against my face. It bounced upward with a giddy *poing* and landed right around my neck.

"I assume you're going to follow your own advice and take off your black thing, the other black thing, and the black thing aside from that!"

"Um...I'm only thinking of what will make it safest for you to swim..."

As a matter of fact, leather and cloth clothing were just as bad as metal—they took on water that added to the weight penalty. Even with our inner-tube secret weapon, it was too risky not to be able to maneuver adequately in a pinch. A pool or lake was one thing, but on a rushing river, we might easily miss our disembarking point and get washed well downstream.

Whether that honest concern of mine registered to her or not, Asuna's anger cooled, and she reached out her right hand. I tossed the yellow tube back so that the hole landed on her outstretched hand, spinning the tube round and round on her arm.

"Fine...We need to go light. I get that. So...am I good with the tunic, at least?"

"Huh? Uh, yeah, I think that should work," I nodded.

She shot me one last glare. "Then let's get going."

Asuna stomped off down the hill. I hurried after her, and within moments, we were back at the riverside to the south.

Asuna stopped and turned for one last look at the pavilion on the hilltop—probably to check that no one was emerging—then opened her window. She worked quickly, turning her back so I couldn't see. First the rapier disappeared, then the cape, armor, and vest.

When the leather skirt vanished into her inventory, only the white tunic was left. It hung low in the front and back, hiding her underwear, but something about that look only seemed to add to its destructive allure...

Lost in thought, I sensed that Asuna was about to turn around, so I quickly spun ninety degrees and hit my REMOVE EQUIPMENT button twice. All of my gear, including my sword, went into storage, leaving me with a single set of underwear trunks.

I was embarrassed to be in such a revealing outfit in front of a very pretty girl around my age, but the dark red boxers almost looked like a short set of swimming trunks. I told myself that anything I felt was entirely in my own head and that it wasn't even my own body.

As I closed the window, I heard a mysterious *pflrt* sound. Turning my head carefully over my shoulder, I saw Asuna with her hand over her mouth, her eyes upturned and wandering. It seemed like a very strange gesture to be making.

"Pff…peh-heh…kaha-ha-ha-ha-ha-ha-ha-ha!!"

The cool, cynical, mysterious fencer burst into uncontrolled laughter. I automatically covered my undies with the inner tube.

"Y-you don't have to laugh *that* hard! Besides, you already said you expected I would be taking everything off," I argued, hurt. Asuna bent over double, holding her sides.

"Ah-ha-ha-ha…I-I mean…seriously, that's just not fair, ha-ha-ha!"

"N-not fair? Look…I know it's a bright color, but…"

"N-no, I'm not talking about the color…pff-hff-hff…Do you really not know what I mean? You should really take a look at your butt!"

"Wh-what…?"

I twisted around in a hurry to check the back of the boxers, but even at the peak flexibility of my avatar's back, I couldn't see my own butt. Struck by a sudden idea, I rushed to the water's edge and stuck my butt over, hoping to catch sight of the reflection through my legs.

"Wh…what the—?!" I yelped.

The rear end of the crimson red trunks was printed with a large, flashy gold bull symbol.

I froze in shock, still in that embarrassing pose, while Asuna finally got her laughing fit under control—down to a simple chuckle.

"So where did you get that underwear? I don't remember ever seeing a pair with such a cool pattern on it at the NPC shops. Or was that your own custom design?"

"…I didn't buy it *or* design it," I grumbled, regaining my poise after the terrible shock. "This was the Last Attack bonus from the second-floor boss…Actually, the sub-boss boss, General Baran. I just assumed it was a plain design. Never occurred to me that there might be a design on the ass…"

"So if it was a bonus, does that mean it has some special effect?"

"Yep. It has a good boost to strength and a little bit of a resistance to debuffs like disease and curses…"

"Ahhh. You know, it's dreadfully boring that you win all of the LA bonuses, but I'm glad I didn't wind up with that underwear. I don't want to have to choose between wearing a stupid cow-print man's boxers for the bonus effects or not."

"You never know—if it dropped for you, it might have been proper lady's underwear. Still with the cow design, though, I bet."

As I inevitably started to imagine the fencer wearing cow panties, she wound up to hurl the inner tube at me again. I shook my head and snorted my nose, and she paused mid-windup.

I sighed to clear my head of that nonsense and knelt down to stick my hand in the river. The water was extremely cold, but I just had to suck it up and deal with it.

Asuna tested the water for herself and murmured, "Didn't you say that some floors of Aincrad are synced up to the actual season outside?"

"That's what it said in a magazine. But that article was obviously before it took us all prisoner, so I have no idea what's going on with Aincrad now…"

"Well, at the very least, this floor doesn't seem to be stuck in midwinter. I was thinking it was boring that there wasn't a more seasonal feeling here, but now I'm glad of it. So, shall we?"

Asuna put the lemon-yellow inner tube on, and I stuck the cobalt blue over my own head. With it fixed firmly in place with both hands, I told her, "Hang on for a moment while I test it out."

I stuck my right leg into the water. Once I was sure that the current right at the shore wasn't too strong, I let my body sink in.

As I suspected, the inflated donut fruit was quite buoyant, and it easily kept my body at the surface of the water. It didn't take too much pressure from my legs to hold my position in the current, either.

"I think it'll be fine," I said, looking up and beckoning her in. Asuna nodded nervously and very carefully entered the water. As soon as she did, the cloth tunic took on a bit of transparency and I hastily looked away, but Asuna didn't seem to notice. When her weight was supported by the inner tube, she even smiled.

"Wow, this takes me back!"

"I-it would have been nicer to swim at the beach."

"Who knows, maybe there *is* an ocean here. If there is, I'll make an actual swimsuit."

"That's right, you're still working on your Tailoring skill. Will you make me one without a bull design? Like…as soon as we get to town?" I added, realizing that we might be forced to use this inner-tube travel for a while.

She grinned devilishly. "Sure. I'll even give you a choice between bear, cat, and frog designs."

"…I'll…think it over. Ready to go?"

"Yep."

We both spun around to join the flow.

The circular area surrounded by cliffs had two exits. One of them was the source of the powerful flow of water, so our inevitable destination was out the other end. I started kicking my legs, keeping a firm grasp on the secret-weapon floaty tube.

After about ten feet, Asuna called out from behind.

"Um…something feels weird."

"The water pressure and texture feels different, doesn't it? That's why you have to practice before you go swimming without a floatation device. Still, it feels like they've made a lot of improvements since the beta."

"I see…This *does* require practice, I can tell…"

"An hour of swimming, and you'll get used to it. Here's the exit—the current will get a lot stronger here, so take care not to drift too far away."

No sooner were the words out of my mouth than I felt Asuna jam her hand between my torso and the swim tube.

"That should keep me secure."

I turned around and asked, "Should I do the same?" The fencer thought it over for two seconds and made a face that said it was special circumstance.

"Here goes, then…"

I stuck my left hand into Asuna's tube and pulled it close.

Unless something really drastic happened, there was no way we'd get separated like this.

We entered the ten-foot-wide canyon, firmly docked. The curves made it impossible to see what lay ahead, but I knew from my beta experience that we'd be heading into a larger canyon soon, one of the main paths of the floor.

As we picked up steam, sure enough, a much wider surface appeared ahead. It was a grand river flowing from west to east. The steep cliffs at the sides were the same, but there was a sense of liberation as the span of the water increased to over thirty feet. The speed of the flow wasn't as rapid as I feared, either.

Once we were out into the center of the river, we stopped kicking and let the water push us along.

"...The landscape really is exactly as it was in the beta. I even remember that rock there," I murmured to myself. Asuna looked around. With her every movement, I felt a pleasurable sensation on my left hand, but the iron wall that was my self-control shut it out of my thoughts.

"Hmm...I wonder why the dusty old canyons are full of water now?"

"Well, if I had to guess about things I have no way of knowing, maybe their water simulation process wasn't quite up to snuff back during the beta. If they were able to get it to a satisfactory level in the three months after that, they might have decided to change it to these rivers, I guess..."

"That makes sense, but it's a boring answer."

"S-sorry."

Asuna shrugged her shoulders, clad in the white fabric of her tunic. The way her skin was visible through the wet material wasn't in the beta, either. I hoped that I wasn't seeing the personal touch of Akihiko Kayaba, the mad director of *SAO* who had trapped all ten thousand of us in his deadly game.

She took another look around the area and wondered, "If all the canyons are filled with rivers now, shouldn't there be other things that have changed aside from the landscape?"

"What do you mean?"

"Things like what the quest NPCs say or the materials you can gather…oh, and the types of monsters you face."

She suddenly stopped, silent. I understood why. If we happened into a monster encounter right now, we were both without any kind of battle equipment on. I quickly shook my head to put her at ease.

"No, we're fine. In the beta, there were hardly any monsters along the route from the staircases to the main city of the next floor…"

"Really?"

"B-besides, the pop rate on monsters in the thirty minutes after the boss is defeated is drastically reduced…"

"Drastically?" she repeated, looking skeptical. "Well, it's certainly been at least thirty minutes."

"Oh, g-good point. But so far we haven't even seen a single fish, much less any monsters. I guess that might mean a real big one gobbled them all up," I added, trying to laugh it off. Suddenly, I heard an irregular *kerplunk*. Asuna heard it, too, as we turned around simultaneously.

About ten yards behind us, something had emerged from the water.

It was a smooth, sleek, triangular fin. There was at least a foot of it sticking out from the surface of the water. The color cursor that appeared was bright red to indicate an enemy, as if that wasn't obvious already. I heard an old familiar movie soundtrack lurch ominously into motion in my head.

"Um, is it just me, or is that…?" Asuna rasped. I didn't wait for the answer—I turned my body back around and tensed my legs for full-power kicking.

"Let's hurry," I suggested. For once, she didn't argue.

"Agreed."

"On the count of three…"

I looked back briefly to check that the menacing fin wasn't closing in yet, then took a deep breath.

"...two, three!"

With a silent roar echoing in my head, I kicked my feet as hard as I could. An enormous splash erupted behind us, and we started racing away downstream, hard enough that the swim tube was tilted nearly vertical.

If my memory was correct, the side path—er, tributary—that led to the main city was maybe a hundred yards off. The canyon twisted right, then back to the left, and I saw an aperture in the vertical cliff face to the right, just as I expected.

"There, Asuna!"

"Got it!"

I doubled my kicking speed for the final spurt and looked back again. Fortunately the terrifying fin was no longer in...

"Eeeeep!" I screeched. The gray fin splitting the surface of the water was barely a dozen feet away. If the body of our underwater pursuer matched the size of the fin, its rows of jagged teeth could be bearing down on my legs right now.

If it caught my toes, I would have to use my Quick Change mod to equip my sword and fight in the water. Meanwhile, I got my legs working up to 120 percent capacity.

"H-hey, what's going on behind us?!" Asuna croaked, too exhausted to even turn around and look.

"D-don't think about that! Just swim as fast as you can!"

"All right!"

We kept our grips on each other's inner tube and paddled madly with our free hands. The entrance ahead grew closer, but I could sense the fin behind us closing faster.

"P-prepare for a hard right!"

"All right!"

I gritted my teeth and flopped to the right. The moment my speed slowed with the turn, I thought I sensed something touching my foot, but our only choice at this point was to race for the goal. I put my full faith in the strength-raising effect of my bullbutt boxers as I stretched for the five-yard-wide tributary.

The side path ended in a small shoreline just twenty-five yards ahead. In the beta, it was another hill, at the top of which lay the gate to the main city. If we could just get to that white sand, we'd win this little game of tag.

"Raaaaah!!"

Roaring with about the seventh-fiercest shout I'd made in the last month and a half, I raced—er, swam—through the remaining distance. The instant my toes touched the sand of the river bottom, I bolted upright and started running, pulling Asuna by the hand. Even when the ground under my feet went from the soggy edge of the water to white, dry sand, I still kept going for another dozen paces before I finally turned back to look.

The dorsal fin that had been chasing us was leaping high above the water. Our fishy foe thought it could tackle us in a land battle. I was ready to oblige and just about to hit the QUICK CHANGE shortcut icon on my menu, when—

"...Hwuh?" Asuna muttered foolishly as she dangled from the swim tube I still clutched with my left hand.

There was no wonder. Beneath the splendid, foot-long fin was a pop-eyed tadpole-like creature just a few inches across and maybe a foot and a half long.

It landed on the wet sand and flapped around. Apparently its dorsal fin was so large and heavy that its tiny limbs couldn't balance properly.

But a large wave rolled in and swallowed the tadpole, pulling it back into the water. Soon the fin poked out of the river again and glided back toward the main current.

"...The hell was that...?"

I fell to my knees in the sand with the disappointment of it all. The inner tube under my left arm came loose and fell, dropping Asuna face-first into the sand. She eventually got up and sat in the sand, seemingly too exhausted to be angry with me this time. The sand stuck to her wet skin, strands of hair plastered across her forehead and cheeks, with the soaked tunic sticking tight to her torso to complete the picture-perfect image of a model at an oceanside photo shoot. The only thing out of place was her empty gaze, which followed the triangular fin.

"...I've just decided. The next time we see that monster, I'm going to kill it, cook it, and make you eat it," she said, her manifesto delivered in a flat voice.

"Why don't...*you* eat it?" I asked.

"It looked gross."

"..."

"Probably poisonous, too."

"..."

Well, as long as you cook it, I'll happily dig in. Maybe it'll taste like shark fin soup, I thought magnanimously, getting to my feet. I extended a hand to Asuna.

"Let's put our gear back on and go into town. I don't think you'll catch a cold sitting like that, but it's doing us no good," I noted. Suddenly, she froze solid, still clutching my hand. Her face, which was pointed down at her outfit, grew much redder. I began to back away, struck by a foreboding premonition much like the one I got upon first seeing that dorsal fin.

But her right hand struck, quick as lightning, and grabbed my left. She pulled until she was on her feet, and with that familiar surgical precision just light enough not to cause damage, she drove her knee into my stomach in the Muay Thai style.

2

"SO WHAT KIND OF PLACE IS THE MAIN TOWN OF THIS floor?"

Asuna strode south up the white hill, the soles of her leather boots grinding against the sand. She was back in her usual outfit of hooded cape and leather skirt.

"Umm…"

I tried to recall the sight of the town. I was back in my customary black coat.

"You know what? Forget it. We'll be there in a minute, and I'd rather see it for myself."

"That's a good idea. It's one of the fun things about MMOR-PGs," I agreed, but the sight of the stone-built town was already flooding back into my mind from memory.

If anything, it was not a particularly memorable town. Compared to the mountain-carved city of the second floor or the monstrous baobabs of the third, this one was structurally quite plain. If there was any odd feature to mention, it was that the entrance to every house was on the second floor, for some reason. In order to get inside, you had to use a set of stone stairs.

"Oh, there's the gate!" Asuna called, her voice about 20 percent more excited than normal. A mossy stone arch was coming into view at the top of the hill. I glanced down at my window, which was still open from putting my gear back on. It was nearly two o'clock.

A few minutes after reaching the fourth floor, a few minutes at the water's edge, a few minutes with the donut tree—these all added up to about fifty minutes since we'd conquered the boss of the third floor. There must be many players down below at this exact moment, just waiting for the teleport gate to open into the new town. I felt bad that we'd taken this long to activate the gate, but they'd understand when they saw the lack of a footpath.

I followed after the fencer as she trotted up the hill. When she reached the arch a step before I did, Asuna bubbled with excitement.

"Wow...It's so pretty here!"

Pretty?

All I remembered was a drab gray town. I strode up the last several lengths, curious now. The instant I passed through the cobblestone arch, countless lights flashed in my eyes. The plain, boring town in the squared hollow I remembered from the beta was now sparkling like a jewel.

The source of the light was the midday sun glittering off of solid blue water.

Everything that had been a stone-paved street before was now a deep waterway. The stone of the buildings had gone from dull gray to bright white, which made the entire place look like a city of chalk floating in the middle of a square lake. On sheer beauty, it easily eclipsed those of the second and third floor. No wonder Asuna exclaimed in wonder.

"...I see...This was supposed to be the finished version all along. That explains the doors on the second floor," I murmured.

My partner waved me over impatiently. "Come on, hurry!"

"Coming!"

We continued along the stone path, which was now descending. On the descent, a thought occurred to me: The theme for the fourth floor had to be "waterways."

Once through the massive front gate of the town, the SAFE HAVEN label appeared in my field of view. Up ahead was a dock a good hundred feet long, complete with a number of small boats helmed by NPCs.

"Oooh, look at the gondolas! It's just like Venice!" Asuna marveled. I started to wonder if she had only seen Venice in pictures, or if she'd actually been there, then snapped myself out of it. It didn't feel right to wonder about her personal life.

The street ended at the dock, so we needed to use a gondola to get anywhere in town. I suppose we had the option of taking those swim tubes back out of storage, but Asuna's eyes were currently gondola shaped, so I took the hint that my idea would be shot down instantly. I didn't exactly relish the thought of showing off my cow boxers, either, even if there weren't any other actual players in town yet.

The gondolas at the dock came in a wealth of sizes, from small one-person boats (aside from the NPC gondolier) up to large cruisers that could seat ten or more. A number of copper plaques listed the prices, indicating that a two-person gondola cost fifty col for a onetime use. It was good to know that the price would be the same no matter where in town we were, but I didn't like the idea of paying fifty col every time we wanted to visit a new place.

For the moment, we didn't have a better option.

"Will this one do?" I asked, pointing to a nearby ivory-white two-seater. Asuna gave it a serious examination and nodded. We headed down the steps of the dock and hopped into the gondola, Asuna first. The burly gondolier, in his traditional straw hat and striped shirt, gave us a friendly greeting.

"Welcome to Rovia, travelers! Fifty col, wherever you want to go!"

"Take us to the teleporter plaza, then," I answered, then wondered if an NPC would understand that terminology. Fortunately, he tipped the brim of his cap in acknowledgment.

"Off we go!" he shouted. A purple payment window appeared briefly, then vanished. The gondolier gave one push of his long oar. The white ship slid away, and at the prow, Asuna pulled her hood back and cheered again.

The gondola left the dock at the north end of the city behind and headed down the cross-shaped main street that split the town into four quarters. Er, no, not a main street, a main—

"Hey, Asuna, what's the English word for a waterway?"

"Channel!"

The main channel of town.

Boats of all colors filled the wide canal, which was a good sixty feet wide, with shops large and small lining the sides. The displays of weapons, armor, and items were very tempting to me, but it would not be easy to take detours in this situation. No doubt we could change destinations on the fly, but I had a feeling that every time we stepped off the boat, it would cost another fifty to get on again. On top of that, I didn't even know if the gondola would wait for us there.

I told myself that we had to prioritize activating the town's teleporter and asked the gondolier a different question.

"Will this boat take us outside of the town as well?"

Fortunately, this question was part of his recognized list, and he gave a proper answer as he rowed the powerful oar.

"I'm afraid I can't do that. I only work here, in the town of Rovia."

"Would another ship take us out of town?"

"Sorry, I can't answer that."

Either the question didn't fit his recognized parameters, or there was a reason he couldn't answer it. There were plenty of other things I wanted to know, but based on my experience in the beta, the most in-depth information on a town had to come from the right NPC—like a bearded village elder, a fishy informant, or a know-it-all child.

For a moment, I was reminded of the Dark Elf knight and her stunningly realistic vocabulary, but there were things to be done before I could dwell on my loneliness.

We'll open the gate, take a short rest, then go about collecting information, I told myself.

A large wharf appeared ahead. It was the teleport gate plaza at the center of the town. The gondolier drew our boat level to the dock at the southern end of the square with expert skill, then put his hand to his cap again.

"Safe and sound! Hope to see you again!"

We thanked him and stepped off the boat. As I feared, the gondola immediately pulled away from the wharf and headed back to the entrance of the town. But there were other gondolas at the dock here, so we could use them on the way back. Opening the teleporter quickly was the matter at hand.

When I turned, I found that Asuna still had stars floating in her eyes.

"That was so, so much fun!"

"Um...I'm glad you enjoyed it."

"Let's ride another one back!"

"I...don't think we have another option."

I almost had to wonder if she really was the same coolheaded, snarky fencer I'd been working with all this time.

An hour after defeating the boss of the third floor, Asuna and I activated the teleport gate for the fourth floor and retreated to a corner of the plaza to watch the swarm of players that came barreling through the wavering blue portal.

The rush of tourists, here for the custom of "town opening," stood around in clumps within the plaza and marveled at the beauty of the town, but more than a few seemed to have a clear purpose in mind already. Middle-of-the-pack swordsmen who headed for the market area in search of better weapons, merchants after more valuable items to stock, and even a short-haired girl with a blacksmith's hammer at her waist, poring over the map of the town.

Glad to see that there were more fighters trying to catch up to the frontier group and crafters offering player support, I joined Asuna in entering a small inn at the outer edge of the plaza.

We got two rooms this time, to avoid the mistake that happened in Zumfut down on the third floor, but we needed to have

a meeting about our plans for the near future before we could lie down for a rest, and therefore, ended up on the sofas in my room. As usual, I had to be wary that her unnecessary danger radar was at max sensitivity, but with the gondola effect still active in her expression, her features were relaxed.

I took a sip of tea from the set that was left in the room and looked at Asuna across from me.

"Do you...like ships?"

She blinked a few times and smiled shyly.

"Not ships as a whole, really...but I've always wanted to ride in a gondola. I just never thought that dream would come true in Aincrad."

"I see. So it's not all bad that the fourth floor got filled with water, then," I noted. She seemed to realize something.

"Oh...so there weren't any of these canals and channels in the beta?"

"Correct. It was just a boring, dusty, gray town. I barely remember anything about it."

"Then I like this one much more. I know the gondolas don't go out of town, so we'll probably have to deal with more swimming...but I can deal with it."

Despite being totally entranced with the boat ride, she'd still taken in every word of the conversation I had with the gondolier. I couldn't help but smile at her capable nature.

"That's right. As for what's next, we should take a break, then resupply, repair, and replace our stuff here in town; accept all the available quests; and find out as much info as we can about the fourth floor. Eventually we'll have to leave the town for other locations, which means using those swim tubes again..."

The dreamy look steadily faded from Asuna's eyes, replaced by her typical cool expression.

"I can handle the swimming—the problem is monsters. That lizard-tadpole thing earlier was a bit of a letdown when the body was barely larger than the fin, but it still had a bright red cursor, right? That meant it was a pretty high level..."

"Exactly. And obviously that won't be the only species of monster on the floor...We'd better try to outfit ourselves for underwater combat."

I only had a tiny bit of experience with that from the beta. Not only did a player have to deal with taking and holding breaths, but the resistance from the water was fierce as well. Fighters with big weapons had to be able to handle those weapons, while those with smaller weapons could only be so agile in the water. The most suited to water were spear-type weapons, with their long reach and jabbing attacks that met with minimal resistance from the water. And neither Asuna nor I had any spear skills.

It was unrealistic to start training now, but Asuna could do her best with the spear-like jabbing of her rapier, and I could limit myself to thrusting skills...

Suddenly, Asuna set down her tea and shouted.

"Oh, right! I forgot, I need to make a swimsuit!"

"Y-you were serious about that?"

"Of course. I think I saw them selling some at the shops, but it would be a waste to spend that money when I've already got the Tailoring skill."

"W-well, you've got a point...Can I ask you to make me some swim trunks, too? Nice plain ones, no bull mark."

"Should I design it with that finned tadpole instead?"

I was going to plead against it, but something else occurred to me first.

"Uh, wait, hang on."

"Wh-what do you mean? I haven't even started."

"No, I mean, I'm thinking..."

I squinted, trying to pull the relevant information out of that conversation we'd had about tailoring back in the Dark Elf camp on the third floor.

On the second floor, I'd seen the mountain of underwear that came out of Asuna's inventory. Those weren't meant to be worn, but were a by-product of her training to raise her skill proficiency.

Afterward, she'd mentioned that she had already taken the Tailoring skill out of its slot.

"…No, it won't work."

"What won't?"

"You don't have Tailoring in one of your slots anymore, do you? This might come as a shock if you didn't know already…but once you remove a skill from its slot, the proficiency goes back down to zero," I explained.

She nodded without batting an eye. "I might be a beginner, but even I know that. Besides, it pops up that warning when you remove the skill from the slot."

"Oh…good. Er, I mean, are you going to train it up from nothing again?"

She shook her head, exasperated. "I might be a hard worker, but I'm not that patient. As a matter of fact…"

Asuna opened her game window, a skeptical look on her face. She flipped over to her inventory storage and materialized a small item.

The small crystal bottle shaped like a nut thunked down onto the coffee table. There was a small amount of faintly glowing blue liquid inside the thick, transparent bottle.

"…What's this?"

"You didn't see one in the beta?"

"No…not that I remember."

I reached out to pick up the vial, but she quickly cut me off.

"Stop, if you don't know what it is! Don't you dare open it up."

"I-I know, I was just gonna read the description."

"I'm serious about that!"

Her stern admonition made me just want to pop it open and gulp it down in one swift movement, but I wasn't trying out to be a stage comedian, so I behaved myself. Carefully picking it up so as not to disturb the glass lid, I was surprised at how heavy it was for being just three inches long. I tapped the side of the glass with a fingertip and examined the properties window that appeared.

"It's called a...Crystal Bottle of Kales'Oh? Never heard of it. Let's see here...*This bottle allows you to save the proficiency of any skill currently equipped in a skill slot*...Aha..."

About three seconds passed.

"Wh...wha...wha...huwhaaaattttuh?!"

The shock wave of my scream put cracks in the walls, tears in the down blanket, and shattered every window in the room.

Okay, in reality, it just caused a mere ripple on the surface of the teacup, but it certainly *felt* like it had that kind of destructive impact. My mouth was frozen open in shock. Asuna pulled the bottle out of my fingers and fiddled with the settings in the properties window, then promptly pulled out the stopper.

The liquid at the bottom of the vial turned into a blue light that floated up into the air. She took a deep breath and sucked it into her nostrils, then breathed yellow light back into the bottle before replacing the cap. The contents now looked like lemon oil. She put the bottle back onto the table and smiled at me.

"Now my Tailoring skill is back to its previous level, and my Sprint skill level is saved in the bottle."

"...I...I see...Erm, so, if I might ask, where did you get that item...?"

"It was kind of chaotic so I couldn't tell, but I think it was that one time. Remember right after we reached the third floor, and we helped Kizmel fight that Forest Elf knight? I think it must have dropped from the elf knight."

"Ohhh," I nodded, still not over the shock. Now that she mentioned it, Kales'Oh was the name of the Forest Elf nation that once existed down on the surface, according to Kizmel's tale.

In fact, that overwhelmingly powerful elf warrior—strong enough that players should normally be unable to win, as it was a story-event battle—had dropped a number of fairly rare items for me as well. But I was so startled by Kizmel's very un-NPC-like dialogue that I never went back to check the loot out.

Asuna couldn't have figured out the properties of the crystal bottle until later that night at the earliest. We didn't describe or ask for each other's skill choices or inventory contents unless it was absolutely necessary, so a week had passed without me ever knowing that Asuna had such a tremendously valuable item.

"Are you just going to sit there in shock the whole time? If we're done talking, can I go to my room and start making swimsuits now?" she asked. It broke me out of my paralysis effect.

"Oh, uh, ummm," I mumbled, trying to organize my thoughts. I held up my hands. "Just…just hang on. There are a few more things I want to be sure of."

"…All right, but why don't you settle down first?"

"Y-yeah."

I gulped down my cold tea and let out a long breath. The Crystal Bottle of Kales'Oh was still sitting right there on the table. I stared at the sparkling yellow liquid made of pure skill proficiency.

The liquid filled about one-twentieth of the capacity of the vial. Assuming that Asuna's Sprint skill had been around 50 or so, and the amount of liquid directly correlated to the proficiency, then this bottle could even save a completed skill at the maximum proficiency level of 1,000.

I took one more deep breath and looked up at her.

"Have you told any other player aside from me about this bottle?"

The fencer shrugged and shook her head.

"You're sure? Not even Argo?"

"Listen, you've been traveling with me for the entire week since I got this item. When would I have had a chance to meet with Argo behind your back?"

"Oh…good point…"

I felt relief flooding into me, but Asuna was still shooting me a skeptical look.

"What's with this overblown reaction? All this bottle does is let you put your skill level in and take it out—you still have to do the work to raise it. You're acting like drinking it will automatically give you one hundred skill points or something. Is it that big of a deal?"

"..."

I was both stunned by what my temporary partner was saying and resigned—apparently this was just how non-RPG players thought. I tried my best to make her understand my surprise and apprehension.

"The thing is...like I said, you lose your skill progress in *SAO* when you remove a skill from its slot. So at level sixteen like I am now, I can only improve four skills at any one time."

"I know that. You've got One-Handed Swords, Martial Arts, Search, and...Hiding, is it?"

She knows!

But it was too late to be alarmed by that at this point. I cleared my throat and continued.

"Y-yeah, anyway, I'm seriously wondering if I should remove Hiding so that I can equip Swimming, instead."

"There's a Swimming skill? What happens if you use it?"

"You can swim faster, there's not as much water resistance, and you can move longer underwater. It'll be a real help on this floor, but I probably won't end up using it. The terrain is bound to change on the next floor, so I would be giving up on all the hard work I've put into Hiding, just for the sake of this one floor."

"Ahh...So with that bottle there, you could save one of your other skills where it already is and temporarily set the Swimming skill in its slot just for this floor."

"Exactly. Every single player who comes to this floor is going to have to face that hard choice. If word gets out that there's a player with a magic bottle that can save your skill progress, you're going to get harassed by people looking to buy it, snooping around, and prying for information, and so on."

There was another much darker possibility that I could see arising, but I chose not to mention it. Asuna reached out and picked up the crystal bottle to stare at it, appreciating its true value for the first time.

"I see...Now that I think about it, Nezha from the Legend Braves could have used this bottle to earn Martial Arts without having to give up on One-Handed Swords. Since it effectively gives you an extra skill slot, I guess I can see why people would make a big fuss about it..."

As usual, she latched onto concepts very quickly for a beginner. Asuna looked up and went on, speaking faster than usual.

"What if we just went ahead and released all the information we have about this thing? If we tell Argo, she'll put it in her strategy guides, right? Then no one will need to come ask us."

"Yeah...I'm not saying that we should cover up its existence... but..."

I leaned over and rested my chin on my folded hands, thinking hard.

"The problem is, the Forest Elven Hallowed Knight that you got the bottle from is only available to fight during that event battle in the Forest of Wavering Mists on the third floor, at this point. You basically only get the one opportunity. I'm guessing that the major players on the front line like Kibaou's Aincrad Liberation Squad and Lind's Dragon Knights Brigade have already beaten that event in the normal way by now..."

"I see...So it's kind of too late to publicize that info now."

"Yeah. Plus, it's not like it's easy to beat him, even if you still have the opportunity..."

"We managed to do it, didn't we?" she said simply.

I had to admit that she was right, but I had my doubts. I scratched at my bangs and admitted something that had been on my mind all along. "...How do you suppose we were able to beat that Forest Elf, anyway...?"

In the short silence that followed, I remembered a conversation I had with Kizmel in the bathing tent of the Dark Elf outpost.

She claimed that she'd been having a strange dream lately.

In the dream, Kizmel was fighting a powerful Forest Elf knight. In the middle of the duel, I showed up with a number of companions, none of which were Asuna. We helped her fight, but no one was able to handle the Forest Elf, and the group fell one after the other—until Kizmel was forced to release the protection of the Holy Tree to save our lives, thus perishing herself.

Aside from the questions of why an NPC would dream or if an NPC actually "slept" in the true sense of the word, one thing stood out—the content of that dream was eerily similar to my experience with the "Jade Key" quest during the beta test of *SAO*.

Kizmel was an extremely special NPC with a highly advanced AI. That much was clear.

Was that the reason that she maintained memory from as far back as the beta test? Or was it the presence of that memory that turned her special? Was it because of Kizmel that Asuna and I were able to beat the deadly Forest Elf knight in the retail game at all...?

"...I think it's because we all tried our hardest," Asuna murmured. I looked up with a start. "You and Kizmel and I all fought as hard as we could, believing we could win. That was the hardest I've concentrated in any battle since I came to Aincrad—even more than the floor bosses."

"..."

As a gamer, I was used to the idea that an "auto-lose event" could never be overturned, no matter how hard one tried, but I couldn't come out and put that into words.

"...Yeah...exactly. You were really something during that fight. And after putting that much effort into it, you'd expect to get a really great piece of loot or two out of the deal."

"Just so you know, I wasn't doing it expecting to be rewarded with items!" she retorted, raising a fist. I laughed and apologized.

Sword Art Online wasn't like all the other RPGs I'd ever played. It was a deadly game with no log-out button, and the world's first VRMMORPG. If I stuck to my preconceived notions of how things should be, I was missing out on what was in front of my own eyes.

I gave Asuna a serious look and asked, "Can we at least take some time to think about what to do with the crystal bottle info?

Like I said, I don't want to just keep it a secret forever. But as long as I know it might be a source of trouble, I want to keep your safety first and foremost."

I expected her to bite back with a snarky reassurance that she wasn't a newbie anymore and could take care of herself, and I even went so far as to prepare a further statement to back my case. But Asuna only looked back at me in silence, then turned away in a huff. I could just barely see her mouth move behind the long hanging bangs.

"…Well, if that's what you want to do, then fine."

"Oh…y-you're okay with that?"

I was so surprised by her answer that I wondered what she was thinking and leaned over onto my right side to see around the side of her face. Instead, Asuna turned harder to her left, evading my gaze until she was seated completely backward, facing into the sofa.

What's going on here?

I had a feeling that if I didn't take it easy, the fencer was going to explode, so I sat back up properly and said, "A-anyway, let's take a little rest now. How about we meet up at…the café on the first floor at six o'clock?"

Asuna nodded silently and slipped off of the sofa, her back still facing me. She got up and placed the Crystal Bottle of Kales'Oh into her inventory, then left the room without ever facing me.

What button of hers had I pressed?

I sank into a sitting position.

Five seconds after I had removed all my gear, sent a single instant message, and laid down on the bed by the window, I fell asleep.

When the alarm I set rudely woke me up, the light in the room was the color of sunset. I slowly sat up and pulled open the curtain to look down at the teleport plaza of Rovia from my second-story vantage point.

In just three hours, the square had filled up with countless players. Frontline members peered at the NPC shop wares, tourists noshed on food from the carts, and romantic-looking couples sat on the benches facing the water.

This was the forty-fifth day since the game of death had begun. It felt both long and short, but I considered it a good thing if matters had settled down enough for people to consider themselves a couple—this was my most magnanimous opinion as a frustrated middle school boy. Meanwhile, I noticed a particularly long line at the gondola dock to the south.

"Ugh…Crap, I forgot," I moaned, kneeling on the bed.

I should have expected this. There were only so many gondolas, so if too many players appeared, it was inevitable that a line would form. I had to get accustomed to the idea that moving around Rovia would take much more time than usual.

At the very least, I was relieved to see that so many people could be crammed into a limited space and lining up politely without any trouble.

No sooner had the thought occurred than a group of five armed players attempted to push their way to the front of the line and get on one of the larger gondolas that was just pulling in. Naturally, the group that was being cut protested. But the large, greatsword-wielding leader of the offending group was shouting back just as angrily.

I couldn't hear them from my distant second-story inn room, but I could imagine what was being said.

"We're fighting to liberate you normal players! Our needs should come first!"

The tourists in their simple cloth gear had no choice but to unhappily let them go. The man and his partners brandished their gleaming metal equipment in a show of might and leaped onto the gondola.

As the boat left the wharf, I muttered to myself, "That was a bad move, Haf."

The quintet that had cut in line were all wearing blue doublets. They were members of the Dragon Knights Brigade, a front-line guild that had just been established on the third floor. And the man with the greatsword at the lead was Hafner, one of the guild's officers.

They'd probably just finished resupplying and opening quests in town and were ready to start conquering the floor in earnest. I could understand how warriors on a mission might be frustrated with waiting around in line behind tourists with no greater purpose.

But if there was one thing to avoid, it was the frontline population acting like it was special and earning the disdain of everyone else. One never knew if those who hadn't been swinging swords yet might one day emerge from the safety of town and reach the frontier of their own will and ability.

In fact, if that never happened, we couldn't beat the game. The frontier group was barely fifty strong at this point and would certainly get bogged down eventually. We needed as many people as possible helping to advance the human progress in the game.

I stifled a sigh and checked the time. Only three minutes left until our meet-up at six o'clock.

Crawling out of the bed, I outfitted myself in all the usual gear and plodded out of the room. When I came face-to-face with Asuna for the first time in three hours below, she was back to her usual cool attitude.

"Sorry about the wait," I said, taking the seat across from her. There were no other players in the café aside from us—clearly the view paled in comparison to what was outside.

"I just got here," she said flatly, then slid the menu over to me. I saw that aside from drinks and sweets, they had a few items that looked like fish.

"...Should we get an early dinner here?"

"I want to get something to eat from the carts outside."

"Okay. Drinks only, then...or would you rather just leave?"

"That's fine with me."

It did seem like there was something different about her, but we hadn't been working together long enough for me to be sure, so I set it aside as I got up. It was poor form to meet up at a coffee shop in the real world and leave without ordering anything, but the NPC waiters here just watched us off without a complaint.

We left the inn without checking out. The underside of the floor above was somewhere between rose and indigo. Within another thirty minutes, it would be properly dark out.

But if anything, the gondola line on the other end of the square was even longer. The stone buildings were lit up with lanterns whose light reflected off the water in an entrancing display. Perhaps nighttime was considered the peak of the boating business here.

"Well, uh, you can see the line...Still want to queue up? Or should we forget the gondolas and just swim for ourselves—"

I stopped as soon as I felt the cold glare from under her hood.

"...Or not. I guess we should line up for a trip to the market area."

"But first I want to visit the food carts."

"Oh, right."

We made our way over to the east end of the square, where five or six stylish little carts were arranged. From what I could tell, only three of them were selling food that might make for a dinner. There was a meal set of fried fish and cooked veggies, a seafood pizza with squid and shellfish, and a panini sandwich with grilled fish and herbs.

"I see. So the main style of food on this floor is fish," I noted.

"Don't like fish?"

I shook my head hastily. "No, it's not that. It's more that I was hoping for...a few traditional choices. Like boiled fish or sashimi."

"You know you're not going to get choices like that in a town like this."

"Good point. I'll have to hold out hope for the tenth floor...I think I'll go for the panini. What about you?"

"That sounds good to me, too."

"You wanna wait on the bench while I buy them?"

Asuna gave me another upward glance beneath her hood, then turned away.

What's going on here? It feels like the time when she ate the cream bread down in Tolbana on the first floor.

The paninis were twelve col each at the cart. I bought two and returned to the bench. I handed one to Asuna, then stopped her when I noticed that she was opening her trade window to pay me for the sandwich.

"No, it's on me."

"...Why?"

"Because, um...Oh, because I'll owe you for making me the swimsuit."

"..."

Fortunately, she nodded and accepted my offer. She was still acting weird, but at least she wasn't angry with me.

I was just about to sit down next to her, shaking my head in confusion, when someone's hand snuck out from the darkness behind us and a teasing voice sounded in my ear.

"Thankee kindly, Kii-boy. I've been hungry."

I wasn't sure whether to play it cool (*"Your Hiding's as good as ever"*) or be honest and reject her (*"No! That's my dinner!"*), so the result had a bit from both columns.

"Your Hiding's as good as ever, but that's my dinner and no you can't have any!"

"Hmph. So you'll buy one for her, but not for me. I see how it is."

"Wha...? I...You heard what I said, that was thanks for her making me an item! It has nothing to do with showing favor on anyone!"

A short female player materialized out of the darkness wearing a plain beige hooded cape much like Asuna's. Her eyes were hidden behind her curly bangs, but the three whiskers drawn with face paint on either cheek left no uncertainty about who it was.

Argo the Rat, information dealer, leaped over the back of the bench with a grin on her face and sat next to Asuna. She looked to her left and lifted the hood back a bit.

"Evening, A-chan. Good work with the third-floor boss and the fourth-floor gate."

"G-good evening, Argo. Um…would you like some of this?" Asuna asked, offering up her own panini. Argo cackled and shook her hand in denial.

"No, no, I appreciate the offer. Eat up."

"Uh, okay…"

Asuna looked as if she wasn't sure whether Argo was hungry or not. I sighed and decided to set her at ease.

"Don't worry about it, Asuna. Her Teasing skill is the best in Aincrad."

"Teasing…?"

Asuna recognized something about this scene, looking up at me, then at the panini in her hands, then to Argo on her right-hand side.

"I-it's not like that, Argo! We are *not, at all, in any way,* like that!"

"Nyo-ho-ho, I get it, I get it," she laughed creepily.

I plopped down on the bench to Argo's right and quietly clinched the message. "It's true. Don't go selling any funny rumors."

"Why, that hurts. You know it's not my style to sell rumors and gossip."

"Yeah, sure. Anyway, the fact that you're here must mean you've got all the intel you needed."

"You bet. In fact, it took just three hours from your message to look up what you wanted, so I figured that might earn me a free meal in addition to my fee, but…"

She had me over the coals. After all, I'd told her I wanted it ASAP, just before I passed out for a quick nap.

"F-fine, fine. What do you want?"

"Gosh, I could sure go for a nice cheesy pizza," she started.

Before the sentence could finish, I had dashed at a sprint to the seafood pizza cart, bought one with three times the cheese, then bolted back to the bench.

"Sorry about all the trouble. This is a mere token of my gratitude."

I presented the pizza with a flourish and Argo grinned back at me.

"Very good, sir."

"Then let's talk as we eat...Chow that down before it gets cold, Asuna," I called to the fencer on the other side of Argo. The three of us said grace and started scarfing down our Italian-style dinner.

I had never eaten a true panini in real life, but between the crispy and chewy bread, the fragrantly grilled whitefish, and the herb-scented tomato sauce, it seemed like this was probably a pretty good re-creation of one. Now if only the main ingredients were a nice thick slab of meat and a thick teriyaki-and-mayo sauce...

Both Asuna and Argo were hungry, and we each gobbled down half the meal before finally stopping to breathe.

Before I could prompt her, Argo pulled out a scroll of parchment from one of the many pouches at her waist and held it out between her fingers.

"Normally I'd charge you an extra fee for quick service...but I'll go with the normal rate this time as thanks for the pile o' cheese you bought me. That's five hundred col."

I pulled out the gold coin I'd stored in my coat pocket for just this occasion and handed it to Argo. Tapping the scroll she handed over caused it to automatically unfurl.

"What information did you request from her?" Asuna asked, leaning over. I showed her the illustration on the scroll: a detailed map of Rovia. Argo herself hadn't drawn this map, however. Anyone could produce the same thing by simply walking all over the town, then copying the map data to a scroll item like this.

The difference was that Argo's map had about twenty exclamation point markers placed all over the town. *This* was what the five hundred col paid for.

"Are those...all of the quest NPCs?" Asuna wondered, as astute as ever. I nodded silently and got back an exasperated glance in return.

"Well, I hate to be hard on Argo, since she did all the work... but you could find all of this stuff just by walking around town. And we'll need to visit these spots to start the quests anyway."

"That was my assumption as well. And didn't you already finish all of these quests in the beta, Kii-boy?"

"That's the thing," I murmured, my mouth full of panini. "I feel like the longer I walk around town, the more my old memories will fade...I just wanted to be able to see the locations all at once like this."

"...Ohhh?"

There was more than a hint of entertainment in Argo's voice. I chose to stare at the map of the town rather than indulge her.

As I suspected, the layout of the town itself was exactly the same. I tapped each icon in turn, remembering the dried, dusty form the settlement used to take. With each tap appeared a quick quest rundown written by Argo.

Once I had examined all of them, I pointed out a single marker in the northwest corner of the map.

"This one."

"...What about it?" Asuna asked, suspicious. I grinned at her.

"This quest wasn't there in the beta. This is the spot that's the key to this town...no, to conquering this entire floor."

"If you get all the intel on this quest, I'll buy it off you," Argo had offered, and with a lingering whiff of cheese, she melted back into the darkness.

Asuna and I finished the last scraps of our sandwiches and got up from the bench to watch the dock to the south. The line looked a little bit shorter than before, but it was still a good thirty-minute wait.

Thanks to the power of a full stomach and a conversation with Argo, Asuna had recovered her normal mood. She noted, "I don't mind lining up...but that dock has a terrible system."

"Oh? What about it?"

"The little two-seaters and the big ten-person boats both stop at the same place. It's taking extra time because one person will end up riding the big gondola, and then the larger groups have to split up and take multiple smaller ones. They ought to at least split the people up into three different lines."

"Good point. So...should we propose that idea?"

"...That's not really my style."

"I don't know. You've got that class rep–style attitude, so I bet people will..."

I let the rest of the sentence hang when I felt Asuna's chilling laser beam stare on my face.?

The nighttime sights of Rovia were truly enchanting now, as the colorful lamps and window lights of the town glimmered off the surface of the dark water. Even the gondolas full of smiling players had lanterns of their own, sitting on the prow and stern of the small ones and the overhanging roofs of the larger ones. The sight of the gondolas crossing in the canals was so beautiful that...

"—Ah!"

I snapped my fingers, a sudden idea lighting up my brain.

"Wh-what?"

"This way! I'll explain later."

I prodded Asuna's back and trotted toward the wharf at the north end, the opposite direction from the dock. There was no boat landing here, so the drop from the piled stone fence to the water was quite far. But that also meant the gondolas were floating quite low.

"I have a bad feeling about this," Asuna muttered, trying to back away. I grabbed the hem of her cape tight.

"Don't worry, it's fine."

"It is not fine! I don't like it!"

"You'll be perfectly all right."

"Do it by yourself if you're so keen on it!" she shouted.

I glanced left and right. Within a few seconds, one of the large twelve-seat gondolas came chugging closer on the right. Luckily enough, another gondola of the same size was approaching from the left. I calculated where the two would pass, given that traffic seemed to move on the right side here, then moved us three yards to the left and five yards back.

"I'll give you a five-second countdown."

"I-I told you, I don't want to do this!"

"That's funny, Asuna, I could have sworn you had a higher agility than me."

"Rgh...y-you know that's not fair to bring up..."

"This should be easy for you, Asuna. I mean, since you have the Sprint skill and everything."

"But I just switched that one out...Arrgh, oh, fine!"

"And five, four, three, two, one..."

At zero, we started running. I hit the low fence in stride and launched off of it with my right foot.

All the traffic in the canals of Rovia traveled on the right side, so I leaped and stretched out for the gondola approaching on the left. Once I had just barely landed by my tiptoes, the gondola shook fiercely and the passengers below shouted in alarm. I yelled a quick apology and cut across the roof to leap again.

In midair, I glanced back to see that Asuna was keeping up. She had better jumping power than I did, so she should be able to make any jump that I did, but I was secretly relieved when I landed on the second gondola coming from the right.

The people riding this gondola must have already noticed the display of ninja acrobatics going on overhead, as they applauded and whistled at the sight of Asuna leaping gracefully through the night sky. Glad that we weren't being yelled at, I raced across the roof and jumped for a third time.

But...

"Ugh!"

The far bank was farther away than I thought. I scrambled my limbs in midair, stretching my arms as far as I could, until I just barely caught the lip of the wall with my fingertips.

As my entire body slammed up against the wall, I heard a light footfall over my head. When I looked up, I saw Asuna standing safe and sound above me, her hands on her hips and a disappointed look on her face.

"If you weren't sure you could make it, you shouldn't have tried," she scolded. I couldn't be bothered to answer her. I had a very sudden and clear understanding of exactly why the passengers on the gondola had been cheering.

"Um, Asuna?"

"...What?"

"You're, um, in a bit of danger...angularly speaking."

"What do you mean...?"

Asuna trailed off, looking down suspiciously at me as I hung there next to her feet, then suddenly went red enough that I could see it, even in the darkness. She quickly put her hands down over the hem of her skirt, then smiled for some reason and lifted one of her boots.

"Better climb up quick before I step on you."

"O-okay, okay, I'm coming up!"

I scrambled up the wall in a hurry.

Rovia had a square layout with main channels that intersected—technically, the teleport square was in the center of town, so there was no actual intersection—and split the town into quarters.

If north was the "top" of the town, then the top right was the sightseeing area, with a park, a plaza, and an outdoor theater. The bottom right was the market area, crammed full of a variety of businesses. The bottom left was the lodging area with inns large and small. And the top-left quadrant, where we were now, was the downtown area where all the NPCs lived.

Naturally, each quarter had smaller canals that split it up, requiring the use of a boat to get around farther. But circling gondolas passed by every stretch of water, so we decided to flag down a two-seat boat.

This time, we gave the NPC gondolier coordinates instead of a name, paid the fee by an automatic half-and-half calculator, then wearily sat down in the two seats.

The fencer in the miniskirt was in a much better mood the instant she sat down at the prow, and she began taking in the sights of the town with sparkles in her eyes. This was the most plain of all the areas in Rovia, but even the practical, homey residential sector had its own charm.

Children played with toy boats at the waterside of their entrance porch, while a mother and baby bird somewhere between a duck and a seagull swam past. Evening sounds and smells wafted through kitchen windows, and warm orange light shone off the water.

"Ooh, that house is for sale!"

I looked where Asuna was pointing and saw a small two-story house with a wooden For Sale sign.

"Hey, you're right. So there are player houses here."

"I wonder how much it costs," she wondered, her eyes sparkling even brighter.

I snorted wryly. "I wouldn't look at the price if I were you. You can only be disappointed."

"I know it'll be expensive. But I'm free to keep it in mind as something I can get if I work hard enough!"

"Su-sure, that's true...but I wouldn't recommend buying in this town. It's a fun, pretty place for sightseeing, but actually living here would be tough when it comes to getting around," I noted. Asuna took that advice to heart surprisingly fast.

"Good point. I wonder what the people here do for their daily shopping and such."

"Maybe they just swim around when we're not watching."

"Come on, don't ruin the illusion. But...if I do decide to get a house, I'll save up for a normal one with a view of a lake," she announced, then faced forward again.

I was more of the opinion that the money you could use to buy a player house was better spent on cheap inn lodgings and better gear, but given Asuna's proactive nature, I could certainly see her landing a lakeside residence someday. Maybe she would even let me crash on her couch...No, definitely not.

Meanwhile, the gondola wove its way through the narrow channels right and left and deposited us at our destination in under ten minutes.

Beyond the tiny dock was a very large but very old building. Aside from the large double doors facing the water, it appeared to be just a plain old house without any notable features.

I approached the building cautiously and peered into a dirty window. Inside was an equally messy room, and in the back was what looked like an old man sitting on the floor, facing the other direction. I thought I could see a faded golden *!* mark over his head. This was our quest NPC.

"...I'm surprised Argo was able to spot him," Asuna commented. I agreed.

"This is more than just good instincts...Anyway, let's go inside."

I went to the front door and knocked twice. After a good five seconds, a brusque voice replied, "It's not locked. Come in if you want something."

This one feels like a real pain in the ass, I thought to myself as I opened the ancient door.

Inside, we were greeted by an old man in a rocking chair that seemed ready to fall apart at any moment, with a bottle of booze in one hand and a pipe in the other. Technically all he did was glare at us with one eye, so it wasn't even a greeting.

His wispy, balding hair and scraggly beard were bone white, but his skin was well burned by the sun, and the muscles of his arms and chest were taut. He looked like an old sailor who'd once boasted of his strength and was now retired and drowning in liquor.

Asuna and I shared a look, in which I saw the message *This one's all on you* in her eyes. I hesitantly tried to say the magic quest words.

"Um...sir, can I help you with anything?"

The old man took a slug from his bottle and grumbled, "Nope."

There was no change in the mark over his head or in my quest log. If he didn't respond to the usual prompt, that meant this was the type of quest you were supposed to arrive at after hearing stories from all over town. Following the proper trail would give us the right keyword to engage him, but since we'd used Argo's supernatural sense of smell to sniff out the quest, we'd bypassed the natural process, and I didn't know what I should say to advance the story.

Perhaps we ought to withdraw and go collect information. But since we'd spent our time and fifty col to get here, it would be a waste to leave empty-handed.

I looked around the large room, hoping to find some kind of hint.

In a properly cleaned place, anything out of line would be apparent quite soon, but this room was anything but. There were so many weird items, it was impossible to tell which one might be a hint to the story. Wall hangings of huge fish, stacks of animal pelts, rusty harpoons, lumber of all sizes, pots with unknown contents, oars snapped in the middle...I couldn't make any kind of guesses, other than that he was a former sailor.

Just as I was about to give up and do this thing the right way, Asuna spoke.

"You really shouldn't leave things like this on the floor, sir."

She picked up something off the ground right next to the leg of the rocking chair—a half-rusted nail about four inches long. It had probably fallen out of the decrepit old chair.

The man took a look at the nail in her hand and snorted angrily

for some reason, then tilted back more of his drink. Asuna looked
back to me for help, but I could only grimace.

"Just put it on the table or something."

"Okay..."

She nodded and moved her arm to drop it.

But I snatched the nail away without thinking.

"Ack! Wh-what?!"

"Hang on...This isn't just a nail. It's...not a throwing pick,
either. It's a square nail...Where have I seen something like this
before?" I muttered to myself, pieces of information connecting
within my brain.

Large double doors facing the water. Leather and wood inside
the room. A collection of items I'd seen in a real-life museum
years ago. A quest that didn't exist in the beta.

This old man's not a former sailor.

I faced him head-on and took a deep breath.

"Sir, can you build us a boat?"

3

I HAD THOUGHT THIS QUEST WOULD BE A PAIN IN THE ass, but I was wrong.

It was more than just a pain in the ass. It was an indescribable, monumental, unprecedented pain in the ass. That was the only way to classify our first quest on the fourth floor: the "Shipwright of Yore."

"Listen…we can't take this thing with us to any other floor, so what's the harm in a little bit of compromise?" I pleaded, but Asuna would have none of it.

"No. If he's going to make us a ship, it's going to be the best it can possibly be."

"Fine, fine. By the way, the word *ship* is a bit ostentatious for what we're getting. A gondola is really more of a boat."

"Fine, it'll be the best boat it can possibly be!"

We were making our way through a forest at night.

Unlike the dry, desolate tinder of the beta, the large forest to the southeast of Rovia was now brimming with life. The way the branches and leaves practically blotted out the sky was very similar to the forests of the third floor, but the ground underfoot was much different. The thick, wet moss swallowed the soles of our boots with every step, making traversal quite difficult. On top of that, little springs were everywhere, and I'd already stepped into deep water four times in our three hours of searching.

The reason I wasn't paying attention to my footing was because we were looking up above us as we traveled. Asuna was doing the same, but I never saw her step in water or trip on any tree roots. Had to be a high-resistance value to stumbling or an excellent real-life Luck stat.

If it was the latter, we ought to be finding our target by now, I thought resentfully. We were not on the hunt for delectable fruits and nuts or bee's nests full of sweet honey. We were looking for four-pronged claw marks on the tree trunks—territorial markings of the gray bear that ruled over this forest.

We'd already defeated over ten normal-size black bears since entering the woods. It was "bear fat" that the old shipwright demanded from us, so the quest would obviously proceed perfectly fine with the fat those ordinary black bears dropped. In that sense, the amount of trouble this quest represented was determined by the player him- or herself.

And Asuna was dead set on the fat of the king of the woods, whose existence the old man had briefly hinted at. It was highly likely that the quality of the item we brought back would have an effect on the quality of the boat.

"Still, I'm a bit surprised. I didn't think that you would feel so strongly about this sort of thing, Asuna," I said, scanning for claw marks by the light of the moon. Her response came from the right.

"What sort of thing?"

"Oh...this sort of scenario happens a lot in RPGs. You don't have to get the best possible result in order to beat the challenge, but if the player wants to, she can strive for it. I guess it's a completionist thing?"

"Well, I don't like the way that it sounds like I'm being taken advantage of...but I wasn't thinking about any game mechanics or design. I just thought, that old man might be gruff and

unfriendly, but he probably really wants to make one more perfect boat."

"...I see."

At that point, there was no use demanding compromise
from her.

Just over three hours ago, once we'd successfully turned the *!*
mark over the old NPC's head into a *?*, he exhaled a long pull of
smoke from his pipe.

"I'm not a shipwright anymore. The Water Carriers Guild controls all the materials a shipwright needs to build boats. But if
you still want one...first go to the forest to the southeast and
get some bear fat, to seal the wood against water. But if you run
across the bear king, best run and save your own hide. I'm sure
his fat would be best of all, though..."

There was plenty in that opening speech to be curious about,
but the old man closed his eyes and showed no interest in elabo-
ration, so we left the house, hailed another gondola on the move,
then left the town via the south gate en route to our current
location.

The king of the bears did exist in the beta, and I did track down
his claw marks back then, but I never ran across it in the end. But
from what I heard, there were a number of full six-member parties who were scattered by the bear's wrath.

It was nerve-racking to be tracking down such a deadly foe
with only the two of us, but we were already a far higher level
than I'd been at this point in the beta, and a bear was a bear. It
wasn't going to be blowing fire or venom at us and had no sword
skills. The attack patterns wouldn't be much different from a normal bear...hopefully...but it would be best if Asuna gave up on
this crazy idea...and I was getting hungry again...

And after hundreds of times looking up at the trees, my mind
vacillating between optimism and pessimism, I finally saw...

"..."

A clear pattern of four deep horizontal grooves. I looked ahead at Asuna's back, and after a brief moment of hesitation, I made up my mind and called out to her.

"Hey, I found it."

"What, really?!"

She raced back instantly and looked up at the spot where I pointed, face bright with expectation.

"You're right! So if we just wait next to this tree, the bear will eventually pop nearby?"

"Supposedly."

"Let's take a break here, then. We'll need to check...our... potions..."

Her high-speed chatter slowed to a halt, so I looked over to see what was the matter. Her slender eyebrows were knitted in concern as she stared at the fresh markings. When she spoke again, her voice was 30 percent quieter.

"...Um, Kirito? Those marks are a whole lot higher on the tree than I was expecting..."

"Eh?"

I looked back at the claw marks and calculated their height from the ground. Seven...fifteen...twenty...twenty-five feet tall.

"...What kind of bear scratches a tree at that height?"

"Well, it would have to be a bear that stands...twenty-five feet...tall..."

"...That doesn't sound like a bear anymore..."

As our conversation got quieter and quieter, a heavy *thud* behind us shook the forest.

I slowly turned around, terrified of what I might find, to see the shadow of a small mountain just inches away.

Each gray hair was as thick as a needle. Two red eyes gleamed in the dark. Fierce fangs poked from its mouth. Claws like daggers protruded from limbs as burly as logs. And on its forehead, black, sharp, gleaming...horns.

"...Yep, that's not a bear. It has horns," I muttered. Above the head of the creature that looked like a bear, but was not a bear, a deep crimson red cursor appeared with the name MAGNATHERIUM.

"Grglololo..."

The growl it uttered was nothing at all like a bear's. It shuffled and stood up vertically. The beast's trunk, which seemed to extend forever, blocked out the moonlight and shrouded us in darkness. Those gleaming eyes at the very top of the black shadow did indeed seem to be at least twenty-five feet tall.

"...Stay calm, Asuna," I whispered frantically. "It can't be that agile with a size this big. Keep a tree between you and it at all times, so it can't charge you."

This order came from the knowledge that the black bears we'd been fighting until now had liked to perform direct charge attacks. My partner nodded and we both drew our blades. Asuna's Chivalric Rapier +5 and my Anneal Blade +8 began to glow faintly.

The Magnatherium growled again in response to the light and opened its massive jaws. Asuna and I both hopped backward and retreated behind a large, ancient tree. If the Magnatherium charged headfirst into the trunk, that should stun it for a brief moment. Then we could each hit it with a single skill and gauge how much damage that caused.

Within a single second, my idea was shot to pieces.

Red light flickered deep in the Magnatherium's throat. It was a beautiful but deadly effect that I had seen on a far higher floor in the beta—but for the first time since we'd been trapped in this game of death.

The pre-effect for fire breath.

I immediately abandoned the option of hiding behind the shelter of the tree trunk. Unlike the lightning breath of Asterios the Taurus King on the second floor, fire could make its way around obstacles to an extent. Even if the tree itself stood tall against the blaze, we could easily be charred to a crisp behind it.

Perhaps a sideways dash, then. But the Magnatherium's red eyes followed us perfectly. If we ran to the side, it could simply change the direction of its blast. There must be a more reliable method of evasion...

"This way!"

On a sudden burst of inspiration, I grabbed Asuna's slender body with my left arm and jumped directly backward. One, two, three steps, and I was at the right spot. It was one of the little natural springs, small but deep, that had plagued me during our search.

At the same moment that I jumped into the water without hesitation, orange flames burst from the Magnatherium's jaws.

Just after my entire body was engulfed in chilly water, the surface of the water turned red. I pushed Asuna down to the bottom of the spring and tried to shrink down as much as I could.

The flames licked and howled for close to five seconds, bringing the near-freezing spring water up to lukewarm. For a moment, I was afraid it might eventually reach boiling temperature, but the breath finally abated right as it reached the point of a hot bath. As soon as the surface above us went dark, we leaped out.

As soon as she stepped onto solid ground, her long hair and cape hem dripping profusely, Asuna muttered, "That is *definitely* not a bear."

"Definitely not," I agreed, scanning the surroundings.

The Magnatherium hadn't moved spots, but the terrain in front of it was blackened and smoking. The tree I'd thought to use as cover was still standing, but it was charred and ashen now. As I feared, the flames had covered the backside.

"What do you think? Should we run?" I asked, recognizing that it was very dangerous to challenge such a deadly foe without any preparation or forehand knowledge. But Asuna didn't bite immediately.

"...We don't have to force ourselves to fight it, but I at least want to collect a bit more intel. We should learn more about the bear's attacks so we can beat it next time."

"..."

I thought fast, watching the Magnatherium closely as it slowly stirred sixty feet away.

As long as there was a nearby spring to jump into, we could evade those fire attacks without damage, and it probably didn't have any other special skills to watch out for. Its physical attacks were no doubt quite dangerous, based on those knifelike claws, but we could shield ourselves with trees against those.

"...All right. Let's start retreating back for town and take down some good data."

"Deal."

Meanwhile, the Magnatherium began advancing. It started off as gentle four-legged ambling, but then, as though a switch had flipped, it began to charge. The sight of that imposing figure, over twelve feet tall at the shoulder—about the size of the Bullbous Bow from the second floor—racing along and pounding the earth, was nothing short of sheer terror.

"Not only does it have its own name, I'm starting to think it's actually the field boss!"

"At the very least, it's definitely not a bear!" Asuna hissed as we ran. We circled around to the right of the Magnatherium, hoping to evade the path of its charge, but it simply turned and followed.

We weren't just running blindly, though. Once we'd maneuvered so that a large old oak stood between us, we held that position.

"Come on...do your worst!"

If it charged headfirst into the six-foot-wide tree, that should at least stop it for several seconds. But two seconds later, my bracing challenge turned to shock.

"No way!"

As I expected, the Magnatherium charged straight for us and collided with the tree at maximum speed, but like some horrid giant's hammer, the thick, short horns on its forehead crushed the wide trunk of the tree into splinters.

Thankfully, it did stop the charge short, but the demon bear wasn't stunned. It roared powerfully on the other side of the tilting tree.

"Gyazgruoahhh!!"

My ears ringing with the tremendous volume of its bellowing, I whispered to Asuna, "Hey, what are a bear's natural enemies?"

"First of all, it's not a bear...but in real life, the larger bears have no enemies. They might be brought down by a tiger or killer whale every once in a while, though."

"W-well, that's just great. Any weaknesses?"

"Why are you asking me? Um...I think I read in a book once that their snouts are sensitive..."

"The snout," I repeated, staring hard at the Magnatherium as it began to move again.

The beast's forehead was protected by those hardy horns, but its black snout was defenseless. On the other hand, even on all fours, it was at least ten feet off the ground, so I couldn't even hit it with my sword. I might be able to hit it with a jumping-type sword skill, but if it reacted to my attack and stood up, we were screwed.

"What I wouldn't give for a good magic spell, some ice magic with physical effects, slamming down giant icicles or something. At least then I'd be able to crit him a few times..."

"How about rather than imagining things that will never happen, you decide what we should do?!" Asuna demanded, shattering my fragile hopes and dreams. Somehow she had opened her window to the map screen. It was set to be visible to party members, so I leaned in for a look.

We were currently smack in the center of the woods to the southeast of Rovia. There were sheer cliffs to the north and east, beyond which was the usual river. The map was grayed out, but if my memory from the beta served, there were cliffs to the south as well. There was a good fifty yards of distance from the forest to the surface of the water, so even if it was the river below, I didn't know if we could survive the fall.

In other words, jumping into the river to escape wasn't an option. We had to leave the forest to the west and escape into the safe haven of Rovia...

"Hey." Asuna tugged on my sleeve, drawing my glance from the map to her face. "It seems like the bear goes immobile for a little bit after blowing its fire breath and knocking down trees."

"…"

I looked at the Magnatherium on her suggestion. The giant bear, which had just knocked over a giant tree with its horns alone, was not exactly stunned, but stood in place, grunting and growling. It would surely attack if we got closer, but as Asuna noted, after both the breath attack and the tree charge, it had stopped moving for a time.

In other words, if we could make use of that habit, it might not be that hard to escape.

"That's weakness number one…if you can even call it a weakness," I mumbled.

It was a useful habit to take advantage of when escaping, but it was no use when trying to defeat the beast, because we still needed to get closer to attack. Besides, there were only so many major trees with enough bulk to stop the bear. If we stayed in one area, it would eventually knock them all over…

At that point, I noticed something odd.

It had nothing to do with me, Asuna, or the Magnatherium. Over near the creature, the fallen tree trunk was still partially there, even though its roots and branches had shattered like glass and disappeared already.

It was a game object that fell to the ground but stayed there rather than vanishing. That meant it was an item that could be picked up.

"Um, Asuna, how much storage space do you still have?" I asked, then remembered that she had filled her capacity with small articles of underwear.

But Asuna seemed to understand exactly what I was thinking about.

"I've got enough space. Remember when I told you that I'd returned most of the clothes I sewed to train my Tailoring skill back into cloth?"

"Ah yes. Of course. Well, if you don't mind, when I lead the bear away, can you go and pick up the log at its feet and check the item name and whether or not you have enough room for it?"

There was suspicion in her eyes, but Asuna didn't argue.

"Sure."

At that exact moment, the Magnatherium burst into life again. About fifty seconds had passed since it crashed into the tree. I recalled a pause of around twenty-five seconds after its fire breath, which certainly left enough time for us to escape if we made use of it.

I patted her on the left arm in a show of support and darted out of the undergrowth we'd been using as cover.

"Over here, you overgrown teddy!" I shouted, running around the right side of the monster. The Magnatherium spun with an agility that belied its massive bulk and stomped after me, rumbling the ground with every step.

When not using its special charge attack, the monster was just a bit slower than me. The problem was the treacherous terrain of damp moss and tangled roots that threatened a slip or trip at any moment. I guided the bear to the north, paying as much attention as I possibly could to the ground before me.

Once I knew I was at least thirty yards away from Asuna, I stopped and turned around.

I didn't expect to beat the creature on my first attempt, but I at least wanted to get a sense of how to fight it. I clutched my Anneal Blade and waited for the bear to descend on me.

"*Gyoglrugul!*" it roared, utterly nonmammalian. The Magnatherium's front right arm swung up high, the limb thicker than a human body.

The claws gleamed hungrily as they caught the pale moonlight.

As the paw came roaring down at me, I shot back the sword skill Slant. The thick blade, glowing light blue, clashed with the four claws in midair. A tremendous shock wave ran through my avatar's arms, shoulders, hips, and legs.

I was knocked back by the powerful collision and my back smashed against a tree, but I was still standing.

The Magnatherium would not have been knocked over, of course, but its front paw was still floating in the air from the momentum of my strike. So at the very least, I could use a sword skill to deflect an ordinary attack. On the other hand, given that my Anneal Blade +8 had four extra points to sharpness and four to durability, a lesser blade would probably not stand up to the shock.

I checked my feet and glanced at both HP gauges. The enemy was unharmed, of course. I'd taken a bit of damage from slamming into the tree behind me, but it was nothing serious.

"Now it's my turn," I growled and stepped forward.

The Magnatherium's eyes flashed red, though it couldn't have recognized my challenge. It snorted and pulled both front legs off the ground, slowly standing to an erect position.

I sensed that more fire breath was coming, and I looked behind me. There was a small blue water surface gleaming to the back of the grove. If I jumped into it, I could evade the fire breath like the last time, but fear rooted my feet to the spot.

The massive, twenty-foot-plus gray monster sucked in a wheezing breath like a bellows and opened its jaws wide.

In that instant, I darted *forward* rather than back. I knew that it could follow flanking maneuvers without a problem, but I hadn't tested its backside yet. Once I was halfway to the bear, I sensed a red light above. I kept running at full speed, evading the breath as it bore down with another earsplitting roar.

When the flames hit the ground just behind me, they created a burning tailwind that buffeted my back.

"Yeowww!" I wailed, but made good use of the extra boost to close the last few yards and burst right through the Magnatherium's tree-trunk-size legs. Once I was behind the bear, I hit the brakes and spun around.

As I was hoping, the bear didn't turn around, but stayed forward, blowing its fire breath.

This is my chance!

I pulled back my trusty sword and set my target. Aiming right for its barrel-size but still short and bearlike tail, I readied the thrusting sword skill, Sonic Leap.

Glowing yellow green in the darkness, I let the game system's automatic assistance propel me forward until my sword met the bear's tail about ten feet off the ground.

There was a satisfying resistance to the blow. The bear's massive bulk arched and the fire attack abruptly stopped, leaving little traces of flame that fell through the air to the ground.

As I did a backflip and landed, the beast let out a high-pitched squeal.

"Zigyawrl!!"

It lowered its paws to the ground and began to run straight ahead. Once it had taken a considerable distance, it finally turned to look back.

There was red burning rage in its eyes now—while it wasn't the snout, the tail seemed to be a critical point of its own. I checked on the Magnatherium's cursor as it retreated and noticed that the HP bar was lowered—not much, but enough.

"...Nice!"

I pumped my fist at the first proper chunk of damage I'd inflicted so far.

"No, it's not nice," came a familiar voice from the rear. I spun around to my left and saw my temporary partner with a cold gaze on her face.

"You said you were running away, and now I see you fighting the thing?"

"Er...no, I'm just collecting info," I started to explain, then remembered what I'd asked her to do moments before. "Oh, right. What about the log?"

"I picked it up and put it in my inventory. I can probably fit another five logs in there. It's called a Noblewood Core."

"..."

I processed that information within a second. "I'm betting that's another gondola material, just like the bear fat."

"Huh...?"

"Listen, you might be tired of me trying to predict these things, but I can tell that this is one of those quests that forces you to visit the same spot several times. We take the bear fat back to the old man, he tells us we need wood next. There's probably one or two other ingredients we need in these woods on top of that."

"Meaning...just like with the fat, there might be normal and fancy versions of wood?" Asuna asked. As usual, she was a quick learner.

"I bet you can get the normal type of wood by cutting down any old tree with an ax. But I bet the fancy stuff can only be harvested from trees that are big enough that you'd need the Lumber skill to chop them down."

"...Then we have no choice but to build up that skill."

Asuna really was dead serious on taking every last step to ensure we got the best possible boat. "Oh, but the log I picked up did say it was 'Noblewood.' Does that mean it's actually pretty fancy?"

"Yeah. See, they set up a way for you to get the luxury stuff without needing the Lumber skill. You just have to use the overgrown teddy..."

Right as I said that, the overgrown teddy was recovering from the damage of its hurt tail. It started loping toward us on all fours, then lowered its horns for another charge attack.

"Here it comes! Find a big tree..."

"Over there," Asuna said, pointing to the southwest while I was distracted watching the bear. She had indeed found a tree that was just as big as the one the bear had pulverized minutes ago, looming black against the night sky.

"Okay, now we need to get it to—"

"To charge into the tree, I know. Then I'll pick up the log, and you go and guide it toward the next big tree. Got it."

"Uh...r-right."

* * *

Driven in a way that I'd never seen before, Asuna gave most of the orders as we coordinated to eventually cause twelve bear-on-tree collisions.

The number of Noblewood Cores that dropped from each tree was randomly determined between zero and three, which caused us both frustration and elation, and once we were comfortable with leading the bear around, both of us had essentially maxed out our storage capacity. I couldn't help but fall back on that old curse, *If only I'd chosen the Inventory Space Expansion...*

"I don't know if this will be enough for the shipwright, but we can't carry any more than this anyway. Once we get him sitting again, let's break away and return to town," I whispered to my partner.

"We still don't have the fat, though," she pointed out.

I grimaced at the sky. "R-right...crap. And the quest won't advance unless we give him that. And I suppose compromising with normal bear fat is—"

"Out of the question."

"Of course," I agreed, crestfallen. I used the Magnatherium's current post-charge sitting state to check on its HP status.

I'd taken the time to attack its tail and legs a few times during our careful manipulation, and while it was tempting to think that I'd *already* got it down to *only* 90 percent, the truth was that it *still* had almost 90 percent left. If I was serious about defeating the creature, I had to abandon the evasion-centric plan we'd been following and risk danger to challenge it in close combat.

The Magnatherium would only charge when there was enough distance between it at the target, but I knew from experience that it would breathe fire at point-blank range. I wasn't guaranteed to successfully dash through its legs each time, and neither was there any guarantee that I'd find a spring nearby. Based on how much heat the water had absorbed in those attempts, I couldn't just stick close to one particular well and reuse it.

Asuna read my mind. "There's a series of four springs in close succession over there. If you use them in order, you might be able to keep evading the fire."

"Ah, great."

Her powers of observation and decision making were second to none, as usual. But I had my doubts. I asked the fencer something that was weighing on my mind.

"Asuna. You're not just...being stubborn, right?"

"Huh...?"

I glanced over at her and elaborated.

"The old man wants to build the best boat possible. So you want to get him the best materials you can—that's what you said. But if that sentiment is something the game is making you say, because you don't want to let it win, to make you feel like you're not good enough...then I don't think we should fight that bear. Victory in this game, in this world, isn't completing quests with the best result..."

"It's to survive," she finished in a faint whisper. "Don't worry, I'm not focusing on the results. The biggest motive for doing this is that I think you and I can beat that bear."

My only response to that was to smile awkwardly.

"Then promise me one thing. The next time I tell you to run, you do it instantly, without argument."

"All right," she responded instantly. I was ready—we'd observed the deadly Magnatherium for over twenty minutes, and its patterns weren't really that complex. We could win, as long as we kept our concentration strong.

"When it comes to close combat, I'll deflect its attacks with sword skills, and you can switch in for a single attack. Don't push your luck, even if you think you can get another sword skill in."

"Got it."

"So...shall we?"

We readied ourselves at the same time that the bear recovered from its prone position. I stared down the giant beast as it lumbered closer on all fours, shutting all unnecessary thoughts out of my head.

I squeezed my trusty sword and launched off the soggy ground toward the concentrated spring area that Asuna had found.

4

I HAD BEEN NAIVE.

I never realized it was quite that strong.

Truly astonishing precision and power. It was the only possible description for the combination of Asuna's sword skills and Chivalric Rapier +5.

"See? I told you we could win," she commented with a grin at the end of our fifty-minute battle with the beast—half of which was simply running around to get it to knock over trees. I could only gaze up at her.

While she did seem a bit tired, it was nothing compared to my slumped exhaustion. She spryly checked on her dropped items. When she hit the newly acquired items tab, she let out a brief squeal of excitement.

"Ooh, wow! I got four Legendary Bear Fats. There's also some pelts, claws, and...what's this? Fire-Bear's Palm?"

"I wouldn't materialize that if I were you. It's bound to be disgusting," I warned, heaving myself up to a standing position to open my own window.

I had three more deposits of bear fat. That had to be enough for the quest. I also had fur and claws, though no paw, for better or for worse. Instead, there was one Fire-Bear's Horn. That must be one of the horns from the Magnetherium's forehead.

With one last glance at the time, I closed my menu and yawned.

It was past eleven at night, and though I'd gotten some sleep in the afternoon, I was now completely fatigued.

"Umm...Asuna?"

"What?"

"When we get back to town, are you going to report on the quest immediately?"

"Of course I am."

"Of course you are."

If only the old shipwright is actually awake, I thought.

On the way back to town, we only had one enemy encounter against the plant monster Gaudy Nepenthes, so the return trip to Rovia's southern gate was rather painless. We hailed one of the gondolas, which were apparently open for business twenty-four hours a day, and headed to the northwest sector of town.

By the time we reached the old man's house, it was 11:50, but the window was still lit, so we knocked without hesitation. As usual, the ancient shipwright was sunk into his rocking chair, alternating endlessly between bottle and pipe.

"We brought the bear fat," Asuna said, producing the bear fat, which fortunately materialized in a small jar, rather than open to the air. The old man twitched an eyebrow.

"That stink...You got the king's fat, didn't ya?"

The whiskey bottle fell to the floor. His sinewy hand snatched the jar of grease away, and with a little jingle, our quest logs updated.

"Hmph. But this ain't enough."

He set the jar down on the nearby table with a *thunk*. I shared a look with Asuna and brought out a jar of my own this time. The old man still shook his head, and for a moment I was terrified that we might have to fight the bear monster again, but at last, at the fourth jar, the chime sounded again.

"Hmph. Very well. You really want this old bag of bones to build you a ship, eh?"

"Of course. We need your help, sir!" Asuna pleaded, not that he could truly be moved by that. The old man set his pipe on the table and raised his hands. His fingers, scarred and tattered, wiggled in the air vibrantly for a moment, then fell and dangled again.

"...As I told you, the Water Carriers Guild controls all of the supplies now. To make you a boat, I'll need a whole lot of lumber. And that's solid birch or oak from the southeast forest."

He paused for dramatic effect, then continued.

"But the greatest of shipbuilding lumber is teak. I can make you a truly sturdy craft if you can deliver me the solid core of a massive, aged teak. Then again, it might be beyond the ability of amateur lumberjacks..."

The quest log updated, initiating part two of the "Shipwright of Yore." Asuna and I promptly went to our menus, producing Noblewood Cores.

The instant the reddened logs clunked down in a big stack, I thought I detected the old man's eyes briefly going wide. Nah, had to be my imagination.

By the time the elderly shipbuilder got up from his chair to start building the two-seat gondola we ordered, Asuna and I had unloaded four Legendary Bear Fats, eight Noblewood Cores, six Fire-Bear Claws—to be treated and carved into nails—and two Fire-Bear Pelts for upholstering the seats.

I watched the old man carefully, relieved that we had enough of everything we needed. He crossed the cluttered room and stopped in front of a door on the south wall, then pulled a key from his pocket to remove the sturdy lock.

The heavy door thunked open to reveal a carpentry storeroom. I spotted massive saws, hammers, chisels, and planes crammed into the space, all of them polished to a shine.

"To think I'd have a chance to use these again one day," the old man muttered wistfully.

You'll probably have a flood of orders by tomorrow, I thought to myself. Asuna and I appeared to be the only ones currently working on the "Shipwright of Yore," but we weren't going to be keeping it a secret. The members of the Dragon Knights and Liberation Squad were out there swimming in the canals and rivers to complete the various quest tasks outside of town.

I couldn't help but wish I could tell those proud front-runners, chanting in a line with their swim trunks and floaty tubes, but we ought to report our findings to Argo soon so she could disseminate the information. As a beater already, I had no fear of a bad reputation, but I didn't want Asuna to suffer on my account.

After all, she'd already earned a lot of attention for the power of her Chivalric Rapier in the third-floor boss battle. If the word got out that she had a de facto extra skill slot thanks to the Crystal Bottle of Kales'Oh, the two main powers of the front line would get truly serious about recruiting her. They might even...

The old man's returning footsteps snapped me out of my thoughts. I looked up to see him laying out a massive scroll on the tabletop. He smacked the pure white parchment with a hand and said, "Tell me how you want your boat built."

The quest log updated and brought up a purple window before our eyes. It appeared to be a gondola design dialog, full of text input fields and pull-down menus. At the very top, my name and Asuna's were listed under the "owner" field. The quest must have been designed to give shared ownership rights to the entire party.

"What is this?" Asuna asked, craning her neck over. I thought I detected a glint in her eyes. "Oooh, wow. So even on a two-seater, we can decide its shape and color and name and everything!"

She reached out with a finger to explore the options, and I scooted over to make room for her, but the window followed me.

"Hang on," I said, bringing up the party settings menu and switching the leader position to Asuna. The quest progress was shared between all party members, but in many cases, spots where detailed decisions had to be made were restricted to just the leader.

Now that she had inherited control from me, Asuna had stars in her eyes.

"What color should we go with? It looks like we've got a whole RGB circle to choose from."

"I don't care about the color...You choose, Asuna."

"Nuh-uh, the ownership is for the both of us, so we have to discuss and choose properly."

"Er, right...In that case, I pick bla—"

"No black! I feel like it would just sink right away."

"Oh...okay. Well, then..."

I just wanted to get it over with so we could return to the inn, but she would know—and be angry—if I didn't take it seriously, so I tried to be logical.

"Umm...well, the ship isn't going to fit into our item storage, which means we'll need to tie it up wherever we leave it. Perhaps a color that sticks out at night would be good. Something white or orange..."

"I see. I think white would be nice—but not pure white, that's boring. Maybe something closer to ivory."

"I-I don't see why not."

"Let's see...right about here," Asuna said, tracing the color circle with her finger until she had selected a regal ivory white. No sooner had I sighed with relief than several other submenus appeared, asking for the off colors that would adorn the prow, stern, decorations, sides, and seats of the ship.

"Um, I'll just leave the rest of these up to you."

"Oh, fine...I'll pick them all out, then," Asuna said in apparent annoyance, despite the continuing presence of stars in her eyes. I backed away from her and sat down on a round chair next to the table.

The old man, who was still patiently holding open the ship plans on the table, grumbled, "It's always been said that a young lady takes three times as long to design her ship."

"Uh...I see. That's...good to know," I remarked.

Ultimately, it wasn't until one o'clock in the morning that the detailed coloring, ship design with various cosmetic features, placement and shape of seats, and other details were finalized. But when Asuna turned to me, she didn't seem tired in the least.

"Lastly, let's give our boat a name."

"Uh…a n-name, huh…?"

To be honest, I had zero faith in my naming ability. Even my character name, Kirito, was just a rearranging of my real name.

"Umm…I will *also* leave that to your discretion," I offered hopefully, but to my surprise, Asuna looked deep in thought already.

"As a matter of fact, I had a great name come to me earlier."

"Oh…like what?"

"Well, I read that in many foreign countries, they give boats female names…and it occurred to me that we should name it after Kizmel's sister."

My eyes went wide with surprise.

The Dark Elf knight Kizmel, whom we met on the third floor, had told me the story of her past in front of a gravestone in the back corner of their camp. She had a younger sister, an herbalist, who died in a battle with the Forest Elves.

And her name was…

"Tilnel, right? So it would be the *Tilnel*…Why not?" I said, nodding. Asuna beamed back at me.

She typed in the letters into the field at the top of the window one at a time, then beckoned me over.

"Is this spelling right?"

I stood up from the chair and looked at what she had typed: *Tilnel*. I nodded.

"Then let's push the FINALIZE button together."

"Whuh?!"

"What? You don't want to?"

"Er, no, it's not that, of course," I said, shaking my head. I reached out my index finger toward the button on the lower right. Asuna did the same, then looked over at me, mouthing the words, *"Ready, set…"*

Just as we were about to slam on the button together, I grabbed her hand and shouted, "No, wait!"

"Wh-what?!"

"Look, this field is still empty..."

I pointed out a drop-down menu titled Optional Equipment. Asuna looked at it and shrugged.

"Oh, that. Well, it didn't have any options in it."

She poked the menu to show that the listing that appeared was indeed empty. It probably meant that we didn't have items that could be equipped on the boat.

"Hmm...Do you mind if I check it myself, just in case?"

"Go ahead."

With her permission, I reverted back to leader. When I checked the drop-down menu for myself—

"Ooh, there's something there!"

"Huh? What is it?!"

We stuck our faces together cheek to cheek to peer into the small window, which featured a single option.

"Fire-Bear's Horn...?"

I felt a terrible premonition rise in my chest as I read the words. Asuna looked concerned as well.

"Horn...like the kind of horn that the old galleys used to feature? Why would a gondola need something like that?"

"I don't know that you would *need* it yet. Especially since it seems like the options don't show up unless you have the necessary items already..."

After thinking it over, I figured that it was best just to ask, so I looked to the old man at the side of the table.

"Um..." I started, then realized that I didn't know what to call him. I checked the NPC's color cursor and saw that his name was Romolo.

"Um, Mr. Romolo. Will we need this optional horn?"

I tried to make my question as simple as possible just in case, but old Romolo did not respond at once. I was afraid I'd asked him something his parameters were unable to answer, but he snorted before I could rephrase the question.

"You won't need it if you're only going to ride around Rovia. But if you row out there, you might need it eventually."

"Meaning...we might need to fight monsters with the boat?"

"Perhaps you will...perhaps you won't," he said unhelpfully. He smacked the spread-out parchment again. "At any rate, this is your ship. It's your decision whether to attach the horn or not."

"..."

My partner and I shared another look. Asuna spoke up first.

"You're the one who has the materials, Kirito, so I'll let you decide."

"Uh, r-really?"

"Well, you let me pick out pretty much everything else about the boat, so I'll let you have one thing at the end."

It sounded snarky coming out of her lips, but there was real concern somewhere in her heart. Or at least, I imagined there was.

"Hmm...I'm not sure if I like the idea of putting a big ugly weapon on our gondola. But it would be worse if the ship got sunk because we didn't put it on. Maybe it was fate that we happened to get an exclusive bear-horn drop. Let's do it."

"Okay," Asuna agreed.

I added, "Plus, since I'm sure the horn is likely to be attached beneath the waterline, we won't have to look at it most of the time. So let's set the horn as active, and..."

I put my hand over the FINISH button again. We counted down again and actually pressed it this time.

The window closed with an imposing, stately noise and the old man began to draw a three-dimensional model of the ship on the parchment. Within just a few seconds, he was done, and the word *Tilnel* was written at the top in dark black ink.

Romolo ceremoniously picked up the parchment and nodded in satisfaction.

"Now I will retreat into my workshop. Be patient, and I will inform you when I'm done with my work."

And rolling up the parchment into a scroll again, the elderly craftsman disappeared into the tool room. The door shut and a very heavy vibration ran through the floor. Apparently his entire storeroom was an elevator.

I *really* wanted to see his workshop, but I didn't want to risk getting yelled at and possibly ruining the quest, so I gave up on sneaking in and yawned instead.

"Mmmm...Man, this has been a long day."

"I wonder how long it takes to finish up a boat," Asuna wondered impatiently.

I grinned wryly. "In the real world it probably takes months, but here it might be a day at the worst...even shorter, I bet—three hours, five hours. If we announce the details of the quest, people will be beating down his door trying to get their own ships."

"I wonder what happens in that case. Will it be like the Dark Elf camp on the third floor...an instance thingy? Where there's as many versions of this house as there are players?"

"I don't know, this is the middle of town...I bet that if someone's currently in the middle of the quest, the door just won't open..."

"Wait...you meant that if it takes three hours, the next person just has to stand there and wait outside the house?"

"More like three and a half, when you count the time for design choices. So that means at maximum, he could only serve six or seven groups in a day...Then again, three hours is just a hunch, so it might be shorter..."

I shrugged and Asuna gave me an indescribable look.

"The thing about your hunches is they're eerily correct."

"S-sorry..."

"Don't apologize to *me*. Thanks to you, we got ours out of the way first...Well, let's trust that three hours is right and make our way back to the inn."

"That's the problem. It just occurred to me while I was talking to you that if we leave this house, it might treat the ship transaction as its own new quest..."

"...Meaning that if we find out it's ready and race over, and another party's already in progress with their own quest, we'll just have to wait outside the house until they're done?"

"I think it's quite possible. I mean, if the door remains closed until the person comes back to get the completed ship and nobody ever returns, it would mean no one can ever start the quest after you."

"...I see," Asuna nodded slowly. She took a look around the messy room. "Which means...we have no choice but to wait here until it's finished."

"Yep..."

I looked around as well and wondered where Mr. Romolo slept. There was no bed, sofa, or blanket to be seen. The doors went to the entrance and the workshop, and I didn't get the sense there were any secret doors.

After a scan of the room, both of our sets of eyes eventually landed on the large rocking chair that Romolo had been sitting in not too long ago. It was the only spot in the room that seemed to support any kind of sleep.

I brushed aside a brief moment of temptation and made a gentlemanly offer.

"I can just sleep on the floor if you want the rocking chair."

"...But..."

In her profile, I saw even more hesitation than when we were deciding whether or not to attach the horn to the gondola. She was probably trying to be considerate to me, but didn't have the courage to sleep on the dusty floor. It was a very fitting concern for fastidious Asuna.

"It's fine, really. Compared to camping out in the safe rooms of the labyrinths, I'm just glad this place has a roof. Besides, I have a personal skill of sleeping wherever I want. You just relax and take the rocking cha—"

"We can both squeeze into it," she said, cutting off the second part of my gentleman's offer.

"Eh?"

"It's a big rocking chair. If we turn sideways, the two of us can fit on it."

Sideways?!

Wait, not that part.

The two of us?!

My memory of the inn room in Zumfut on the third floor was still fresh, where Asuna pitched an unidentified fruit directly into my head. She already had a powerful personal barrier to begin with, and now she was suggesting that we squeeze together into a cramped rocking chair.

I couldn't decide: to thankfully decline or to take her up on the offer? Eventually she turned away in a huff, put her rapier into her item storage, then sat on the leather rocking chair and turned ninety degrees to face the outside.

"I'll go ahead and start getting some sleep. If you want to use the empty space, you're welcome to it," she announced, her back to me, then fell silent.

After a full two minutes of standing still, I snuck over to the chair. I was curious to see if Asuna was actually sleeping or not, but that would require circling around to her side and that seemed like crossing a line.

Inside, I put a hand to the bars of the backrest and pushed slightly. The chair rocked back and forth with a faint squeaking. Asuna did not move or react.

At this point, I truly had no idea what to do. My mind was a blank as the chair continued to swing, when—

"Mmh..."

Asuna grunted and fell over in my direction. Her eyes were shut firmly. If I focused, I could hear the sound of sleep breathing coming from her barely parted lips. She was definitely asleep now.

It was a wonder to me that the fencer, who'd been so sensitive when I met her on the first floor, was now so bold...but then I changed my mind.

At the time she'd been telling me I had a choice whether to use the chair or not, the fatigue must have been beating her down. She only made that offer because she didn't want me to realize how close she was to a sleep log-out—though that MMO term did not apply to Aincrad anymore.

I couldn't blame her. In the morning, she'd left the inn and raced through the third-floor labyrinth tower until we reached the floor boss. After the battle, we climbed to the fourth floor, floated down the river, and engaged in that mad chase with the sharklike tadpole thing; had a brief rest in town before starting the shipbuilding quest, battling several monsters, and finishing it off against a giant fire-breathing bear as powerful as a boss on its own. She never once said a word about being tired, but she had to be exhausted enough to fall to pieces as soon as we got back to town.

"...Enjoy your rest," I whispered, and pulled the round stool from the table over toward the rocking chair.

There was not enough space there now that Asuna had rolled over, and even if there were, I didn't want to risk waking her up.

I put a hand on the backrest and rocked it gently again. A slight smile snuck onto Asuna's childlike face in her sleep.

Maybe she was dreaming of the finished *Tilnel* sailing along on the channel. I'd guessed three hours for old Mr. Romolo, but as I silently rocked the chair, I didn't mind if he took just a bit longer.

The quest log buzzed into life at around four thirty in the morning, when the darkness outside the window was just showing the first signs of lightening.

The window said, THE SHIP YOU ORDERED IS COMPLETE. HEAD TO THE SHIPWRIGHT'S WORKSHOP. It was at one thirty that Romolo had descended into his workshop, so the time of construction was three hours on the nose, exactly what I'd guessed.

Asuna must have heard the sound effect, too, but she was still zonked out on the rocking chair, eyes closed. I was of a mind to keep rocking it gently for another hour or two of sleep.

But I had a feeling that if I did, she'd scold me later for not waking her up. I decided that once we got the finished boat, we could return to the inn for some proper sleep. I stood up and leaned over Asuna.

"Um, hello? I think our boat is ready."

Her eyebrows twitched in her sleep, and she murmured something inaudibly, but did not wake. I put a hand on her shoulder and shook it gently. It occurred to me that I'd been gently rocking her for the last three hours, so a little more vibration wouldn't do the trick.

I decided to gradually increase the pressure of my rocking and started calling out, "Good morning, rise and shiiine…"

Suddenly, Asuna bolted upright with a bizarre sound.

"Hwulyuh?!"

I had to fall backward to avoid getting a head-butt right to the chin. The fencer looked around, bleary-eyed, until her eyes focused on an empty spot in the air just in front of her.

"…Was that weird noise…from this window…? What is this…?" she mumbled. I shook my head.

"No, it's just the quest log updating…No, wait…"

That didn't make sense. She would have heard that sound the same time I did, and that was far too long ago for her to be waking up now. So whatever window Asuna was seeing had to be…

"Oh, I see…So I can just close this, then," she muttered, reaching out with her finger extended.

"Aaaaah! Wait, wait! Stop! Stooooop!!" I screamed. That bellowing had bumped her up to 70 percent wakefulness, and her hand jumped and stopped.

"Wh-what?!"

"Don't press it!!"

"Huh…? Umm…"

She looked back in my desperate, screaming face with suspicion, then glanced more closely at the window only she could see.

"…Activate automatic teleportation of subject due to harassment code violation…?"

She suddenly clutched her body and looked at me. The remaining

30 percent of sleepiness evaporated instantly, and her eyebrows shot up into the air.

"Wh-wh-what did you do to me while I was sleeping?!"

"I didn't do anything!! I was just trying to wake you up!!"

"If that was all, then the harassment code wouldn't have gone off!!"

"I-it's your fault for not waking up!!"

Before we could go further down that spiral of pointless argument, I held up a hand.

"W-wait. Something's not right...The order of the harassment code deployment is wrong..."

"What do you mean?" she asked, still wary. I chose my words very carefully.

"W-well...When the harassment-prevention code activates upon inappropriate contact, it delivers both a warning and knocks the offending hand away, eventually developing into forced teleportation if the contact continues, from what I understand..."

"...Meaning that when you were touching me, you should have been getting warnings too?"

"B-but there weren't any. And it didn't knock my hand away... So I just kept shaking you, trying to get you to wake up, until you just leaped up like that."

"...Hmm..."

She was finally settling down a step below her stage of nervous caution. Asuna looked down to reexamine the details of the warning window, but I was still beside myself with nerves. If she hit the YES button, even on accident, I would be instantly teleported down to the prison area beneath Blackiron Palace, all the way down on the first floor.

Fortunately, she just pored over the details of the window before shrugging.

"It doesn't say anything aside from asking if I want to activate the code. So I should press NO, then?"

"P-please..."

"Fine, pressed."

I let out a long sigh of relief that I had evaded the danger of prison and slumped down onto the stool. She just shook her head and stood up from the rocking chair.

"I have no idea what all of this is about...but we can ask Argo, I suppose. Anyway...did you even sleep?"

I honestly wasn't sure what kind of response Asuna would have if I told her that I'd spent three hours just rocking her chair for no good reason while she slept, so I kept it vague.

"Erm, I might have nodded off for a bit."

"...Where?"

"On the stool there."

"...Oh."

She looked back down at the rocking chair where she'd slept, then decided to change the subject without further comment. "And why did you try waking me up so vigorously that it set the harassment code off?"

"B-because the boat's finished."

She instantly glared at her quest log with ferocious concentration, and her face lit up.

"You should have said that earlier!"

"It was the first thing I said..."

But the fencer ignored my rebuttal and rushed back to the front door, then hit the brakes on her third step.

"Wait, the log says to go to the workshop, but this isn't the shop itself."

"Good point. And it doesn't seem like old gramps is coming back here...which means..."

I walked over to the door to the tool storeroom on the opposite wall from the entrance and gripped the dimly gleaming handle. It turned slowly, heavily opening just a crack.

"I think this is it, Asu—"

Before I could finish, something pushed my back and tipped me forward into the storeroom. Asuna had essentially delivered a body blow in the process of rushing into the room. No sooner had I closed the door than she turned on me and demanded, "Well?!"

I looked around hastily and found a suggestive lever on the wall. It would be one thing if this was a dungeon, but I decided there couldn't possibly be any traps in the middle of a town. It was safe to pull.

The entire room rumbled to life and started descending. The storeroom was indeed a giant elevator leading down to the underground workshop.

After about twenty seconds, the rumbling stopped and Asuna pried the door open impatiently.

"Ooooh!" she marveled. I whistled.

It was huge. The room above felt fairly spacious, but this was closer to an entire factory in scope. The floor, walls, and ceiling were all made of solid stone, and there were massive work platforms, wooden hoists, and various stacks of large-scale ship materials with plenty of room to spare.

But the feature that most drew my eye was a pool—no, a dock—installed in the center of the room. It was a channel about five yards wide filled with clear water that passed across the room and to a massive door on one side. It must have been connected to the town's canals through that door.

Romolo was standing at the side of the dock, hands on his hips. He gazed over the surface of the water at the graceful form of a two-seat gondola that glittered bright under the workshop's countless lamps.

I followed Asuna over to the brand-new boat. There was a *?* mark over the old man's head, which meant we needed to talk to him to advance the quest, but I couldn't help but look at the fresh new gondola.

It was about twenty-three feet long and just over four feet wide. The body was painted a gleaming ivory white, while the sides and prow were a deep forest green. The two leather seats and the rest of the interior were calm shades of brown. As I expected, the horn was probably affixed beneath the prow and was barely visible through the water.

Lastly, I couldn't help but stare at the beautiful, flowing cal-

ligraphy of the name *Tilnel* on the side. I finally turned to the elderly shipwright.

"…Thank you very much for this fine boat, Mr. Romolo."

"Hmph. It's been a long time since I was this satisfied with a vessel," the old man muttered happily, scratching at his whiskers, before suddenly adding, "However! After driving this poor senior citizen into his workshop, you'd better not let her sink!"

"We're not going to!" Asuna cried. She looked like the blood was rushing to her head, and those stars were back in her eyes. "We went through hell to gather the supplies to create this boat. We'll treat her well, Grandpa! Thank you!"

I was afraid the cantankerous old shipwright would object to being called "grandpa," but Romolo snorted in apparent satisfaction, then took a step back.

"In that case, the ship is now yours. I'll open the gate for you, and then you can row it wherever you like."

"Yes, sir!" Asuna bubbled and hopped into the gondola. I lifted my leg to step into the boat after her, then stopped it in midair.

"H-hang on a sec…Mr. Romolo, where's the boatman?"

The *Tilnel* was built with two seats, just like we ordered, but the space at the prow for someone to man the long oar was empty. There was no sign of any other NPC in the spacious workshop.

"Kirito, the person who rows a gondola is called a gondolier," Asuna said prissily from the front seat, but I didn't care about that.

The old man raised an eyebrow at my question, then spread his knotted hands.

"Boatman? There is no boatman."

"There's not?! Then…how will we move the ship?!"

"That's obvious. You stand there and pull the oar."

"P-pardon me?!" I screeched, stunned.

Asuna was entirely unfazed. "Oh, so that's how it works. Well, let's get going, Kirito!"

Either I should be really happy that there's an in-game manual on ship control, or I should be really angry at the corners cut by whomever decided to sink the fourth floor in water, I thought as I timidly gripped the long oar.

If the manual that came with the gondola was to be believed, controlling the boat wasn't that complicated. If you tilted the oar forward, it would advance, and if you held it straight up, it would brake. Tilting it backward would cause the gondola to back up, and pushing left or right resulted in the proper turn. The gondoliers in Venice no doubt needed much more complex skills in real life, but they'd simplified the process for the game to make it more fun.

Still, I had no more experience piloting a boat than the old paddleboards at the Kawagoe Water Park with my little sister when we were kids—I was terrified that I would suddenly smash the boat to splinters against the side of the dock. Only once I had tried regripping the oar several times was I confident enough to look over at Romolo and nod.

"I'm opening the gate!" he warned, and pulled the lever. The massive double doors facing the dock opened left and right. The pale light of impending dawn and a roil of pure white mist poured into the workshop.

"H-h-here goes, then! Hang on tight!" I called out to Asuna. Her response was utterly devoid of any kind of nerves. I took one last deep breath.

"Now launching the *Tilnel*!" I announced, fulfilling the dream of every boy who had ever wanted to be a captain, and pushed the oar forward. The boat proceeded so easily, it was almost disappointing.

Hey, this might not be so hard after all, I thought for the briefest of moments.

"Left, Kirito! You're leaning to the left!"

"Huh? L-left?"

I pushed the oar to the left in a panic, which only caused the prow to turn harder.

"No, the opposite! Go right!"

"R-r-right?"

I tilted the oar the opposite direction, but its reaction was slow. There was a feeling of heavy resistance for a moment, then once the boat actually started turning, I felt an unpleasant grinding through the floor. Apparently the horn sticking out of the prow on the underside of the boat had scraped against the dock wall.

"Um, is everything all right?!"

"I, uh…I think it's all right," I mumbled in a tone that suggested it was not all right. Clearly I needed to look farther ahead than just where my hands and the prow were pointing.

By the time I had properly straightened out the direction, the boat was through the water gate.

"We'll be back again, Grandpa!" Asuna called out, waving to Romolo. I tilted the oar to make a right turn.

Out in the waterways of Rovia at last, I turned the *Tilnel* to the east and rowed as hard as I could. The gondola peeled through the morning mist and picked up momentum. Asuna spread her arms and cheered.

"Aaah, this feels so great! Let's just head straight out of town!"

"I'm not sure that going out is a good idea…I was kind of hoping to get some steering practice in the safety of town. Remember, we promised Mr. Romolo we wouldn't crash it," I suggested. The fencer looked back in dissatisfaction, but she agreed when she saw my uncertain control of the oar.

"Oh, fine. Then take us on a little tour of the canals."

"Aye-aye, sir," I replied, facing forward with a sigh of relief.

The shadow of another craft came imminently racing toward us through the thick mist. I tried to remember which side the traffic used here and started to turn to the left before remembering that it was right—*right!*

We weren't going very fast, but the craft clearly handled slower than an automatic car. My only experience driving was in other VR games, but this gondola was just as fake as they were, so the comparison worked. Once my desperate turn was complete, t'

large gondola piloted by an NPC rushed past to the left with just inches to spare.

"Watch it, clown!"

I ducked my head in embarrassment and straightened out the ship. At this rate, it was clear that I ought to stick to the right edge of the channels.

"He doesn't have to shout just because his boat is bigger," Asuna snorted.

I tried to calm her down. "There, there. He's probably just programmed to react like that if the gondolas get too close for comfort."

"So he would have said worse if we actually collided, then."

"Ha-ha, I'm sure he would have..."

No sooner were those words out of my mouth than another gondola, this one the same size as the *Tilnel*, came racing by to pass us on the left.

"Outta the way! Don't clog up the canals!" the boatman roared before disappearing into the mist.

"Wh-what was that for? Chase him, Kirito—I've got to give him a piece of my mind!"

"I-I can't. I won't be able to make the turn if I go that fast," I complained to the aggressive shipowner, then stopped to wonder.

When a player got his own boat, did that mean that the NPC gondoliers he shared the waterways with became his enemies? Technically, one would be drawing the ire of the NPC's passengers, so it wasn't nothing, but this seemed to be developing into more trouble than I wanted out of a video game.

"...No, hang on," I muttered, pushing the oar carefully.

Romolo had claimed that he quit the shipmaking business because the Water Carriers Guild had monopolized the building materials. Why had the guild been so desperate to exclude Romolo, who clearly wasn't a member? Was there some reason that they needed to control both the shipbuilding and water transport industries here in Rovia?

In fact, that reminded me that the first gondolier we met in town had said something curious. When I asked him if any other boats might take us out of the city, he claimed that he couldn't answer the question.

What if that response was not a cut-and-paste reaction to a question he didn't understand, but something related to the Water Carriers Guild?

Perhaps there were ships that would go out of town, but circumstances prevented him from talking about it...?

"...!"

Struck by a sudden thought, I reopened the log window for the "Shipwright of Yore" quest, which I'd assumed was over. Just as I suspected, there was a new line of text right at the very bottom.

THE BOATS FROM THE WATER CARRIERS GUILD ARE ACTING STRANGE. TALK TO THE OLD CRAFTSMAN AGAIN.

"Sorry, Asuna, we've got to go see Gramps again!" I shouted, and slowed down the ship. She nearly pitched forward out of her seat and turned back with eyes blazing. Her mouth closed when she saw my face, though.

Once the stationary gondola had finished its 180-degree turn, I made full use of my strength stat to row us forward.

Thirty minutes later, the *Tilnel* was back in the waterways of Rovia. Asuna and I faced each other, our heads tilted at the same curious angle.

"...His story didn't really make sense..."

"I agree...but the quest is still going..."

Asuna straightened her neck and yawned adorably. It was 5:40 in the morning, about the time that the nocturnal players would return to town and the early birds would be waking up. If anything, I was a night owl, but sleeping in the Dark Elf camp had fixed my schedule to being more of a morning person. I was dead exhausted.

Once I had joined her in yawning, my partner gave me a light-hearted scolding.

"I told you we could have shared the rocking chair."

"...Well, you still seem plenty tired after using it."

"It's because this ship rocks you to sleep...but if you want to return to the inn and get some proper shut-eye, I won't argue."

"Thanks for being considerate..."

I pondered our situation. Romolo didn't explain exactly what the reason was for the other gondoliers' antagonism or what happened between him and the guild. Instead, he gave us a mystery to consider.

If you really want to know, find the big boat carrying wooden boxes instead of passengers, and follow it without drawing notice. It should leave town to the southeast around nightfall. Just be careful not to let them spot you. They've got ruffians on board—then again, after the bear king, you've got nothing to fear.

"What do you think, Asuna? We've got our ship already. Should we keep going with the quest?" I asked, banking on the fact that the fencer had enough good luck to earn two unbelievably rare items already.

She blinked in surprise and nodded as if the answer was obvious. "Of course we are. I wouldn't feel right otherwise."

"Ah, okay. Well...I'd feel bad about submitting incomplete info to Argo...Let's go back to the inn, then..."

"Mm," she replied. I waited to continue rowing until she was back in her seat.

We made our way south down the main canal and headed for the teleport square, enduring the continuing insults of the gondoliers. I was planning to leave the temporary inn overlooking the square to move to a proper hotel in the southwest quarter, but it occurred to me that keeping our base in the town center would make it more convenient for travel.

After several minutes of rowing, a massive stone wharf came into view. The NPC-run gondolas only docked at the south end of the center island, while the east- and west-facing docks only featured a few little boats tied up. The western dock was straight ahead, so I eventually backed the gondola up to a pier with great difficulty.

Asuna got up and offered a word of thanks for my piloting, then seemed to have an idea.

"Hey…can't we put the *Tilnel* in our inventory somehow? Do we have to leave it behind?"

"According to the manual, we can fix the boat in place by dropping an anchor or tying it to a bitt on the dock. Once it's affixed, only the owner can unlock the ship, it says…so I don't *think* we'll need to worry about it being stolen…"

"I was hoping for a more confident answer," Asuna complained. She picked up a coiled rope sitting at the front of the gondola. "Is this the rope we use?"

"I think so."

"And is that the bitt?"

She pointed at a fat, rounded post at the side of the pier.

"I think so."

"I'll do it, then," she announced, and leaped onto the pier, placing the rope noose over the post. That was all it took—a game message appeared letting me know that the *Tilnel* had been fixed in place.

I set down the oar and hopped over to the pier to enjoy a good long stretch.

It had been a very long day. Despite a few breaks here and there, I'd essentially been active for a period of twenty-four hours following the third-floor boss fight.

But as I gazed at the beautiful ivory-white and forest-green gondola, it seemed to me that the time had been well spent. It never occurred to me that I might have my own vehicle that I could control in Aincrad.

"Do you like the combination of white and green?" I asked.

Asuna looked down at her own outfit. "Hmm…In terms of personal preference, I'd go for white and red."

That made sense, given her white tunic and dark red cape. I sent her a questioning look, and she put on a rare gentle grin.

"The signs for safety or the environment are usually a green cross on a white background, right? The colors just popped into my head once we decided to use Tilnel's name for the boat. Then again...that green cross symbol is only recognized in Japan."

"...I see..."

I pictured an image of Tilnel the herbalist, a person I'd never met but heard about from Kizmel on several occasions. When I spoke, it was in a deliberately cheery voice to cover up the rare lump that rose in my throat.

"Once I realized that I had to row it myself, we should have made it a one-seater. We could have saved on materials, and it would be easier to maneuver..."

"Just think of it as a bargain: We built a two-seat gondola that can actually hold three."

"Is that really...a bargain...?" I wasn't sure, but with my brain working at a decreased capacity, I had no choice but to hesitantly agree. "Umm...yeah. Sure. Anyway, let's go back to the inn..."

I let out an enormous yawn in the light of the morning sun from the outer perimeter, and this time it was Asuna who caught it from me.

"*Fwah*...What time should we meet up?"

"Ummm...Ten—no, eleven, please..."

"Roger that."

Both low on sleep, we turned our backs to the steadily stirring teleport square and plodded off to our temporary lodgings.

My mind went blank the instant I fell onto the bed, and it seemed like the alarm was smacking me awake just moments later.

It wasn't quite enough sleep, but at any rate, it was time to start Day Forty-Six. I noted the date (12/22) on my menu window and couldn't help but feel like something important was coming up, but I was out the door before I latched onto what it was.

Asuna and I met up on the first floor and headed out to the Italian food carts in the square for a meal. My hunger overrode my sleepiness the instant I caught a whiff of melting cheese. I'd chosen the panini sandwich yesterday, so I was trying to decide between the pizza or the fried fish or perhaps getting both to make up for the lack of breakfast—oh, but that would leave nothing new to try tomorrow...

"...What is it?" I heard mumbled next to me. I thought over my answer.

"Well, I was eyeing the fried fish meal..."

"No, I mean *that*."

She reached out and grabbed the back of my head to turn it eighty degrees to the right.

I saw more than a few players running straight through the square to the west. The looks on their faces did not suggest an emergency, but clearly something was up. I tuned my ears and thought I heard an even larger rumbling coming from the direction they were running.

"We should probably go see what's happening," Asuna noted seriously. I longingly gazed side-eyed at the three carts before sucking it up.

The teleport square here was an actual square surrounded by water, so while there were inns, carts, and other structures in the corners, it generally had an excellent view all around. So the instant we circled around the gate itself and walked into the western half, we noticed the crowd up against the wharf. There were at least fifty players there, but there couldn't be anything beyond them except for the dock. And the public gondolas didn't stop at the east or west docks.

"...I have a bad feeling about this," Asuna murmured. I nodded my agreement. We picked up our pace and closed the remaining distance at once.

Upon slipping into the right edge of the crowd, we saw that our expectations were half-correct and half–completely wrong.

The cause of the uproar appeared to be a brand-new gondola moored on one of the piers—the *Tilnel*. But what drew the attention of the onlookers was not the boat, but two groups that were facing off at the start of the pier. Both seemed to be made of six members: the max for a single party.

The party on the left-hand side was entirely decked out in blue doublets. There was no mistaking the uniform of the Dragon Knights Brigade, one of the elite guilds of the front line.

Meanwhile, the party on the right was in moss green. Like the other team, they were one of the well-known guilds in the game: the Aincrad Liberation Squad.

As I watched in silence, a man with spiked chunks of hair just like a morning star at the head of the ALS stepped forward and growled.

"You still don't get how things work around here, do ya?! Listen, *we* found this ship first, and that means *we* got the right to investigate it first!"

The target of his rage was a slender man at the center of the Dragon Knights with long blue hair tied behind his head. Though his irritation was plain to see, he kept better composure than the cactus-headed man.

"You claim you found it first, but as the man in charge over there, you arrived two minutes later than I did. We've already started our investigation—why don't you save your baseless complaints for another time?"

"Baseless complaints?! No, you stuff that nonsense logic up yer ass! You don't get the right ta act all high-and-mighty, when it was you who shoved my guard outta the way!"

"We're inside the town. You know full well there's no way we could have forced your man to move. These excuses are laughable!"

Neither of the two guild leaders showed the least sign of backing down. A voice with the perfect blend of apprehension and exhaustion sounded in my right ear.

"...I don't even know what to say..."

I thought it over and offered her my best advice. "In this situation, I think a simple *ugh* will suffice."

".........Ugh."

I glanced over at Asuna and decided to be a bit more constructive this time.

"While there's not much you can say about this other than

'ugh,' perhaps we should come up with a plan...Here's Plan A: We go back to the square, eat our lunch, and sneak the ship away once they've all calmed down. Plan B: Butt right into their argument, reveal everything we know about the shipbuilding quest, and get them to see the light."

"...Do you really think they'll calm down?" she responded instantly. I considered that.

The *Tilnel* was locked to the pier by the game system itself. No other player aside from me or Asuna should be able to move it. With that in mind, I supposed that both of the guilds would have to give up eventually, but I didn't know that for sure. If I was in their position, I could imagine the sight of that fresh new boat begging for a ride driving me crazy until I figured out how to get it.

On top of that, the leader of the rival guild was right there. They weren't likely to give up and withdraw, knowing that the other side might find out a way to move the ship.

"Hmm. Maybe they *won't* calm down..."

"That's what I think."

"Which means we have no choice but to explain the entire quest to them," I said, resigned, but Asuna did not agree.

"...And you can imagine what will happen after that, can't you?"

"Huh...? What do you mean?"

"Y'all aren't allowed ta slip ahead of us! You gotta help us with the quest until we git our own boat!"

Her imitation of Kibaou's Kansai accent was so accurate, I couldn't help but get a shiver up my spine.

"Yep, that's definitely more than just an *ugh*...And we're supposed to be tracking down that big gondola for Old Grandpa Romolo..."

"There's another thing that worries me, too," Asuna said, looking pensively at the *Tilnel*. "The boat is currently classified as an Immobile Object, right?"

"Should be."

"Does that mean it's also an Immortal Object?"

"Should b..."

I stopped before the last *e* left my lips.

In an ordinary RPG, vehicles that the player could obtain were essentially never destroyed unless it was part of the main story line. In many MMORPGs, mounts were impossible to attack. After all of the passion Asuna poured into the *Tilnel*, I desperately hoped that this was the case in *SAO*—but the ship's optional equipment worried me.

That ram made of Fire-Bear's Horn had to be for the purpose of sinking other ships in a collision. If that function was programmed into it, then it stood to reason that all ships had a durability rating that would sink them when it reached zero.

I regretted not checking the *Tilnel*'s property window when I had the chance, but it was too late for that now.

"...Actually, maybe it's not labeled immortal. I feel like it's probably protected here in town, but I don't want to say for sure until I check the manual again..."

"In that case, we should probably move the ship before those people decide the investigation requires whacking it a bunch."

I didn't think that even they would stoop that low...until I remembered the scene at the public dock to the south last night. The Dragon Knights had barged in front of the lengthy line of tourists as if it was their God-given right. Certainly there was a greater-than-zero chance that they might feel entitled to not just smack the ship, but destroy it if it couldn't be theirs.

"So that would be...Plan C: Burst through by force?"

"I don't like sticking out for bad reasons, but it'll save them from wasting their time. Let's go with that one."

"All right. I'll hop into the boat first to prepare for rowing while you remove the rope."

She nodded silently, and we shared a glance to get our timing right before leaping from the wharf down to the dock about five feet below.

I politely shouted, "Excuse us, coming through," as we raced down to the pier. The blue and green parties were taken aback just enough for us to slip through and leap onto the *Tilnel*. Asuna pulled the mooring rope off as I yanked the oar off of its U-joint to prepare for sailing.

Upon seeing the previously immobile rope removed from the bitt without issue, Kibaou, the leader of the green Aincrad Liberation Squad, shouted angrily. But Asuna simply hopped into the gondola without looking back. The rope in her hand was automatically snapped into a coil at the front of the boat, and I promptly began rowing as hard as I could.

The instant the *Tilnel* left the dock, it was the leader of the blue Dragon Knights, Lind, who spoke up.

"H-hey, you there! How did you get that—?"

I finally turned back and shouted, "The details on the shipbuilding quest will be in the next strategy guide! Just wait for that!"

"N-no, you git back here! And…not *you two* again!" Kibaou ranted, brandishing his fists.

I cut a salute with my right hand, then raised our speed.

Once we had made a half lap around the south end of the main canal and headed into one of the smaller waterways of the southeast quarter, I stopped the boat and checked the operation manual that was accessible from the gondola's property window. In doing so, I learned a few facts.

The *Tilnel* was not, in fact, an Immortal Object—it had a set durability value. As I feared, that value would be diminished by attacks from large monsters, collisions with obstacles, and battle with other boats. If it reached zero, the ship would capsize, but it could be restored by visiting a shipwright or using the Carpentry skill.

Fortunately, the durability value was protected when anchored and unmanned. So there was no need to fear the ship being destroyed when we weren't there to watch it, as with the previous incident.

"I don't know whether to be reassured by that information or not," Asuna remarked.

I agreed. "I think it's pretty unlikely that we'll get into collision wars with other boats, but I feel that it's pretty likely I'll have a few run-ins with obstacles…"

"Practice defensive driving!"

"Yeah, sure. So…as far as the quest goes, he said that the ship in question will appear in the southeast quadrant in the evening, right?"

She nodded.

"Then let's get something to eat for now, then meet up with Argo and give her the quest details. I was hoping to do that after we finished it for good, but I'm afraid of what might happen if we delay any longer."

"Agreed. I was hoping to see them all swimming around in their inner tubes, though."

"Ha-ha, yeah. Me, I was hoping for one last As—"

I stopped unnaturally the instant that I realized the mistake I was about to commit. But the fencer's preternatural hearing—practically full mastery of the Eavesdropping skill—kicked in, and she turned to me with a smile.

"What was that?"

"I was hoping for one last…bite of asparagus…" I finished lamely.

Her smile went from lukewarm to below the freezing point.

"Why not have something like that for lunch, then?"

The southeast quarter of Rovia was a business district split up by its countless canals.

When we were using the guild's gondolas, I couldn't be bothered to check each shop, knowing that every time we set foot on solid ground, we had to pay the fee again. But now that we had our own, I was free to spend as much time browsing as I wanted. We could stop the boat and peer at the displayed wares and dock at a pier if we were interested in buying. The time simply flew by.

Asuna was mostly drawn to the shops selling minor goods and accessories, which put a thought into my mind.

"Hey, what would you say to upgrading your armor? You've been using that breastplate since the second floor, right?"

Asuna pulled away from the display case of the item shop, her expression lost in thought.

"That's true, but...I don't really want to increase the weight of my equipment. The ones with really high defense are all so heavy."

"Well, there's nothing you can do about that," I admitted, then analyzed her outfit from top to bottom.

The only metal item she wore was the thin breastplate; her gloves, boots, and skirt were all made of leather. I had no issue with her philosophy of keeping the weight down so she could focus on evading rather than defending, but it was scary to consider what might happen if she got paralyzed, stunned, or fell.

Plus, wimpy monsters whose patterns could be recognized were one thing, but the third floor had taught me that not only did you have to deal with boss monsters with shifting patterns, but the even more terrifying prospect of foes whose actions couldn't be predicted.

I brushed my chest lightly, remembering the feeling of that critical hit ax combo, Double Cleave.

"Take this for what it's worth, coming from a guy who wears nothing but leather and cloth. If you have the Light Metal Armor skill, why not make more use of the 'metal' part? You'll find that just switching your gloves or boots to studded or plated armor will make a big difference."

"Studded? Meaning...it has metal studs stuck in it?" she asked.

Now it was my turn to be confused.

"Studs? You mean, like...those punk fashion spiky things?"

Neither of us seemed to be following the other's point. She pursed her lips.

"I don't really understand. Can I see the real thing in a store before I decide?"

"Of course. Now, I think the recommended shop for the fourth floor was..."

Even soaked in water as it was now, the layout of the town was the same as it had been before, so I consulted my beta memory banks, pointing east-southeast.

"...That way, I think. There's a nice little restaurant tucked away there, so we can eat after we shop."

Though I'd never paid much attention to the English term before this, I found out that the name "studded armor" did indeed come from metal studs hammered into the armor, and they didn't necessarily need to be spiked.

"So that's why they call it studded leather...Man, it's hard to say," I grumbled. Meanwhile, Asuna's voice came drifting over about 20 percent faster than her usual speaking pace.

"Kirito, have you decided what you'll eat? I was thinking of the crab gratin, but it's hard to pass up the steamed clams. Want to order both and share them?"

The reason for her excitement was probably the new set of armor. Her breastplate had been upgraded from bronze to a sturdier steel make, while still keeping the weight low. Her leather skirt was now plated leather, which meant that flat steel plates had been sewn into the sides. Her gloves and boots were now studded, but they were smooth and rounded, not spiked, so it didn't make her look imposing.

The white tunic she wore beneath the armor and the red hooded cape were still the same as before, but it was clearly the biggest onetime gear upgrade she'd ever had, and it was kind of adorable how she would occasionally look herself over and chuckle with satisfaction...

"Listen, if you don't want the steamed clams, then order something. I'm starving over here."

"S-sorry. That'll do fine."

"Then I'll put the order in. I'll just pick out something to drink."

Once Asuna had finished giving the NPC waitress her food and drink order, she looked back down at her breastplate and traced the subtle plant design. Her voice was finally back to normal.

"As a matter of fact, I've always had a dislike of really *armory* armor."

"Oh...? Why's that?"

"It's heavy and bulky...and I always felt like wearing serious armor meant giving in and finally being a true resident of this world in body and spirit..."

"What? But by that logic, your weapon would..." I paused briefly. "Oh, does that mean you chose a rapier because you had fencing experience in real life?"

Asuna grimaced and shook her head. "No, not at all. But there was a similarly thin sword above the mantelpiece in my home growing up. When I was a kid, I took it down and swung it around. Boy, did I get in trouble for that."

The very first thought that sprung to my mind was, *What's a mantelpiece?* But I only motioned for her to go on with my eyes.

"So...because of that, maybe I did think that the rapier had some kind of connection to my real self. Something just barely within the realm of acceptability...which is hilarious to consider, at this point."

True to her word, she giggled.

I asked, "Then why the breastplate? Did you have one of those at home, too?"

"No way. This was my compromise between stubbornness and weakness. I didn't want to wear a big honking suit of armor, but I was too scared to go out of town in just clothing. Before I met you, I lost a lot of HP from kobold attacks in that first labyrinth tower, so it was probably a good thing that I got the armor after all."

"...No kidding," I murmured, letting out a long, slow breath. "In this world, weakness and cowardice are practically virtues. You can never have a large enough safety margin."

"I don't want to hear that from someone with lighter armor than me," she said, annoyed. I had no defense: My only metal armor was an ultrathin protector that couldn't even be called plate armor and shoulder guards on my coat. I had to admit that

I wouldn't be here if not for the protection of that slim piece of metal when Morte hit me with his ax on the third floor.

"A-anyways, I'm going to be sure to keep this on at all times," I assured her, pointing to my own chest briefly before flipping my wrist over to point at her new breastplate. "Don't be so picky about armor, Asuna. You want to cover that spot at the very least…Oh, and by 'that spot,' I mean your heart."

I snapped my hand back down to my knees. Asuna glanced down at her chest, then put on a smile at least fifty degrees chillier than the one after the asparagus remark.

"Of course. You picked it out for me, so I'll take good care of it."

Thankfully, the gratin, steamed clams, wine, and bread arrived to melt her icy aura. She drew her spoon as quickly as her rapier and stated, "We'll switch after eating half of each dish!"

And with a huge mouthful of crab gratin stuffed into her cheek, her eyes narrowed with pleasure.

While there were still occasions that my careless remarks prompted a terrifying response from Asuna, it seemed as though I'd seen her smile more often since we reached the fourth floor. Some of that had to be attributed to the city of canals, the gondolas, and the seafood cuisine, but I suspected that Asuna might finally be accepting her life in a virtual world.

If that was the case, I hoped that I could at least keep her away from anything frightening or sad while we were on this floor.

I jammed a large, meaty clam into my mouth, praying that it would give me the strength to achieve that hope.

5

IT WAS A NEW DAY: 12:15 AM, FRIDAY, DECEMBER 23.

Once again, we crossed over into a new day while outside of town—and it was unlikely that we'd be back at the inn by morning.

The sunken dungeon in the eastern mountains of the fourth floor was far larger than I expected.

"Here comes the claw attack from the right, Asuna!"

My partner nimbly ducked in her position at the prow. The giant crab claw just grazed her long hair as it flew through the air.

Its passenger brilliantly evaded the attack, but the boat itself was not quite so agile, and the claw clipped the right side of the craft. *Gachunk!* A shock rattled through the wood and rocked the boat.

"Hrrg!"

I gritted my teeth, feeling the loss of the craft's durability as if it were my own health. I wanted to switch spots with Asuna at once and ram my Anneal Blade +8 into a soft crevice in the giant crab's shell, but I couldn't let go of the oar that controlled the *Tilnel*'s course.

Asuna must have sensed my panic because she turned back to me for just a moment.

"Don't worry, I'll break its next attack and give us an opening! Just hang on!"

"R-roger!"

Her bracing voice, untouched by fatigue after our many battles, whipped me back into shape. I put my trust in her and waited for the right moment.

The Scuttle Crab, one of the tougher monsters in this watery dungeon, measured a good four yards wide if you included its two pincer claws. It reared that giant bulk backward and opened its jaws wide, complete with disgusting little wriggling legs. That was the sign for its bubble breath. If that hit us, we'd be unable to see the space in front of us, and it wouldn't go away until we jumped in water to wash the effect away.

Just before the crab could shoot out the blast of fine suds, Asuna leaped up from her crouch, timed to the rocking of the ship, to unleash a Streak diagonal slash.

This was a basic rapier attack, just like the horizontal thrust Linear and the low thrust Oblique, but it was still deadly with the power of the upgraded Chivalric Rapier. Because the powerful move hit it right in the mouth, the Scuttle Crab's weak point, the creature lost more than 40 percent of its HP in one go.

"Now, Kirito!" she shouted from the postattack frozen position.

But I was already pushing the oar forward with all of my might. The *Tilnel* pushed ahead at full power, driving the Fire-Bear's Horn affixed below the surface into the crab's fleshy belly. The material of the Magnatherium's horn emitted terrible heat when it attacked, producing a great billow of steam from the water and turning the unpleasant dark green crab shell redder by the moment.

At the same time, its half-depleted HP gauge shot down to zero. The red shell exploded into blue polygonal shards and Asuna stood up from her delay to flash me yet another V-for-victory sign.

The Scuttle Crab dropped a material item called Great Crab Shell, a few gems for some reason, and two food ingredients: Great Crab Leg Meat and Great Crab Claw Meat.

Asuna sat down on the railing of the boat for a break and checked out her item listing with apparent dissatisfaction.

"...Please tell me that crab gratin we ate back at the restaurant in town wasn't using this crabmeat..."

The immature boy in me wanted to say yes, but I decided to be kind and assuage my partner's concerns.

"NPC restaurants don't need to import ingredients, so I very highly doubt the chef goes out to gather Scuttle Crab meat. I'd be careful about any steamed crab buns you find at a player-owned shop, though."

"I'm never buying them. I'm also not selling this crabmeat to any player merchants."

"G-good luck with that. But it is a D-class ingredient, so I feel like it's probably pretty good...That crab gratin was awful tasty, remember?" I noted. She turned her face away. She was probably still feeling weird about sharing our lunch.

About ten hours earlier, we ordered crab gratin and steamed clams at that little restaurant in Rovia, splitting the two dishes halfway. Once the excited Asuna had cleaned out exactly half of the gratin and slid the dish over to me, she seemed to realize the forward nature of her actions.

Her face went red and she told me to wait just a second after I'd boldly scooped a massive spoonful of crab into my mouth. The dish itself was quite good, and I didn't notice the change in Asuna's behavior until I'd cleaned the dish down to a quarter left, and by then it was too late.

If a boy and girl in middle school who weren't romantically involved shared a cafeteria gratin meal from the same plate, they'd be engulfed in an inferno of teasing and catcalls in class.

But just a moment. This was a virtual world, where that barbaric, childish, boorish, and inefficient value system was rendered pointless. The employee would probably not bring us separate plates to share, even if we asked for them. We didn't have a choice but to share the food in that manner, I told myself.

"Um, listen...Like I said at the restaurant, Aincrad is a virtual world. I think it's pointless to get hung up on things like half-eaten food or reusing utensils. You can even drop a steamed bun on the ground, and as long as you pick it up before three seconds, it won't lose durability points or pick up any dirt effects..."

"That's not what shocked me," she said quietly. I blinked.

"Huh? Then what was it?"

"It was the fact that I thought the same things you just said. That there wasn't any problem because this is a virtual world. But the more I think about it, that *is* a problem..."

"Um, why would it be? This *is* a virtual world."

"I'm saying I don't want to mimic that same insensitive side that you have!"

"I...insensitive? What is that...a bonus effect or something?"

"Shush! In-sen-si-tive!! You can look it up in a dictionary once you're done beating the game!"

She turned away with a powerful huff. I knew enough at this point to realize that the situation wouldn't right itself for another thirty minutes, so I shook my head and picked up the oar again.

"S-so...setting the gratin aside for now, shall we keep going?"

I waited for the fencer to sit down in her front seat before I started up the *Tilnel* again. The wide waterway was dim, and the way forward was shrouded in darkness, so there was no way to guess how much of the dungeon still waited ahead of us.

Once we'd finished eating and resupplying yesterday afternoon, I sent off a number of instant messages to Argo with information as we circled around the market district of Rovia. Around four thirty, we finally spotted a boat that matched the description we wanted.

It was at least twice as long as the *Tilnel*—a good fifty feet in all. It was even larger than the ten-person sightseeing gondolas, yet there were only four NPCs on board. Two large men with wide daggers stood at the prow, while a burly oarsman rowed on either side of the craft. In the center was a stack of about ten large wooden boxes covered with a sheet.

The bluish-black ship proved itself to be fleet for its size, winding through the narrow channels quickly enough that following at a distance proved to be quite a task. I felt like my piloting skill as a player rose by at least a hundred points during the chase.

The large boat slipped out of the market area without using the main channel and left the town via the south gate, melting into the darkness. We had no choice but to follow it, and therefore, we weren't able to celebrate the *Tilnel*'s first trip outside of town due to the task at hand. Through the winding natural waterways we went, eventually ending up passing through a large waterfall into this submerged dungeon.

The crew on the big gondola must have traveled regularly between Rovia and this dungeon, as they rowed along in the darkness with familiar ease. We steeled ourselves for trouble when we entered the dungeon, trying to follow the ship ahead, but were soon interrupted by our first encounter with a Scuttle Crab. We managed to win our first ship battle despite knowing nothing about what to do, but by the time it was over the bigger boat was long gone.

It had been around six o'clock in the evening that we entered the place, which meant we'd been wandering the watery halls for over six hours now. There had been a few breaks here and there, but it was getting to the point that our concentration was faltering.

I kept the speed at a crawl so I could switch my window to the map tab and check our location. The full dimensions of the dungeon were still unknown, but I felt as though we were nearly upon the core of the place.

"Oh, there's a door to the right," Asuna pointed out. I looked up and saw a small landing about ten feet ahead, plus a metal door set into the wall.

"Though it figures to be yet another dead end," she added in frustration. We'd found countless other doors just like it and prepped ourselves for a possible boss fight each time, only to find more confusing paths unrelated to our quest.

"W-well, at least there's usually a treasure chest at most dead ends," I offered, the type of player who couldn't stand *not* exploring every last branch in a dungeon to fill out the map. Asuna was not cheered by this advice.

"Probably just more rusty swords and armor…"

"Never discount rusted gear. Every once in a while, you can take it to a blacksmith for repair, and it turns out to be a legendary find! Like, once in a hundred times…"

"Yes, yes, I get it…No, wait, stop!"

She held out her left hand urgently, and I promptly stood the oar upright. The gondola ground to a steady halt.

"Wh-what is it?!" I murmured. Asuna leaned out over the front of the ship, then turned back with a deadly serious look on her face.

"I think there's a big space up ahead. And…I hear a whole lot of voices coming from up there."

"Um…of people, or crabs?" I asked. Asuna's eyes briefly contained a hint of murder, so I shook my head rapidly. "People, of course. How silly of me. Let's take it slow on the approach, then."

She nodded without a word, and once she was crouched at the prow, I carefully pushed the oar forward.

We passed by the door and down the dark waterway, praying that no monsters would interrupt. There was indeed a large open surface visible ahead. It looked like a much larger hall in which a number of paths met.

I stopped the *Tilnel* just before the pathway dumped us into the open space and snuck up the length of the boat to peer over Asuna's shoulder.

It was even larger than I expected. The half-circle hall had to be a good hundred yards across. The curved wall on this side of the space featured at least five or six tunnel mouths, including the one we were currently perched in. The wall opposite us was flat, however, with a wide staircase in the center that stretched upward from the steps. Below it was a pier with—

"…!"

Asuna sucked in a sharp breath below me.

Tied up at the pier was the very same gondola we had followed out of Rovia, moored with thick ropes. They were exactly in the middle of unloading those wooden boxes.

The same four sailors were unloading the boxes themselves, while imposing warriors with slender scimitars at their waists took the boxes and carried them up the stairs. They were thin but tall, clad in dark gray leather armor, and wearing eerie masks that covered their faces.

I couldn't help but feel that I'd seen them somewhere before… and when I noticed the long ears, I was sure of it.

"…!!"

This time it was my turn to hold my breath. I lowered my head toward Asuna's ear and whispered as quietly as I could, "They're Fallen Elves."

There was tension in her profile as she nodded.

Fallen Elves—a race that served as the foes at the climax of the "Elf War" campaign quest on the third floor. Asuna and I and the knight Kizmel had engaged in a number of fierce battles against the elven creatures.

According to the Dark Elf commander, the Fallen were the descendants of elves who plotted to gain immortality to blades with the Holy Tree's magic, well before the Great Separation, and had been banished accordingly. They were experts in underhanded means such as poison, traps, and blindness, and even with the formidable presence of Kizmel, it was not easy to defeat the Fallen Elf Commander.

They were supposed to be after the Jade Key from the campaign quest, so why did they have a secret hideout set up here and why were the men from Rovia transporting supplies here? Asuna was clearly entertaining the same questions I was.

"What happened here in the beta test?" she whispered. I was expecting that question.

"I don't remember ever running across the Fallen here. In fact, this dungeon didn't even exist in the beta."

"Meaning...this is all part of one self-contained quest? Or does it fall under the umbrella of the campaign?"

"...I don't know. But I can say that I fought Fallen Elves on several occasions in the beta, and I never once saw them cooperating with human NPCs like this."

"I don't like it...If those sailors are with Rovia's Water Carriers Guild...then the guild itself could be aligned with the Fallen Elves," Asuna pointed out.

I squinted and frowned. My imagination was rusty from my long career as a beater, but I managed to get the wheels turning again.

We could extrapolate from Romolo's statements that craftsmen like him were once free to build ships as they pleased in Rovia, until some point in time at which the guild monopolized that work, forcing him out of business. At the same time, civilian gondolas were forbidden from leaving the town.

Meanwhile, the Water Carriers Guild was sending this ship meant for hauling out of town to the Fallen Elves' hideout, carrying a great many mysterious boxes.

It was natural to assume that the guild was embarking on these policies to hide their dirty business from the town. But we couldn't assume anything further, because...

"...We need to find out what's in those boxes," I finished aloud. Asuna agreed.

As we sat and watched, the sailors hauled the last box off of the boat, and one of the Fallen warriors picked it up. In order to learn the contents of the box, we had to charge the scene with the *Tilnel* and defeat all of the foes present, but that was too foolhardy and extreme.

For one thing, the Fallen Elves had red enemy cursors, but the sailors were the yellow of NPCs. They might turn red if they spotted us, but I wasn't sure if I wanted to lead an unprovoked attack.

As I waffled about what to do, the Fallen Elf with the box reached the top of the stairs and disappeared through the large door there. The particularly large and imposing masked Fallen who appeared to be their leader handed a small bag to one of the sailors. The man looked inside to check the contents, then nodded satisfactorily and motioned to his fellows to leave.

"Well, I know what's in that bag," Asuna whispered.

"Cold, hard cash," I agreed. "If they're all thousand-col gold coins…that could be 200,000 in all…"

She shut me down at once. "Don't you dare think about attacking and robbing them on the way back."

"N-no way! They looked really tough, anyway."

Meanwhile, the four sailors undid the mooring rope and piled onto the gondola. The two oarsmen pushed off, and the large craft lurched into motion.

I quickly leaped to the stern, hoping they weren't actually coming back the same way. I had the oar in my hand, ready to throw the boat into reverse if necessary.

"They're coming this way!" Asuna hissed in a panic.

Crap! I needed to think. We could wait here for the large ship and prepare for battle, if need be…but that wasn't an option. The fact that we'd been shown the scene of the sailors accepting the bag of money was surely a warning that if we fought with them, the quest would end in failure.

That left the option of retreat, but the canal we were in now was just five yards wide, too narrow for the *Tilnel* to turn around. Going in reverse was too slow; the large gondola would catch up to us before we could retreat to the first side tunnel.

That left just one option.

"Hnng!"

I tilted the oar backward with the quietest possible grunt, putting the boat into a full-speed reverse. Once we were back at the door that Asuna had claimed was just another dead end, I hopped onto the narrow dock and held out my hand to the dumbfounded fencer.

"The rope!"

Once she caught on, she was blindingly fast. She picked up the coiled rope at the prow and hurled it to me. I tossed the end around the bitt, making sure it notified me of the ship's location being locked, then turned around and threw the door open, leaping inside.

Unlike the countless side paths we'd explored earlier, this door opened into a large storeroom. Various goods were stacked up against the walls, but there were no chests. Wait, that wasn't the point of this.

"Does it even matter if we hide in here? Won't they just see the *Tilnel* outside?" Asuna whispered as she tried to shut the door without making any sound.

I nodded and added, "Good point, but there's no other escape for us. If they float past without noticing, great, and even if they disembark, they can't destroy the unmanned boat while it's tied up."

"But what if they come in here?!"

"Then we'll just have to hide…"

I looked around the room and picked up a folded piece of cloth from the ground a short distance away. Upon unfolding it, I found it was surprisingly thin and light and large enough to hide two.

"Just get under here," I suggested, but Asuna grabbed my wrist.

"Wait! This isn't just a piece of loose cloth."

Her slender fingers tapped the surface of the silvery-gray material, popping up a property window. I immediately noticed that the description was too long for a piece of junk.

ARGYRO'S SHEET: A CLOTH MADE OF SILK FROM A RARE AQUATIC SPIDER. THIS CLOTH WILL HIDE ANYTHING IT COVERS, BUT ONLY IN A PLACE SURROUNDED BY WATER.

The instant those words registered in my brain, I raced to the door of the storeroom and opened it just enough to see the exit of the hallway. The silhouette of the large ship was much closer, but it hadn't entered the tunnel yet.

There was no time for hesitation. I ordered Asuna to stay here with a look, then slipped out of the door and dashed to the ship, hunched over. Within seconds, I had placed the silvery sheet over the *Tilnel*.

The instant the airy material covered the boat from prow to stern, it took on the exact same color as the surface of the water, and even when I tried, I could hardly make out the boat at all. The sailors wouldn't notice it now—assuming they didn't ram right into it.

That would all come down to luck, though. I rushed back into the storeroom and shut the door. Asuna and I pressed our heads together to peer out of the peephole in the door at the same time. Even at this close distance, there was no way to see the *Tilnel* moored just feet away.

"If we'd just searched this room first, we wouldn't have had to panic like this," Asuna murmured regretfully.

I couldn't help but grin, despite the circumstances. "See? It pays off to explore the nooks and crannies. Let's shoot for a hundred percent map completion in the next dungeon."

"Shh! Here they come!"

She elbowed me in the side to shut me up. A few seconds later, the prow of the large ship appeared to the right, followed by the massive length of the craft, then its stern. The sailors did not notice the invisible *Tilnel*, nor did they crash into it. They just passed by, much faster now that their payload was lifted.

Only once the ship had traveled an appropriate distance away did the two of us let out long breaths.

"Ahh...I don't like these...what do you call them? Stealth quests?"

I had no disagreement with her on that one. "The tension is so much higher in a VRMMO...If you hadn't noticed the special properties of that cloth, they'd have found us."

It was meant to be an idle observation, but the fencer blinked several times in surprise, looking conflicted.

"Wh-who cares about that? What's our plan now? Will we follow the ship again?"

"No...I'm guessing it'll just go right back to Rovia," I noted, bringing up my window to check the quest log. The latest prompt was still the vague command to FIND THE SECRET OF THE TRANSPORT SHIP. "Looks like we still need to find out what's inside those wooden boxes."

"...I suppose so. And that means sneaking up those stairs crawling with Fallen Elves."

"The stealth mission continues. If you're tired, we can probably turn back to town and resume tomorrow. What do you think?" I asked, just in case, but Asuna refused at once.

"Thanks, but I'm fine. I'd rather not have to fight all those crabs and turtles and shellfish again."

"Good point...Let's put in some more good work, then."

When I returned to the dock, I had to reach out and feel for the Argyro's Sheet in order to take it off the boat. Even limited to the waterside, its all-encompassing hiding ability seemed too convenient to exist at such a low floor in the overall game. When I checked the properties tab again, sure enough, it had already lost close to 10 percent of its durability, just from five minutes of use.

"I should have figured...If you get carried away with this thing, it'll break down in no time."

The sheet folded itself up automatically, so I shoved it into the luggage space at the rear of the boat. Asuna removed the mooring rope and looked downcast.

"What will the people who do this quest after us do, then? There's no more of that whatever-sheet in the storeroom, is there?"

"It was on the floor, not a special treasure chest...so I'm guessing it will probably generate every time a party in the midst of the quest passes by. If that's the case, then the bigger guilds with plenty of players can probably take advantage of that to earn themselves a whole bunch of sheets, but we'll have to make do with just this one."

"We'll probably need to use it when tying the boat up in front of those stairs, too. Let's try to get back as quickly as we can."

"All right. Here goes."

I tilted the oar forward, easing the boat forward until we stopped at the mouth of the tunnel again. The hundred-yard-wide, ten-yard-tall chamber showed no hints of any aquatic monsters or Fallen Elves.

Asuna looked back at me. I nodded and pushed the boat onward. The only light came from torches in ten wall sconces. I kept up moving carefully across the water, as fast as I reasonably could.

When we reached the boat landing at the foot of the stairs, I hid the *Tilnel* under the Argyro's Sheet again. If five minutes was enough to consume 10 percent of its usage time, that meant we had forty-five minutes before it was gone.

"Let's hurry," I whispered.

Asuna nodded and fiddled with her equipment mannequin in the menu. Within moments, her familiar red hooded cape was replaced with an expensive-looking violet cape with elaborate woven patterns on it.

"Huh…Oh yeah, that was a reward from the third floor, wasn't it? Why didn't you use it until now?" I asked as we climbed the steps.

Her shoulders shrugged, brushing the silky, half-glossy material. "Well, its maximum durability is very low, and my Tailoring skill isn't high enough to repair it yet. So I was saving it for when it was really needed."

"You can't fix it up at an NPC tailor?"

"I tried that in the last village of the third floor, but she said, 'Sorry, 'fraid I'm not good enough to mend this.'"

"Hmm…It's possible that the NPCs on this floor could handle it, but it's convenient to be able to repair things yourself. There were plenty of combat-first players in the beta who picked up crafting skills for that purpose…"

We reached the hefty-looking metal door at the top of the staircase. We never found any keys while exploring the dungeon, so if this was locked, we were out of options. I grabbed the rusty red handle and pulled gingerly.

Fortunately, I didn't get that special feedback that always came from those system-locked doors, as if they were glued in place. But once they were an inch or two open, there was a stubborn resistance—probably the kind of trap that would creak loudly and alert the foes inside if I pulled too hard. If I just had some lubricating spray, I could put that on the hinges, but such an item didn't exist here. I just had to be very slow.

Once the door was open four inches, I was able to peer inside.

A dim, gloomy hallway stretched ahead for a good sixty feet before stopping and branching left and right. Halfway down the hall was a slender silhouette walking away with its back to us. I didn't need to see the scimitar at its side to know it was a Fallen Elf guard. Sure enough, the name on the pale red cursor read Fallen Elven Guard.

Our expedition into the Fallen Elf hideout on the third floor was also a stealth mission, but we had Kizmel with us, so I wasn't particularly worried about being spotted. But the elite knight was not here to help us now. Asuna and I had a healthy safety margin, and he didn't seem to be that tough based on the color of the cursor, but I wanted to avoid all the battle I could.

Don't turn back, don't turn back, I prayed as I watched him go. Thankfully, the wish worked, and the guard turned right at the end of the hall, walking out of sight.

But if he was walking a set route, he would be back. There was no time to wait around. I pulled open the door a little bit farther so that we could slip inside. Once the door was shut behind us, we raced down to the intersection as silently as we could.

I peered around the right corner and spotted the guard's back as he walked down the hall, his boots clacking. It looked like a dead end ahead of him, so he would certainly be coming back soon.

The hallway to the left turned to the right after a short distance. There was no telling what was around that corner, but it was our only choice. I gestured to Asuna and ran left.

We turned that blind corner at the exact moment that the retreating guard's footsteps paused. Within a few seconds, the footsteps resumed, approaching this time, but at the same pace. We had made it past the first checkpoint.

There were no guards in the hallway we'd just entered, at least for now. It proceeded forward as far as the eye could see, with a number of wooden doors to the left and right along its length. We'd have to try all of the doors, since there was no way to know where the wooden boxes had been stored.

"This'll be a long job, but we'll just have to take it slow and careful," I whispered.

My partner nodded back.

Ultimately, all of the doors were busts.

There were a number of chests, and we had a nice rest in a small break room, but it did little to ease my heavy fatigue. I was a completionist when it came to mapping, but even I had my limits.

By the time we finished searching the over three-hundred-foot-long hallway, it was nearly two in the morning. At this rate, we wouldn't be getting back to town until sunrise at the earliest, just like yesterday morning.

"Hmm…There's still a long way to go, I think," I muttered, peering down the stairs we found at the end of the hallway. Asuna fixed me with a look.

"Are you tired?"

"N-no…I'm fine…What about you?"

"I'm perfectly all right. I got better sleep than usual yesterday."

I wondered about that. She did get two or three hours in Romolo's rocking chair, but it was hard to recover from fatigue on bits of sleep like that. If that was *better* than usual, how did she usually sleep?

She seemed to sense what I was thinking. "I usually don't sleep all that much anyway."

"...I see."

I wasn't sure whether she was referring to her sleeping habits in real life or just since we'd been trapped in this game of death, but Asuna didn't elaborate.

"Come on, let's go. My instinct is telling me that those wooden boxes we want are down there," she said, patting me on the shoulder. I hurried after her.

At the bottom of the long staircase was a wide-open warehouse completely unlike the tight corridors above. The back wall featured a large double door guarded on either side by heavily armored Fallen Elf guards, by their standards. On the side walls were careless stacks of wooden boxes.

"Ooh, there they are," I whispered from the wall of the staircase. Asuna looked smug for a moment but wiped the grin off momentarily.

"We'll probably draw the attention of the guards if we just walk in there...If we can just sneak behind the boxes to the left or right somehow."

"I feel like we could beat them in a fight, but whatever's behind those huge doors worries me...I think I hear something weird from behind them."

We both stopped to concentrate. There were faint but clearly audible sounds of occasional banging or scraping.

"I wonder if we can distract those guards somehow."

"...Might as well give it a shot," I muttered, and picked up a stone from the ground. If I had the Distraction mod for the Throwing Knives skill that would up my chances, but there was no use complaining about what I didn't have. I aimed for one of the wooden boxes on the right and tossed the pebble.

It just barely clanked against the corner of a box, but it was enough to draw the notice of the guards' imposing masks. At that exact moment, I pushed Asuna forward into the warehouse and rushed behind her. We hunched over and made our way to the shadows behind the boxes on the left as quickly as we possibly could.

Fortunately, we were both in light leather and cloth armor, so our little stunt worked out. I let out a sigh of relief once my back was pressed against the box.

"*Whew*…Now let's see what's in this thing," I mumbled, turning around to check it out. From what I could tell, none of the boxes were nailed shut. I set my sights on a box without anything stacked on top and very, very carefully lifted the heavy lid to prevent any noises.

"…"

"…"

The instant we saw what was inside, Asuna and I shared a glance before looking back again, followed by another shared glance.

"…What does this mean?"

"…No idea…"

There was no other possible reaction. The wooden box was completely empty.

"Maybe they already hauled out the contents of the box," I wondered, and started opening the one next to it. But the result was the same. The next one and the next after that all contained nothing but air.

"Why…? They were treating them so carefully…"

"And paid all of that money…"

No sooner had we expressed our doubt and disappointment than we heard the sound of the giant doors opening beyond the mountain of boxes.

The excitement over my chance to check out what was in the next room soon evaporated into chills. The sound of seven or eight heavy pairs of boots flooded into the warehouse.

For half a second, I considered just hiding in the shadows, but that option was out the window. My in-game event senses were telling me that this scene demanded action. Thankfully, the loud marching and talking gave us a bit of cover when it came to sound.

There was no time to hesitate. I pried open the lid of the nearest box with one hand and pushed Asuna's back with the other.

"Inside!" I rasped, and my fear convinced her to do so. Once she had stepped over the side of the crate, I leaped in after her.

"Hey—"

I felt something soft pressed against the right side of my avatar. It was much smaller than I expected inside, but I couldn't move to the next box now. I pressed as much of my body into empty space as I could and slid the lid into place, leaving just a crack for air.

Before I even had time to breathe in relief, a very confused and upset whisper sounded in my ear.

"Why is this...so tight...?"

"G-good question. It looks a lot bigger from the outside... Maybe the walls of the box are really thick..."

"If they're making such thick boxes and not putting anything inside, maybe the boxes themselves are—"

"Shh!" I cut her off. Through the open slit, I saw a number of figures enter the frame from the left.

Standing at the lead was a large man who was quite burly for a Fallen Elf—more craftsman than soldier, if I had to guess. His plain mask only covered the lower half of his face, and his thick arms were covered with long leather gloves. He carried a very large hammer.

At first, I couldn't tell if it was meant to be a weapon or a tool. His color cursor identified him as EDDHU: FALLEN ELVEN FOREMAN, and I hadn't learned the meaning of the English term *foreman* in school.

The man named Eddhu stopped just five yards away from our box before turning back to his group of about ten followers.

"Thanks to today's shipment, we've now got the total we need."

Total of what? They're empty! I wanted to yell. But Asuna, who was pressed against me in an uncomfortable position, simply shook her head as if to say, "*Hold it in.*"

I nodded and focused on listening.

"Good. Well done," came a voice as beautiful and cold as ice from a tall and slender man who fit every expectation of an elf. His armor was a melding of leather and metal, a rarity for a Fallen, and a crimson cape flowed from his shoulders. His black mask had two horns growing from the forehead, but the eyes beneath them seemed to glow and flicker with red light.

"But the assembly is taking longer than expected," the caped man continued.

Eddhu bowed deeply. "I am very sorry, Your Excellency. We should be caught up within three days."

"Good. Then I may assume that it will be finished entirely in five days, as the plan stated?"

You can't say what *will be finished?!* I screamed silently again, focusing my gaze on the caped man to bring up his cursor. As soon as I did I flinched, shaking my own body and Asuna's as well.

The color was so dark, it was nearly black. Monster cursors shifted in shade from light to dark to distinguish the difference in level from the viewer, but I had never seen a color cursor as dark as the one belonging to "His Excellency." The Fallen Elven Commander from the third floor was nothing compared to him.

The problem was that my level was currently 16, well above the expected difficulty for the fourth floor. How much higher above could the caped man be if it was that black?

"..."

I glanced at the name at the bottom of the cursor, barely aware that Asuna was squeezing my right shoulder.

N'ltzahh: Fallen Elven General.

General!

Wait, how the hell do you say that name?!

Fortunately, Eddhu was there to solve at least half of my mix of fear and confusion.

"I will pledge my life to making it happen, General N'ltzahh."

"Very good. Get to work, Eddhu."

The general—whose name the foreman had pronounced like "Noltza"—patted Eddhu on one of his burly arms and began walking, his cape flowing behind him. Right toward the box in which we were currently hiding.

A chill ran up my spine, and I let the lid down to close properly. N'ltzahh himself would be more than a handful, but if we had to deal with another eight warriors and the undoubtedly strong Eddhu, too, our chances of winning were next to nothing. If they found us inside the box, our only chance of survival would be to leap out of the box and race for the stairs to the right, all the way out of their hideout.

The slow, teasing pace of his boots stopped approximately ten feet away. N'ltzahh's chilly voice cut right through the thick wooden lid of the box.

"…It truly is a farce, isn't it? Eons since we were removed from the blessing of the Holy Tree, yet we are still bound by the taboos of the elven race," he mocked. The first response came not from Eddhu's gruff voice, but a feminine mix of sweet and sharp.

"Yes…if not for that nonsensical taboo, we would not need to strike this deal with the filthy humans in order to gain these materials."

"It is not worth complaining about, Kysala. Pay them as much gold as they want. Once we have all of the keys and open the door to the Sanctuary, even the greatest magic left to humankind will vanish without a trace…"

"Of course, Excellency. The moment of our triumph grows ever closer."

"Indeed. But our initial mission is to recover the first key that the special forces commander let slip from our grasp. The plan begins in five days, once all of our preparations are complete. I have great expectations of all of you."

The soldiers shouted a salute in unison that rattled the lid of the box.

Even after the myriad footsteps faded into the distance and the enormous metal door slammed shut, I couldn't move.

I tried to commit as much detail of that conversation to memory as I could—it had to be written down as soon as we escaped from this bind. That was how much crucial information the Fallen Elves had just revealed. Secret keys and the Sanctuary—both keywords from the campaign quest during the beta, but never revealed in such concrete terms. And I had never met the man named General N'ltzahh back then. Who was he…?

"…Hey."

"Is he the true leader of the Fallen…?"

"…Hey, Kirito."

She pushed my shoulder, knocking me out of my thoughts.

"Huh? Wh-what?"

"What do you mean, what? How long are you going to do this?"

"Oh, crap, s-sorry," I started, then glanced down at my right side. I belatedly realized that my arm was stuck in quite a situation.

"Shry—!"

I nearly screamed "sorry," but clamped my mouth shut. My right arm was jammed right between Asuna's brand-new breastplate and her tunic. I tried to yank it loose, but there was no place behind me for the arm to go. The only result was a continued squishy, soft pressure against my arm.

"Hey, don't just shove me around."

"B-but I'm trying to—this is weird."

"…Ah! Listen, if you're doing this on purpose, I'm going to hurl you into the other room."

"Not at all, Your Excellency!" I wanted to yelp. Meanwhile, I folded up my arm in an acrobatic manner and just managed to pull it out of the side of the armor. Naturally, that wasn't the very end of my peril; I lifted up the lid of the box as much to escape the brunt of the laser beam glare trained at my cheek as anything else.

I couldn't see any of the Fallen Elves. But those two guards had to still be at the sides of the massive doors on the other side of the pile of boxes. I stood up, the lid still clutched in my hand, and helped Asuna out of the box. Once I had straddled the side to exit the wooden prison, I carefully replaced the lid.

Before I could even enjoy a brief moment of peace, Asuna got right in my face. I was expecting her to give me hell over my transgression, but her whisper was actually about a serious matter.

"We need to figure out what the 'materials' they mentioned are before we leave this place. There must be a clue in one of the boxes we haven't checked yet."

"Yeah, I agree...but...it's possible that..." I mumbled, my brain working feverishly over the phrases we heard.

The total needed. Completed as planned. Elven taboo. Deals with the humans. Keys. Recover. Plan begins in five days...

My mind was trapped in that space where inspiration was tantalizingly close yet still out of reach. I put a question into words that had been bothering me.

"Hey, Asuna. That Eddhu guy's class was labeled 'foreman.' Do you know what that is?"

She nodded at once—she'd probably learned the English term in school.

"Yes. It's the leader of a work crew for a factory, for example. Or a head craftsman."

"...Head craftsman...?"

That would mean the hammer he carried was a tool, not a weapon. Whatever he worked on, it must be big...

Suddenly all of the pieces snapped into place in my head with an audible *ka-ching!*

"......!"

I nearly shouted in surprise, but I held it in and glanced over at the stack of boxes.

That's right—I was about to say it to Asuna when we were hiding inside it. These sturdy boxes weren't meant to transport something. They were something else disguised as boxes to hide the secret of the Fallen Elves' dirty dealing.

Everything we were looking at was ship materials.

That had to be a huge workshop on the other side of the door, where they were dismantling the boxes to form pieces of lumber. The faint hammering sounds were evidence of that.

So why did they need to strike a deal with Rovia's Water Carriers Guild to build a ship? Probably something to do with the elven taboo that General N'ltzahh mentioned. The elves in this world were forbidden from cutting down live trees for lumber. They could only take trees that had fallen naturally. So they were making deals with humans for extra materials to speed up the process.

"...Did you figure something out?" Asuna asked, jabbing my arm. My mind ground to a halt.

"Uh, y-yeah. But it'll be a long explanation, so let's leave this spot first. You never know if they might come back."

"If that happens, we're hiding in a bigger box," she announced. I had no choice but to agree heartily.

I used the pebble distraction trick to buy us an escape from the storeroom so we could retreat up the staircase to the first floor. Either through sheer carelessness or mental fatigue, we were spotted by the guard patrolling near the entrance to the hideout but were able to defeat him before he could call his fellows. At last, we were back at the dock in the watery dungeon.

Because the infiltration took much longer than expected, the Argyro's Sheet was at less than 10 percent durability when we removed it. I carefully folded up the sheet in thanks for its invaluable service, then placed it in storage and got the ship moving.

We ran across several crabs and turtles and such on the trip back, but the *Tilnel*'s Burning Charge—as I liked to call it—made easy work of them, and we escaped the dungeon at last.

The moment we left the cave for the black predawn river, the quest log *ding*ed to alert us to an update.

I kept one hand on the oar while I called up the window. The new instruction said to alert the appropriate person of the information gained.

Asuna read the same instruction as she watched the space ahead of the gondola. She turned back and asked, "When it says 'appropriate person,' does that mean Mr. Romolo?"

"Maybe, but the previous instructions always called him the 'shipwright,' so maybe not..."

"Someone important at the Water Carriers Guild, then?"

"Hmm. Something tells me they wouldn't have a very friendly reaction to us..."

"Well, who, then?"

"Let's figure that out once we get back to town," I suggested.

Asuna accepted, although reluctantly. She started to face forward but turned back to add, "Oh, right. Do you want to change inns? The place next to the teleport gate wasn't bad, but I don't want another ruckus raised at that dock."

"Oh, good point. We can look for someplace a little more out of the way. Plus, we need to let the blue team and green team know about the quest soon," I murmured, then stopped in my tracks.

If Lind and Kibaou managed to build their ships and finish the quest, great. But what if they kept going like we were now? What if they heard out Romolo's story, spotted and followed the mysterious ship back to the submerged dungeon, then snuck into the Fallen Elf hideout...and just so happened to get in a battle with General N'ltzahh and his men? I trusted in Lind and Kibaou's strength, but could they really tackle the general, who might be as powerful as a floor boss, without suffering any fatalities?

I thought back to N'ltzahh's pitch-black cursor and trembled. No, defeat was certain if that event ended in battle. Perhaps there was a built-in failure prevention aspect, such as with the battle between the Dark Elf and Forest Elf champions at the start of the "Jade Key" quest on the third floor. But if not, that could result in the death of a full party of six.

"Maybe we should discuss with Argo first about how much info to reveal," I murmured, rowing slowly. Up ahead, the looming sight of Rovia's south gate came into view.

We ended up picking out a tiny inn in the corner of the southwest quadrant for our new base of operations, our choice clinched by the small shack we could use to keep the gondola inside. We collapsed in one of the two rooms we rented, me in the rocking chair and Asuna on the bed.

After sharing a long, luxurious sigh, I lazily lifted a finger to return my weapon and armor to storage. It was three thirty in the morning. We made it back earlier than the previous day, but the ten hours of adventuring threatened to shut off my brain with fatigue.

I couldn't sleep now, though. I needed to put together the information while it was still fresh in my mind, and besides, this was Asuna's room, not mine.

"Well, let's start with the wooden boxes," I began, stifling a yawn. Asuna didn't respond. I sat up and looked over at the bed. She was lying facedown with her face stuffed into the pillow, entirely still. Her menu window was still displayed right above the pillow, too.

For someone who complained about not being able to sleep, she's doing a good job of it now, I thought. I got up from the rocking chair and stood next to the bed.

"Hey, you left your window open," I called out, softly shaking her shoulder. She didn't wake up. The window was set to private mode by default, so it was just a blank board to me, but it still felt a little careless.

"Miss Asuna, wake uuup."

No response. If I kept shaking, she was going to get another harassment notice. Speaking of which, I needed to figure out what was up with the warning order. But for now, it was more important to get her to close her menu.

After thinking it over for a bit, I picked up her right hand from its spot splayed out on the bed. The main menu would disappear with a good, long flick from the top, so I moved her finger to the right spot and pulled down. On the third try, it took for good, and the window disappeared. I set her hand back down at once with relief.

"We can have the meeting later. Good night," I murmured, and left the room as quietly as I could.

6

3:00 PM, SATURDAY, DECEMBER 24—THE NEXT DAY.

I was really getting used to controlling the *Tilnel* and wound the oar around adeptly, exclaiming in wonder.

"You know…it's truly impressive, how much you built…"

A gravelly, deep voice came from the midsize boat moored just to the right.

"Ha-ha! You should have seen the Bear Forest yesterday. We had two axmen with us, so the material gathering didn't take long at all. Then again, we focused on the normal wood, so it's nothing to brag about."

The voice belonged to a large man with a shaved bald head and short beard stubble. He'd been practicing his ship steering until late in the night, so his oarsmanship was quite impressive.

"So you didn't have to line up at the old man's place, then?"

"Nope. We were the first there after the guide came out. Boy, the DKB didn't like it when they showed up second, five minutes later. You were the ones who collected that data, right? I gotta thank you for that."

"N-nah, no big deal," I mumbled, feeling guilty about the fact that we were still covering up half of the quest-related info. He smirked at me knowingly.

The man's name was Agil, and he was the leader of a four-man party that maintained a neutral position among the frontline

players between the twin powers of the Dragon Knights Brigade and Aincrad Liberation Squad guilds.

He and his three companions with their double-handed heavy weapons sat in a midsize gondola painted a calm brown shade. Due to the haste of their construction, the boat didn't have any options such as the battering horn, but the passengers' imposing weapons seemed capable of making up for that. The name *Pequod* was written in black ink along the side.

I didn't recognize the source of that name, but Asuna in her red hood noticed it at once.

"The *Pequod* isn't a very optimistic name for a boat like that."

Agil roared with laughter, and one of his companions bearing a two-handed hammer grumbled, "That's what we told him."

Asuna noticed the giant question mark hanging over my head and turned around to explain.

"The *Pequod* was the name of Captain Ahab's ship. It gets sunk by Moby Dick in the end."

"I-I see...And why did you choose that name?" I asked the bald man, who grinned again.

"Think of it this way: It can't sink until we fight that big white whale, right? And from what I hear, you don't fight a whale here, but a turtle." He pointed a thick finger ahead.

The *Tilnel* and *Pequod* were moored at the entrance to a caldera lake just north of the center of the fourth floor. The pure blue lake, over three hundred yards across and surrounded by sheer cliffs, had to be passed to reach the south half of the floor. In other words, we were waiting here to take part in a battle against the field boss who guarded the path ahead.

In the beta test, this was the mouth of a volcano with red glowing magma bubbling up from cracks in the earth. It was many times more beautiful now that it was filled with water, but I was uneasy about fighting a boss on a boat. After all, if the player steering the boat fell into the water, it could no longer be maneuvered.

The crashing of a gong interrupted my thoughts. The sound

was coming from one of the *many* other boats that I had praised just moments earlier.

Ahead and to the right of the *Tilnel* were three gondolas pointed away from us, their bodies painted blue with white trim. The one in the center was a ten-seater, the largest kind Romolo could make. The other two were four-seaters like Agil's. Each one had an extra space for a gondolier, so in all, they could carry twenty-one. As the blue color suggested, they belonged to the Dragon Knights Brigade.

On the left were three more gondolas, the bodies moss green, with the broadsides dark gray. Each of the three were sized for six, once again totaling twenty-one when boatmen were added. These were the ships of the green-themed Aincrad Liberation Squad.

On the third floor, each guild had numbered eighteen, so they must have both picked up three more over the course of this floor. If I didn't get a registry from Argo soon, I wouldn't be able to keep track of their faces and names anymore. I searched closely for Morte, the mysterious swordsman/axman who I'd dueled against in the dead of night, but his trademark coif was nowhere to be seen.

Even with all the available manpower they had, it was incredible that both guilds had managed three gondolas each in the span of a single day. It took three hours to build one boat, so the final one must have been finished just barely before our meeting time. NPC or not, old man Romolo must have been exhausted from working around the clock.

The clanging of the gong was coming from the DKB mother ship, the largest present. The gong right at the prow must have been an option for the larger size. The ALS looked on with distaste at what they hadn't been able to procure, as Lind held up a hand to stop the gong and address the crowd.

"It's time! We are about to begin our battle against the Biceps Archelon, field boss of the fourth floor! None of us have any experience with a major water battle aboard ships, but there's nothing to fear! As you've seen in fighting ordinary monsters, their attacks are almost entirely absorbed by our ships!"

Easy for you to say, in that giant cruise ship, I grumbled mentally. He raised his right hand high in the air and clenched it into a fist.

"As I explained in our prebattle meeting, the Archelon's attacks are quite simple! As long as we watch out for the direction its two heads are facing, we can avoid taking any charges! We will use this gong to signal the timing of evasion, so please keep an ear out for it!"

And we were the ones who found out that info for you, I grumbled again. Naturally, there was a price for sneaking ahead of everyone to get our ship first, so as a member of this community, I supposed it was my duty to scout ahead and learn what I could.

I figured they might as well saddle us with the duty of charging front and center in the fight, but that role went to the DKB and ALS. In this fight, the minor parties—Asuna and I and Agil's group—had to attack the boss's sides, which were virtually impervious thanks to the creature's thick shell.

"Let's move out! Take formation when the boss appears! Dragon Knights fleet, forward!!" Lind cried, swinging his arm forward. The DKB mother ship *Leviathan* and its two escorts began to move. Kibaou growled to his guildmates on the left side, not wanting to be left behind.

"C'mon, let's get goin'! All ships at top speed, Liberation Squad!!"

With an "Aye-aye, sir," the helmsman of the *Unleash* rowed onward, and their consorts joined in.

"Welp...guess we should get going," I said lifelessly, while Agil smirked and thrust out a heavy fist.

"Let's show 'em that we're not playing second fiddle here!"

His trio of teammates roared in approval, and Asuna nodded with serious intent. It wouldn't do for me to be left out of the group, so I lamely raised my hand and joined in the cheer.

* * *

The field boss of the fourth dungeon was a huge water monster named Biceps Archelon, and true to the name, it was an ancient, two-headed turtle. It had three attacks: a bite attack from both heads, a watery smack from its side fins, and a charge making use of its sixty-foot length.

As Lind had reassured us, the bite and fin attacks weren't that powerful, so letting the ship absorb the damage if necessary was a valid option. The charge attack was the real problem, and it would probably be enough to capsize our ships if it struck true.

According to Lind's report, a capsized boat recovered automatically after thirty seconds, but until then, the crew had no choice but to cling to it, leaving them vulnerable to the bites and fin slaps.

Fortunately, a few seconds before it started one of its massive charges, both heads would point in the same direction. If we watched for that motion and made sure to avoid their line of sight, it shouldn't be hard to avoid the charge.

Bwong, bwong! The *Leviathan*'s gong crashed, and Lind shouted. "Evade!"

Up ahead, four gondolas split left and right from their position directly before the Archelon. We were on the left flank of the turtle, but I backed up the *Tilnel* just in case.

A moment later, the draconic heads of the Archelon rose high in the air, and its sixty-foot-long bulk tore forward.

Spray showered down on us, and the waves in the wake of its passing rocked the boat. I stood the oar up to balance against the rocking so I could look around; none of the other ships had capsized. The boss's HP gauge was nearly halfway gone, and at this rate, the battle would be over in less than twenty minutes.

I sent the gondola after the Archelon's new location, and Asuna turned back to me, rapier in her hand.

"Hey, what kind of boss was here in the beta?"

"Well…it was still a turtle, but more of a giant tortoise. Very tough but slow, and I don't remember us having much trouble."

"Hmm…so I suppose it must have gotten an update along with everything else when they decided to soak this level in water."

"Well, of course. I mean, it's to be expected—all the doors to the buildings in town were on the second floor to start with… *Whoa!*"

One of the ALS's six-man gondolas raced past, knocking the tiny *Tilnel* off-balance. As they passed us, the riders left us a heartwarming message: "Even the great beater ain't gonna win the LA today!"

After it left, Asuna stomped her foot in indignation.

"What's the big idea? This formation was *their* idea to begin with."

"Now, now. As long as we stay to the side, we don't have to worry about the boat getting damaged," I said soothingly, moving us back into position at the Archelon's left flank.

The attacks and the damage caused were fiercest at the heads, where the DKB and ALS kept two ships each. The third ships from both guilds were at the tail, which also suffered some damage—this was all according to our plan. We and Agil had to take the sides, sheer walls of dark, gleaming shell. Even Asuna's Chivalric Rapier +5 could barely scratch the boss's HP.

I watched her shoot off the Parallel Sting two-part combo out of sheer frustration and used half my brain to engage in some idle thinking.

The latter stages of the shipbuilding quest were not mentioned in Argo's strategy guide when the guide appeared in the afternoon yesterday. This was both because of the unknown nature of N'ltzahh's strength and the fierce rivalry between the two main guilds.

There was very nearly open warfare outside the Forest Elf camp on the third floor between the DKB, who were undertaking the Forest Elf side of the campaign, and the ALS, who were aligned with the Dark Elf faction. My arguments fell on deaf ears, and we nearly had player-on-player violence—only the advent of the powerful knight Kizmel succeeded in staying their blades.

After some discussion, both guilds agreed to put the campaign quest on hold, thus averting a collapse of the frontline collective. However, the latter part of this shipbuilding quest seemed to be related to the campaign. If we publicized that information, they might take the teleporter back to the third floor to renew the quest. We had to ensure that the two guilds did not resume butting heads again.

So after discussion with Argo, Asuna and I decided not to release the connections to the Fallen Elves. But Lind and Kibaou weren't leading their guilds for show. It was very possible they would discover the continuation of the quest on their own, and if that happened, there was nothing we could do. Then again, with their great numbers, massive ships, and apparently reckless boating, they might not even succeed at trailing the guild's transport ship.

It was a fact that the pitched competition between the two guilds was speeding our progress along through the game. But the lack of any kind of stopping force, if their competition crossed a healthy line, was terrifying to me.

We needed a third power. It could be small in scale, but something with enough influence and leadership qualities that Lind and Kibaou couldn't overlook it—a linchpin to the frontline force as a whole.

At present, the closest thing to that third power was Agil the ax warrior, currently fighting on the opposite side of the giant turtle shell. But he and his three companions intended to maintain their position as a free-roaming, neutral force. They only joined the group for field and floor bosses and barely ever appeared otherwise.

The only other person with the capability of being that linchpin was Asuna the fencer, with her flashing silver rapier.

After we fought Illfang the Kobold Lord on the first floor, I told her that she could be strong, and if anyone she trusted invited her to a guild, not to refuse. That there were limits to what could be accomplished in solo play.

My instinct wasn't wrong. If anything, I was underestimating her potential. If she got more accustomed to this world and learned more of the game's rules and quirks, Asuna could easily lead a guild of her own. That guild could admirably serve as a third power to balance out the ALS and DKB.

But as long as she was with me, the beater, she would be shunned within the group. She would never be seen as anything other than a willful outsider, showing up where she pleased and leeching hard-earned items and information from more worthy people.

If the sake of the front line as a whole, and Asuna as an individual, were to be taken into account…then maybe we shouldn't be a duo forever. But the existence of Asuna's Chivalric Rapier, with its absurdly good stats, and the Bottle of Kales'Oh that granted her an extra skill slot filled me with unspoken dread. I wanted to prioritize her safety above all else.

Yes, I was concerned for her well-being, but the truth was, there was another bigger reason that drove my choices…an egotistical one.

Somewhere in my heart, I was afraid of her gathering more attention and eventually being called on to take a leadership role…

"Kirito! The gauge is about to drop into the red!"

I was snapped back into the present. Up above the looming, mountainous shell of the Biceps Archelon, the two-bar HP gauge was on its last legs. More than a few bosses changed their attack patterns once in the red zone, so I pushed the boat backward, just in case.

But the four ships trained at the heads of the turtle doing the brunt of the damage were still right there, hammering even harder than before. The players lined up along the sides of the gondolas facing the turtle set off sword skills left and right, enveloping the Archelon's two heads in colored light. The HP gauge dropped further, under the 10 percent mark.

"Hey! Everyone get away!" I heard Agil shout from the other side of the turtle shell.

I was already at a safe distance, just far enough back to take in the entirety of the beast. Its two heads, front and rear flippers, and tail were all twisted up against the sides of the shell. I'd never seen this animation before, but I sensed what it was.

"Watch out, it's going to spin!!"

I very much doubted that it would spin enough to fly like a certain movie monster, but even the largest gondola would certainly capsize if sucked into a giant whirlpool—if it didn't crash into other ships first. But neither guild retreated, even after our warnings. They probably hoped to take it all the way down in this burst of sword skills, but the spinning preparation raised the boss's defense, and its HP stubbornly refused to drain away.

"They're in big trouble at this rate, Kirito!" Asuna cried. That settled the matter.

I ordered my partner to duck down, then rowed madly. As the *Tilnel* raced forward through the whitecaps, the Archelon's massive body tensed powerfully.

If we charge in and take all the glory again, it's just going to make our reputation worse, I thought briefly. But then I changed my mind and pushed on with one last row.

"Screw that! I'm not giving up my position!"

The burning red ram at the front of the *Tilnel* plunged deep into the softer gut of the Archelon just before it could begin spinning. After a brief moment of silence, a few white steam vents burst out of the shell. The entire form of the turtle bulged outward, shrouded in blue light—and exploded.

I looked up at the listing of col, normal loot, and the Last Attack bonus and thought, *Good grief, I did it again.*

Asuna stood up at the prow of the boat and slid her rapier into its sheath, then glanced skeptically at me.

"S-sorry about just charging like that, but it looked like the turtle was about to start something bad…"

"Yes, that's fine. But what did you mean by 'my position'?"

I didn't know if telling her that I meant "my position as gondolier" would fly as an excuse, but fortunately for me, she didn't press any further, so I quickly guided the boat toward the exit of the caldera.

We zoomed past the Dragon Knights and Liberation Squad, who looked mighty peeved, pissed, and petulant for having just defeated the field boss, and waved to Agil's team as they shot us thumbs-up on the way out of the lake. After a brief trip down the river, we would reach a small village called Usco.

"Y'know, I've been noticing," I started to say to Asuna. She was clearly deep in thought, as it took her a few seconds to turn around and respond.

"Huh…? Wh-what?"

"Oh, it's nothing serious…but I was noticing that travel from town to town on this floor hasn't been easy. In the previous few, we could just sprint our way down the path, but here you've got to either swim or paddle."

"Mm, you're right. Plus there's the occasional monster in the river. People coming for sightseeing will be satisfied by Rovia alone, I'm sure, but I wonder how Argo's doing here."

"Speaking of which, I wonder if even she'll be stuck in the main town this time…"

"No looking down on me, Kii-boy."

"I'm not looking down on you, but—*whaaah?!*"

A familiar voice sounded in my ear that should definitely *not* have been present, and I nearly fell out of the boat. I lost balance and caused the oar to slip, rocking the gondola. Asuna abruptly had to regain her balance up front and turned back in surprise.

Traveling just to the left of the *Tilnel* at the exact same speed was the unmistakable face of Argo the Rat.

She wasn't swimming. She wasn't riding on a boat, either.

She was gliding on the surface of the river like a water strider.

"Wh-what the heck is that?! Did you become an apprentice to those doofus ninjas from the Fuma Ninja Force?!"

"Nya-ha-ha, hardly. I found these babies in town."

She slid along the water on one leg, raising her right foot high so I could see. Instead of her usual boots, she was wearing sandals equipped with very light-looking wooden floater paddles. An item that gave the wielder the ability to run on water, no doubt.

"Wha…Th-they were selling those things?! What was the point of going to all that trouble to build a ship…?"

"The rub is, these require a ridiculous amount of agility to equip, and you gotta lower your weight as much as possible when using 'em. Tip your balance even the tiniest bit, and you'll flip over. No way to fight when using these babies."

"Ohhh…Doesn't seem like you've given up much of your gear, though," I remarked, looking sidelong at her. As far as I could tell, she was still in her familiar hooded cape and didn't seem much lighter than usual.

The Rat's face crinkled into a smirk, her painted whiskers twitching.

"Is that how it seems to you? Never know, I might be wearin' nothin' at all under here."

"…O-oh yeah?"

I started to turn my head to check, but felt a stare inflicting piercing damage on my forehead from the front seat and turned to face forward. Argo chuckled again, while Asuna cleared her throat to ask a question.

"Um, Argo, would you like to ride with us to the next village? We have an open seat."

"Ooh, thanks. I'll take you up on that."

The Rat nimbly leaped onto the gondola and took the leather seat just behind Asuna. The two girls abruptly began whispering to each other.

As I picked up the gondola's pace, I silently hissed at old man Romolo. *Gramps, you should have told us that a two-seater actually holds three!*

*   *   *

If the main town of Rovia was a "city of water," then Usco was a "floating village."

It was made of about a dozen shacks, walkways, and open spaces buoyed by balsa-like logs, floating and creaking in the midst of a crescent-shaped lake. It was certainly more picturesque than the plain little run-down village of the beta, but I felt likely to get low-grade seasickness if I spent more than a little time there.

Then again, motion sickness came from the inner ear, so the fact that the signals of movement were bypassing that to the brain directly might mean that there was no seasickness here. In fact, I didn't recall anyone in the front line feeling sick while riding on the gondolas.

We stopped the *Tilnel* at the dock on the edge of town and moored it there, then headed for the center of the settlement to the only restaurant there. It was still early in the day, but surely we could be allowed to a toast to our triumph over the field boss.

I did my very best to avoid looking at the bare legs clad in floater sandals peeking out from Argo's cape as we walked down the boarded, floating walkways. Eventually we came to a tropical-themed restaurant. There were no other players sitting on the open terrace facing the lake, of course.

I sat down at the special seat in the center and ordered drinks and appetizers from the scantily clad NPC waitress, then leaned back in the wicker chair and stretched.

"Ahhh...Finally, we're halfway done with the fourth floor..."

"You say 'finally' as if it hasn't been just three days since we got here. We're on a much faster pace than the second or third floor," Asuna pointed out.

"What, really...? We got up to this floor on December twenty-first, so that makes the twenty-second, twenty-third, twenty-fourth...Oh, you're right."

"You're not old enough to be going senile yet, Kii-boy," Argo chimed in.

I grinned and shot back at her, "You never know. In real life, I might be an old gentleman spending his retirement enjoying a good MMORPG."

"Then I'll have to start calling you Kii-gramps instead."

"...Never mind. Please don't..."

As we bickered and joked, a tray of brightly colored cocktails arrived. We clinked our glasses, and after downing over half of the lychee-scented juice, I let out a very long breath.

Once we'd eaten something, I was pretty much ready to walk next door and fall asleep, but there was business to conduct. I shook my head to get into the proper mood.

"The DKB and ALS will be here very soon, so we should pick up all the quests in the village and start on some of the easier ones..."

We'd finished all of the short individual quests in Rovia aside from the "Shipwright of Yore" yesterday, while the guilds were busy building their gondolas. That had earned us quite a bit of experience, but we were also well above the proper level for this area, so it wasn't enough for a level-up. We'd probably get there with two or three quests from this village, so my proper gamer's instinct said I should hit that point before I slept.

Asuna and Argo looked at each other, then spoke in turn.

"I don't know about Agil's group, but the big guilds are going back to the city for today."

"So there's no need to rush through all of this village's quests today, Kii-boy."

"Huh...? They're going back to Rovia? Did they leave some quests behind?" I said, confused. The two girls shot me questioning looks.

"So...you didn't get invited, Kirito?"

"...Invited to what?"

"Nothin' to be disappointed about, Kii-boy. We'll be here with ya."

"...Disappointed about what?"

"Didn't you *just* say what day it was?"

"What...you mean December twenty-fourth?" I said, then frowned. A few days ago, it had occurred to me that some special day was coming up. December 24...meant the day before December 25, making it...something eve...

"W-wait, you mean...Chrisma-whatever? And *that's* why the DKB and ALS went back? Is that why they were in such a rush to beat the field boss?" I said, flabbergasted. The girls nodded together, their faces sympathetic.

But nothing could have prepared me for what Asuna said next.

"Yes. You see, tonight the two guilds are going to hold a united Christmas send-off party."

"...Wha...u...united...party...? You mean...they're...but...wha..."

My *"What the hell?"* scream turned into a sonic boom that ripped the lake apart and shook Usco with a magnitude-7 quake.

From what I heard later, the Christmas send-off party was a sumptuous, free, all-you-can-eat-and-drink event held in the teleport square of Rovia starting at five o'clock on Christmas Eve.

They didn't advertise it far and wide with bulletin boards and flyers (I would have noticed if they had), but they did manage to draw nearly two hundred non-frontline players through word of mouth alone. Between the first major player-run public event and the unpredictable weather, it caused quite a hullabaloo. Aside from the food arranged by the sponsors, some merchant players set up food carts of their own, and there was even a young female blacksmith who set up a stand for weapon repairs.

The idea came from the ALS, apparently as a way to make good use of all the crab, shrimp, and bear meat they'd accumulated on their questing. Calling it a Christmas party would attract attention from other players, both increasing the guild's profile and acting as a good recruitment opportunity. When the DKB learned of this, they tried to set up a competing event, and after much squabbling over the use of the teleport square in Rovia, the two groups decided to make up and throw the party together.

"Well, I suppose I should be happy that they managed to put on an event together…but calling it a 'send-off party' is a bit weird. Isn't that usually what you throw before a big competition or when traveling somewhere new? It seems backward for the people who are going off to the labyrinth tower to throw their own send-off party," I grumbled as I slurped the remainder of the lychee juice and poked at the food tray.

Asuna looked like she didn't know whether to feel sorry for me or laugh at me. She noted softly, "It wasn't like *nobody* suggested inviting you to the party. You're one of the front-runners, too, Kirito. But some folks in the ALS wondered why they should pay for free food and drinks for the guy who always steals the LA bonuses, and they ended up deciding that you didn't need an invitation."

"Who did you hear this from, by the way?"

"From Shivata in the DKB during the field boss strategy meeting. He also asked me to apologize to you for them."

"…Hmm."

"They did say that I could go, if I wanted."

"…Hmmmm."

"And I got lots of instant messages from other people."

"…Hmmmmmm."

"By the way, Agil's team is going back to the city as well, but only to finish up their quests, not to participate. So you don't have to sulk so much."

"…*Hmmmmmmmm.* So you fancy yourself a solo player, do you?"

Suddenly, Argo burst out with a series of eerie, smirking giggles.

"Wh-what's up with you?"

"Oh, nothing. Now if you don't mind, I'll be getting back to the main town," she remarked, slipping out of her chair.

Stunned, I asked, "Already? If you were going to leave so soon, why did you even come out here to this village?"

"To gather data on quests and shop selections, of course. I'd like to pop in on the send-off party, too. Welp, so long, A-chan, Kii-boy." She waved briefly, grinned, and added, "Oops, nearly forgot. Merry Christmas."

"Merry Christmas, Argo. Take care," Asuna said.

"M...Many Crimmas," I joined in, feeling like I didn't quite have that right. Before I knew it, the information dealer was gone.

After a while, Asuna mumbled, "Argo should have been the first one invited to the Christmas party."

"No kidding. With ultra-elite VIP status," I agreed, finishing my juice.

At this very moment, Argo was out collecting information on the businesses, wares, and quest NPCs of Usco. Her drive for information, whether in the safety of town or hazards of the wilderness, was an invaluable support to our progress in the game of death.

But more than a few players in the two guilds still felt distaste at hearing the name Argo the Rat. They seemed to think that the former beta testers had a solemn duty to provide the information for these invaluable strategy guides that everyone was using.

In the face of this expectation, Argo's policies of selling anything she could and getting her money's worth were distasteful, to be sure. She would even sell what we'd just talked about, if someone wanted it and paid the price. Even a friend like me had to filter what he said around her.

I didn't know why she pursued such unfriendly policies. She would probably sell me the reason if I asked. One day I'd buy that reason from her, price be damned, I told myself, setting the empty cocktail glass on the table.

"So...what do we do n..." I started, then realized that I hadn't checked something with her first. "Er, I mean...if you want to go, I'm not going to hold you back."

My temporary partner looked surprised at that, so I added, "I mean...if you got formally invited to the Christmas send-off party and you're refusing because of me, you don't need to—"

"Oh, that?" she interrupted, cutting me short. She snorted. "No, don't bother yourself. I had no intention of going from the start. I'm not one for flashy parties."

"O-oh, I see. Well, then…umm…"

Before I could suggest that we clear up two or three quests and level up before nightfall, I stopped myself.

I had no particular attachment to Christmas Eve, but that didn't necessarily hold true for Asuna. She knew what day it was—and talented fencer though she might be, she was still a young woman…I thought.

"…Do you…want to try it here?"

"Try what?"

"Having our own…Christmassy thing."

The fencer stared right into me, her eyebrows tensing, as if simulating several possible answers. She ended up choosing the turn-your-head-away-in-a-huff response.

"N-no, that's not necessary. I don't have anything prepared… and it just doesn't feel like Christmas in this tropical island village."

For a moment, I almost thought the weather-controlling system heard her. The onslaught of golden afternoon light abruptly dimmed, and the sparkling blue surface of the lake went a cloudy gray. A chilly wind from across the lake rustled her long hair.

"N-no way," she whispered. I followed her gaze.

There was a tiny white dot falling silently from the cloudy sky.

It caught the breeze and wandered over through the open terrace of the restaurant to land on my gloved hand. The white dot melted promptly, leaving a tiny chill on the palm of my hand.

Then came another and another. Seen there were countless white points dancing in the air.

"…It's snow…" I mumbled. True, it was December, but I'd never seen snow in Aincrad before. In fact, I'd hardly ever felt what I would call a wintry chill.

According to what I read in an article before the game trapped me inside, *SAO* was supposed to re-create the actual season outside, depending on which floor one was on. But the fourth floor couldn't be one of those specially aligned ones. This snow must be from a special holiday event, just for Christmas.

Soon the huts of dried tropical grasses were white with snow. Some NPC children raced along the nearby walkway, giggling and screaming.

As I took in the surreal sight of the tropical island turning to a winter wonderland, I heard a reluctant sigh from beside me.

"Why did it have to do this…?"

I looked back to see Asuna watching the snow with wide-open eyes. I couldn't possibly read the expression on her face.

At the very least, I knew that the little white flurry dancing past her light brown eyes was beautiful. Eventually, she noticed me staring at her and blinked several times.

"…Just when we escaped the main city and came here, so I could avoid thinking about Christmas," she mumbled. "It's not fair."

"Huh…? You were trying not to think about it? But…didn't you say…?"

I pressed my fingers to my temples and dredged up my memory of a conversation from nearly two weeks ago.

"Didn't you say that it might snow on Christmas, when we were tackling the second-floor labyrinth?"

She pursed her lips in mild embarrassment. "I'm surprised you remember that. Maybe I did say that, but I'm in no mood to enjoy the holiday given the circumstances. We should be pushing farther rather than throwing parties. Besides, you didn't even bring it up until just minutes ago."

"Huh? Bring…what up…?"

As soon as I asked, she gave me a dirty look. "If you wanted to have a Christmas event, you should have told me a few days earlier, so I could have prepared. And if you're not going to bring it up until the day, it's only natural to assume you weren't interested in that."

"Huh? Prepare...?"

"Prepare what?" I wanted to ask, but I already knew the answer. The three essential elements to any Japanese Christmas celebration were fried chicken, cake, and presents. The first two could be arranged at an NPC shop, but not the presents.

I didn't have a single considerate item that Asuna might be happy to receive in my inventory, of course, so bringing up the suggestion of a Christmas party was not to be taken lightly.

Then again, if I really inspected my entire item list, there might be a surprise here or there, I thought stubbornly, but it was a meaningless idea. When Asuna said she didn't have anything prepared, she had to be talking about a Christmas present, and knowing her perfectionist nature, she would not want to settle for picking out a present from her unwanted leftovers, rather than something conceived as a gift from the start.

Besides, it was clear from Asuna's explanations that she was pretending to shun the big Christmas party in town and focus on the game as a rationale because I hadn't said anything about the holiday before now.

"...It's my fault. I'm sorry," I said automatically.

"Huh...? N-no, you don't need to apologize," she said, surprised. But I kept my head bowed low.

"No. I brought up Christmas on the second floor and then forgot all about it by the time we got here—it's messed up. If we can't take our mind off the game for this day, at the very least..."

"This is...kind of throwing me off," she said awkwardly. I looked up, half-afraid of what I would see. She shrugged and didn't really look that angry. "Listen, if I really wanted to have a Christmas thing, I should have spoken up about it. But I didn't, so you don't need to apologize to me. I'm happy just seeing all of this."

I looked out at the village again. The steadily falling snow was already piling up two inches high, which made it look like the village of Usco itself was faintly glowing.

It did put me in a traveling mind, but I knew that if snow was falling all over Aincrad, there must be better views for it. The stunning setting of Rovia was no doubt improved even more with a coating of snow, and there would be beauty to spare in the forest city of Zumfut, Urbus nestled in its mountain, and even the Town of Beginnings at the very bottom.

But while it would be easy to travel between these cities with the teleporter, getting back to the gate was too far a distance. We'd have to travel across nearly half of the six-mile-wide floor to get to the gate, and it would be surrounded by all the members of the DKB and ALS in the midst of their party. Now wasn't the time to show up in their midst.

We'd have to find someplace here on the fourth floor to be the setting for our white Christmas...

Suddenly, an image flashed into my head.

A place I visited in the beta. A dusty building jutting alone out of a wide, wasted landscape of sand and rocks. But there were no more dry, dirty wastelands on this floor anymore. Yes, that spot would do...

"...Hey, Asuna."

"What?"

She tilted her head toward me. I cast my hesitation aside and made my suggestion.

"It's not something physical I can give you...but there is something I'd like to give you, to make up for it..."

"..."

She stared at me with large eyes for a few long moments, then mumbled, "Well, you're free to offer it. Just don't expect anything in return."

We refueled on consumable items in snowy Usco and went ahead with accepting quests, then set off in the *Tilnel* again through the falling powder.

If this was happening in the real world, there would be plenty of discomfort: too cold, not enough visibility, snow piling up in the gondola. But in the virtual world, the worst that happened was slightly worse vision and nothing that interfered with our rowing. The boat passed through the evening crescent lake and to the river that exited to the south.

There was no hint of monsters in the water, either due to it being Christmas Eve or just too cold with all the snow. I used that to my advantage to pick up the speed, and we slid smoothly over the placid surface.

Eventually the shape of a faded gray tower loomed in the far distance. It was the labyrinth tower at the south tip of the floor, the means by which we would reach the next floor up. It was still nearly two miles away, but the menace of the boss waiting on its highest level emanated out to prickle the skin.

"You aren't taking me *there*, are you?" Asuna turned around to ask me. I quickly shook my head.

"N-no. Our destination's over here," I said, pointing out the southeast branch of a fork in the river up ahead.

Eventually the cliffs standing tall over us on either side began to change color. The blackened basalt-style rock featured fine horizontal lines carved right across like engraving. Using my memory of the beta and the map in my menu, I took us left and right through several branches in the river.

About an hour after we left Usco, our way was blocked by a nearly pure white wall at the end of a dimming valley.

"Hey, it's a dead end!" Asuna shouted, but I only put more strength into my rowing.

"Don't worry—that's where we're headed!"

"B-but I can't see what's ahead. What if there's a wall—?"

"We're fine! It's just normal mist…Well, not normal exactly."

She turned back, skepticism on her face. I grinned at her and shot the *Tilnel* right into the thick white fog.

Within seconds, I couldn't even see Asuna sitting seven feet ahead of me. When I sucked in a deep breath, the chilly dampness of the air contained the fresh, lively scent of forest.

"Huh…?! Wait, is this mist actually—"

She couldn't even finish before the mist abruptly cleared away, restoring our view.

It was a great circular lake, several times larger than the caldera lake where we fought the Biceps Archelon. The falling snow dyed most of the surface white. I pulled the oar out from the water and let the ship coast forward.

As the *Tilnel* silently glided through a world of white, a black silhouette eventually appeared ahead.

It was a fearsome and grand palace...no, fortress, standing tall in the middle of the lake. Four towers of differing heights stood over the roof of the building thick with snow, each one waving a triangular pennant. They featured a crossed horn and scimitar on a black field.

"Is that...the Dark Elf flag?!" Asuna cried, her voice ragged with surprise and hope.

I already knew that there was a Dark Elf fortress here. In the beta test, the "Elf War" campaign quest resumed here with another series of brief duties before ending in a long dungeon that carried the story over to the next floor.

But here in the retail game, there were already major differences from what I remembered. The Fallen Elves were making deals with the Water Carriers Guild in town to buy huge quantities of lumber, and a shadowy figure named General N'ltzahh was overseeing their operation. These things were not present in the beta.

Because of that, I was planning to only visit this fortress once I had collected as much related information as I could. But given that we'd already passed the field boss's lair on the fourth day on this floor, we'd be heading into the labyrinth tower much quicker than on the second or third floors. Asuna and I were probably the only people actively following the Elf War questline among the frontline group now, so if we didn't act with haste, the two guilds would pass by and leave us behind.

But this reason might have been nothing but an excuse. I just wanted to show my partner this sight.

"...It's beautiful," Asuna murmured, staring at the snowy castle as we approached. "More beautiful than any castle I've seen in real life."

"Are you talking about...so-and-so's castle at the theme park? Or the real thing in Europe...?" I asked carefully. She smiled and didn't elaborate.

Castles were a fantasy RPG staple, but this might have been the first proper castle in Aincrad so far. The building's design was about the same as in the beta, but the impression it left was completely different now that it was in the midst of a picturesque lake, rather than a flat, dried basin. Especially on Christmas Eve frosted with a layer of snow.

The Dark Elf army fortress was walled with white stone, its steeply angled roof gray slate tile. Orange light spilled from its countless arched windows, a perfect counterbalance to the indigo gloom of evening. The building itself was completely isolated from the surrounding land, and several large black gondolas were moored at the long pier straight outside the front gate.

Guided by a lantern emitting bluish light at the tip of the pier, I slid the *Tilnel* into an empty space along the dock. No alarms had sounded or guards had come running yet.

I stashed away the oar and leaped onto the stone pier, then turned to catch the expertly tossed rope and place it over the bronze bitt. Asuna reached over for a helping hand to step off, and we walked to the middle of the pier for a better look.

The front gate was still a distance away, but the castle's grand visage was clear to behold. The highest of the towers had to be more than a hundred and fifty feet off the ground. The scale of the structure rivaled that of the giant baobabs that made up the city on the third floor.

Orange light from the windows spilled onto countless roofs, peaks, and eaves. I stared at the fantastical sight until a small voice hit my ears.

"...Thank you. It's a wonderful present."

"Well...as long as you think so, it was worth rowing across the entire floor to see..."

I glanced over at her and grinned.

"But that's only half of the present."

"Oh...?"

I put a hand on her back and gently pushed, urging her on. She would figure it out before long, so I had to rush my perceptive partner along to preserve the surprise.

Ahead on the pier was a massive gate made of dark and gleaming plates of thick metal, with very large, heavily armed (by elvish standards) guards on either side. I took one look at their stunningly long halberds and had to steel myself to push onward.

The moment I came within twenty feet of the gate, the right guard barked, "Halt!"

Meanwhile, the left one said, "This place is not for humankind!"

They crossed their halberds in midair. I was relieved to recognize the same lines of dialogue from the beta and pulled out what I had prepared from my belt pouch and held it aloft.

"My name is Kirito! I request an audience with the master of this castle!"

The dialogue probably wasn't necessary, but I wanted to play the part, so I stifled my embarrassment and pushed forward with it.

The two guards looked at the sealed scroll I held aloft, bearing the same seal as the one on the castle flags—the invitation given to us by the commander of the Dark Elf forces on the third floor. Their halberds clanked back to a standing state.

The next moment, the massive metal gate split open with a deep rumble. I breathed a sigh of relief and nudged Asuna into the castle grounds.

The next moment, a cry of surprise escaped her lips.

"Ooohh!!"

The castle's front garden enveloped us with all the beauty of a great work of art. Trees, planters, and cast-iron fences all frosted with powdery snow were glittering in the light of the lamps. The long approach to the castle doors was absolutely pristine—not a single footprint. I almost didn't want to step onto it.

If everything was the same as in the beta, we'd be able to walk freely about the castle. Between the dining hall, the various stores, and even the dungeon-like cells, there was plenty worth exploring, but our first destination was already set in stone.

We opened the door and walked inside. Asuna exlaimed in wonder again.

In the center of the main hall with its red rugs was a marble fountain filled with glittering water. Beyond that was a grand staircase, and wide hallways extended to the left and right. Familiar Dark Elf NPCs glided forward on the sound of unseen violins, but unlike on the third floor, very few of these elves had weapons.

"I don't see any players," Asuna remarked, then nodded to herself. "But of course there aren't. That wall of mist we passed through to get to the lake was switching us to an instance map, wasn't it?"

"Good answer. We will never run across another player here, so we're free to laugh and scream and sing all we want."

"I-I wasn't going to do any of that. Anyways, let's take a look around," she said, her aggrieved look giving way to excitement as she tugged on my sleeve.

"Sure thing, but I already know our first destination: this way."

I pulled her hooded cape in return and dragged her down the hallway to the right.

Yofel Castle, the Dark Elf fortress, was laid out in such a way that the main building connected the four main towers in the shape of a rectangle with one open side. For the most part, the right side of the castle was a station for soldiers, while the left side housed the castle's inhabitants and servants. But I wanted the center courtyard.

We walked down the hallway past several soldiers, then turned left at a corner. I found a small door straight ahead and softly pushed it open.

Back out in the open air, we were met by a place less dazzling than the front garden, but somehow much more mysterious and sacred. Thorny hedges sprouting little black flowers blocked the way left and right like a maze, preventing us from seeing farther ahead.

We walked over the snowy cobblestones with the pale lantern light as a guide. I could see that someone had left footsteps down the center of the path. Asuna and I shared a look, and we hurried along the trail before the falling snow covered the tracks.

When we had passed through the thorny maze, we ended up in a beautiful garden surrounding a stunning conifer. Brick flower planters and bronze benches alternated around the tree. Its jutting branches kept the snow back, so the footprints disappeared near the entrance to the garden.

But we didn't need to follow them anymore.

Before our eyes, seated silently on one of the benches, was a frail figure. It was barely more than a silhouette from our location, but there was no need to get closer for a better look or callout or squint to bring up a color cursor for identification.

As soon as I took the first step forward, pulled toward the figure, it noticed us and stood up, leaping over the planter next to it with all the force of a thrusting sword skill.

The person landed lightly in front us and embraced us with open arms.

"Kirito! Asuna!" the familiar, silky voice sounded.

Doing my best to withstand the rib-cracking hug attack delivered with elite-level strength, I managed to grunt, "Good to see you again, Kizmel."

7

EVEN AFTER I WAS RELEASED, ASUNA CONTINUED TO hug the Dark Elf knight for another five seconds. When they let go at last, she traced the side of her eye with a finger and put on an enormous smile.

"...I always believed we'd see you before long...but I'm still so happy to see you."

Kizmel smiled. "So am I. Even after coming here through the spirit tree, I found that I was always thinking of you two."

The Dark Elf seemed to be savoring those words as she said them. I understood right away what made her seem different from before. She was wearing only a long dress of deep purple to cover her slender form, and her usual armor, saber, and cape were gone.

She had never removed equipment in the third-floor camp except for when she was in her own tent, I remembered. Kizmel's gaze moved from Asuna to me, the smile still stuck on her face.

"I'm surprised that you knew to find me here. Isn't this your first visit to this castle?"

"Y-yeah. Just a...lucky guess," I stammered. Of course, I knew this spot because it had struck me deeply during the beta test. At the time there was no thorny hedge maze, just a dusty stone path with a single, dried, dead tree in the middle. But there was obviously *something* more to the place, and thus it stuck in my memory.

Her smile deepened at my answer, and she looked up at the massive tree stretching over our heads.

"My sister loved the oil refined from this juniper. Perhaps that's why I found myself here..."

"Ahhh..."

I looked up at the tree and breathed a deep breath in through my nose. My lungs filled with a cool, pure woody scent.

"So this is a juniper tree," Asuna noted, sniffing the same smell. "In the world we come from, it's also used as a flavoring for alcohol."

"Is that so? I shall have to try it sometime...At any rate, thank you for coming. I suppose you vanquished the guardian beast in the Pillar of the Heavens without trouble."

"Yeah. It helped that the base commander warned us about its poison attacks."

Kizmel nodded sagely. "Yes, he is a trustworthy man. I wish to rejoin the advance party down on the third floor as soon as I can, but..."

She looked down at the dress she was wearing and squinted. The smile came back just as quickly, though, and she patted Asuna on the back.

"Let's go back inside. You must be hungry after rowing all this way, yes?"

"Very hungry," she responded. They started walking for the door.

As I trotted after them, I couldn't help but think, *You know, I was the one doing all the rowing.*

Just as I remembered, the dining hall of Yofel Castle was on the second floor of the west wing.

Inside, there were drool-inducing smells and pleasant chatter atop the gentle strains of string music. All of this had been upgraded since the beta, so I couldn't help but look around with curiosity.

Nearly everyone eating at the pristinely set tables was a soldier in leather armor, but there was also a group of what looked like mages in long robes and even a few small children. That seemed strange—I thought that the power of magic had been lost in the creation of the floating castle Aincrad, according to legend.

As we walked toward an empty table to sit down, Kizmel noticed my stare at the robed figures and leaned in to whisper, "They are priests who serve the Holy Tree. They were dispatched from the palace on the ninth floor to oversee our operation to retrieve the keys."

"Priests..."

I ran a mental search on the term, thinking it was unfamiliar within Aincrad—sure enough, I had no memory of it during the beta. I made a note to look into them more in the future. Asuna asked the next question.

"And the kids?"

"They are the children of the castle's master. Such bright young spirits," Kizmel explained, beaming as she guided us to a table in the back.

NPC maids—Dark Elves, of course—brought us out a full-course meal, starting with soup and appetizer. When they brought out roasted chicken for the main dish, Asuna and I couldn't help but share a look.

I didn't think elves had any reason to celebrate Christmas, but the dish was a little too close to tradition; perhaps it was part of the game's holiday event.

While they didn't follow it up with a cake, we had an excellent view of the snow-covered juniper tree in the courtyard through the hall's large window, which made the meal plenty festive.

Our main topic of conversation during the meal was the waterways that were central to the fourth-floor experience. Kizmel was most interested in our stories about the inner-tube swim from the staircase to the main town and the battle against the Fire-Bear for shipbuilding materials.

During that discussion, I asked and discovered that the Dark

Elves did not cut down living trees, either, but it was not out of any restrictive law, but rather respect for an aged plant. That made them different from the reluctantly obedient Fallen Elves.

Fortunately, she said that collecting wood from trees destroyed by monsters was allowed. I was glad that we'd taken the trouble to get the high-quality material.

Once we finished our fruit dessert, Kizmel took us to the officers' room on the fourth floor of the east wing. It was quite a grade up from the second-floor ten-man barracks of the beta. But this was a suite room, with two bedrooms and a shared living room. Which meant…

"Use this room while you are staying at the castle," Kizmel offered.

"Oooh, what a lovely place!" Asuna cried, racing to the large window in the back and only belatedly realizing the presence of the doors on either wall. She looked left and right, then back in confusion, but was hesitating on immediately demanding a different room.

I had the option of requesting it as well, but I was afraid of the significant downgrade to the barracks, and Kizmel spoke up before I could say anything, either.

"In that case, I will be in the adjacent room to the left. Knock on the door if you need anything. Enjoy your rest tonight; you must be tired."

She shut the door, and quiet footsteps faded away.

"…"

Left alone in the gorgeous suite, we could only stare at each other in silence.

"…Well, hey, at least it's not the first time for this," Asuna started off.

I nodded eagerly.

"It's pretty much unavoidable if we want to prioritize beating the game."

Nod, nod.

"But…I will say just one thing."

Nod?

"Your Christmas present was reuniting us with Kizmel, right? That was a wonderful present. Thank you."

I nodded one last time and mumbled uneasily, "Um, yeah, uh, you're welcome…But in all honesty, I'm glad we saw her again. She seems a little subdued, though."

"Yeah…"

That seemed to have shifted her mind from the sudden suite dilemma to Kizmel's current state, as she wore a slightly different look of concern now.

"The dress looked very nice on her, but I don't think she was wearing it out of choice. I wonder why she wasn't in her armor?"

"Didn't have her sword, either…Perhaps there's some state of affairs forcing her to stay here. Wonder if she'll tell us, if we ask…"

I glanced over at the neighboring room that housed the elf knight.

While I'd never spoken of this with Asuna, I knew that Kizmel was different from the other NPCs. While Romolo the ship-wright, for example, had engaged in very natural conversation with us, that was because we were careful never to say anything unrelated to the shipbuilding questline. But Kizmel had started talking about why she loved that tree in the courtyard, just from seeing me look up at it. That was far out of the norm for an NPC's conversational ability, which only responded properly when it heard statements that fit its content parameters.

But I wasn't so sure if Kizmel had been special from the very start. When we first met her in the third floor's Forest of Wavering Mists, Kizmel said, "Do not interfere! Begone from this place!"—exactly the same thing she started with in the beta, down to the word.

Through some reason I didn't understand, the quest story, which said that both she and the Forest Elf knight would die, had been overwritten. In that instant, *something* happened to Kizmel, and she stopped being a normal NPC. Did the fact that she'd been given memory and thoughtfulness beyond the bounds of an NPC mean…she was a high-functioning AI?

If that guess was correct, it gave birth to a new mystery. Was it the real-life GM who changed her, or was it the system that controlled *SAO*?

In the retail version of *SAO*, the cage that housed this shocking and unprecedented incident, only Akihiko Kayaba controlled the reins. I had no idea where he was or what he was doing now, but I couldn't imagine him taking the time to alter the specifications of a single NPC by hand. But neither could I imagine why he would turn it into an AI.

Meanwhile, I couldn't even say if the game system was advanced enough to allow for such a function. If it was true, the system that kept this virtual world running was far more than just a program…it was equipped with a level of autonomy that encompassed artificial intelligence on its own…

A suspicious voice reached my ears as I stared at the plaster wall, completely lost in thought.

"…Um, hello, Kirito?"

"Whu—ah! S-sorry, what did you say?"

"I didn't say anything."

Asuna was leaning against the window with her arms folded, pointing out the two doors with a look. "Which bedroom did you want?"

"E-either one is fine."

"I'll use this one, then," she announced, pointing to the door on the east wall. Then I realized that the main room had two other small doors aside from the ones to the bedrooms. One was to the bathroom, and the other looked like a closet. The bathroom was next to the eastern bedroom—she probably didn't feel comfortable with the idea of bathing while I was sleeping on the other side of the wall.

I told her to go right ahead, of course, then added something that popped into my head. "But on the third floor of the castle, there should be a super-huge bathing room."

"...Super?"

"Yeah, super."

"...With separate baths for men and women?"

"Yeah...er, wait..."

According to my memory, the bathing hall was at the very tip of the west wing on the third floor. But I didn't remember if it had separate baths for men and women. Back in the beta, I preferred to kill as many monsters as possible rather than waste time relaxing in the bath.

"Sorry, I don't know for sure," I admitted, throwing up my hands.

Asuna sighed. "I have a bad feeling about this. Come on, let's go."

"Let's...? Me, too?"

"Well, I don't know where it is."

This was a castle, not a labyrinthine dungeon, so I could probably explain the directions to her, but she spoke with such direct conviction that I didn't have any option but to accept her command.

We left the suite and used the grand stairs at the center of the castle to descend to the third floor. I had to fight the urge to open and inspect the contents of the countless doors we passed in the hall, but finally we reached the far end of the west wing.

There I saw a familiar arch. Through that threshold, the red carpet turned to white marble tiles—I was relieved to see that the bathhouse hadn't disappeared in the redesign. Beyond the arch, I turned us to the right.

The hallway came to an abrupt end, with another arched entrance to the left, through which floated the echoing sounds of water. We shared a look and peered through the arch at the same time to see a single, grand changing room.

"...They don't split the bath," my partner said. I coughed awkwardly.

"W-well, I guess that was the same for the bathing tent on the third floor. Perhaps that's just how elves do things."

It's probably just a data volume issue, though, I silently added to myself.

"A-anyway, I'll just use the bath back in the room; you should enjoy yourself here, Asuna. I'll see you in a while..."

As soon as I turned around to flee, a hand caught my back collar. I timidly turned around to see the fencer glaring up at me, a conflicted look on her face.

"Rrrh," she grunted. I wondered what kind of nuance I was meant to take away from that, then recalled a similar situation occurring at the bathing tent back in the camp.

Back then, Asuna was afraid of a male Dark Elf wandering into the tent while she was bathing, so I stood outside on watch. That meant she probably wanted the same thing now.

"Umm, it's gonna be pretty hard for me to warn you from the outside of a huge bath like this. Plus, I can't just block the NPCs from going in..."

"Rrrh," she grunted again, looking at the changing room with longing.

It didn't seem like there was anyone in the bath now, but there was no saying how long that would be the case. In this instance, Asuna the bathing enthusiast would just have to give up, it seemed clear to me.

"Rrrh...oh, I know!" she suddenly piped up, leaping into the changing room and sitting in one of the many wicker chairs. She popped up her window and started taking out items left and right.

A lot of colored cloth and a small box of sewing tools ended up clattering onto the long marble table. I was baffled as to what she was going to do and walked through the arch for a better look.

Just the changing room itself was huge. The floor and walls were covered in pure white tiles, a shining chandelier hung from the ceiling, and large potted plants sat in the corners. There were no automatic dryers or massage chairs, but there was a pitcher of iced water and several kinds of fruit on the table in the center.

I nibbled on what looked like a big grape, then tossed the rest into my mouth to watch Asuna work. She used the Crystal Bottle of Kales'Oh to reequip her Tailoring skill and was about to make something with the items she'd just produced.

As a matter of fact, it might have been the first time I'd ever seen the Tailoring skill at work. Asuna selected a plain white piece of cloth out of her mountain of textiles, then pulled a large pair of scissors out of the box.

She tapped the scissors next to pull up a list of items she could create. She made her choice, set the scissors to the cloth, then ripped them through with a brilliant metallic *shwing!* Suddenly, the exact same way as with ingots struck by a blacksmith's hammer, the cloth started glowing and changing shape. What emerged was two pieces of cloth in exactly the same shape.

Asuna put the scissors back into the box and placed the two pieces together, then started poking the hem of the cloth with a silver needle. That action had to be analogous to the striking of the ingot with the smithing hammer. Her handiwork was quick and sure, and the sewing was done in moments.

The cloth started glowing again, then bloomed from its flat state into something properly clothing-like, with actual volume. It was an ordinary one-piece swimsuit.

"Done!" she exclaimed proudly, holding the swimsuit up.

"Um...are you going to wear that...into the bath?"

"That's not against the rules, is it? Or is my wearing this swimsuit in the bath going to inconvenience you in some way?"

"Not in the least," I finished, shaking my head. With the kind of massive bath a castle like this would have, a person could probably treat it like a pool. In fact, it might even be fun.

I wasn't particularly attached to bathing in Aincrad, but I had to admit I was a little jealous in this situation. But the only swimwear I had on hand was the pair of bull-logo boxers I got as the Last Attack bonus from General Baran, and I didn't want to wear those unless it was an emergency.

I side-eyed the swimsuit my tailor partner was holding up happily against her body and groaned with envy when she looked back briefly and put on a foreboding grin. I had a bad feeling about the pleased smile on her face.

"By the way, I haven't given you a present in return yet, have I?"

"Er...n-no need for that. I didn't give you a physical present to begin with, after all..."

"No, but it made me much happier than any store-bought item. So I want to give you back something good. And it is Christmas Eve, after all."

"Um, w-well, if you're offering, I'll happily accept anything you give me," I said, shivering inside at her suddenly gentle tone and smile. Asuna sat back down on the chair and pulled out a black piece of cloth from the pile.

She cut up the smaller cloth with the scissors and sewed it up. When the light subsided, she was holding a pair of surf shorts—black, just the way I liked them.

"Oooh, cool!"

I wasn't afraid to wear these in front of others. I took a step forward in delight, but she held up her right hand to stop me. With that same hand, she selected a brilliant orange scrap from the cloth pile. The three steps of settings, cutting, and sewing took place in an instant, and the swimsuit glowed again.

From what I could see, nothing had changed. She met my confusion with a smirk, then smartly flipped around the black surf shorts to expose the rear.

"...Wh-what the hell is that?!"

There was a brilliant bear-shaped patch on the bum of the shorts, glowing a flaming orange.

"Here you go. Merry Christmas!"

She smiled and held them out to me. I had no choice but to thank her and accept them.

The golden bull on red?

Or the orange bear on black?

While I grappled with the ultimate decision, Asuna changed into her white one-piece swimsuit and pushed open the clouded glass door at the back of the room, only to let out a cry of wonder just as grand as any she'd emitted in Rovia.

I scurried over, shorts still in hand, and peered over her back. Even I had to grunt in amazement.

The size of the bath chamber was the same as in the beta, but it had received a considerable visual upgrade. The tiles in the floor were an ivory white so pure one could see through them. The bath in the back was made of the horizontally lined ebony basalt that surrounded the lake, but polished to a perfect sheen. It was indeed about as large as a pool.

The gold faucet set into the wall was pouring out a considerable waterfall of water that filled the tub already, gently cascading over the lip and onto the tile floor. Even better, the western and southern walls of the chamber were made of glass, offering a huge vista of the lake and the falling snow. There were no elves in the bath before us—it must have been too early to bathe.

"I'm in first!"

Asuna trotted over the tiles in her bare feet toward the massive tub. I watched the wide-open back of her swimsuit go as I hung back at the entrance. With one last glare each at the red and black shorts, I opened up my menu.

With two presses of the UNEQUIP ALL button, I placed the black shorts in my bottom underwear slot, stuck the red shorts in my inventory, then raced after my partner, who was standing at the edge of the tub.

With an enormous leap, I launched myself over her and landed into the bath first, sending up a huge spout of water. The last thing I heard before the water was a strangled yelp.

"*Fgyack!*"

Several minutes later, Asuna's mood had recovered. She was sitting in the southwest corner of the tub, looking at the night lake below.

"It's amazing…The water of the bath and the surface of the lake melt together so that it looks like we're floating in the sky…"

Now that she said it, the sight did resemble that image. I just gazed out at the stunning view.

"You know what they call these pools that look like they connect to the ocean or a lake? Infinity edge pools. You find them at resorts and places like that overseas."

"Ooh…Infinity edge kind of sounds like a sword skill," I said tactlessly.

She giggled. "You're right. Probably a dagger skill."

"No, I'd say rapier."

The conversation seemed light and harmless, but I was actually using all of my concentration and effort to keep my gaze fixed on the lake outside.

How could I be blamed? Just a few feet to the left, a pretty girl in a white bathing suit was lying facedown and stretching her long legs out to float in the water. No matter how far back I dredged up my real-life memories, there was nothing that featured me alone with a girl in a heated pool like this.

The eerie floating sensation helped give the scene a powerful tinge of unreality. I sat there, pointlessly counting the snowflakes falling outside, when I heard the sound of a door opening far behind us.

Asuna promptly sank into the water up to her mouth. I turned around and stared at the entrance to the bathing chamber.

There was a thin silhouette approaching beyond the floating steam, but I couldn't tell if it was male or female. I kept staring until a yellow cursor finally appeared, and I heard a familiar female voice.

"So here you two are."

Oh, it's just Kizmel, I thought with relief.

In the next instant, Asuna's hand shot like lightning to the top of my head, clenching my hair and forcing me down under the water. She used that boost to leap out of the tub and run over to Kizmel.

I popped my head half out of the water, feeling aggrieved, only to see Asuna trying to push Kizmel back through the steam. I couldn't tell what they were murmuring about from here, but within moments they were both retreating to the changing room for some reason.

Before I could make up my mind whether to join them or wait here, the door opened again, and they returned to the bathing hall. Asuna looked smug again in her white one-piece, while Kizmel wore a purple bikini over her dusky skin.

That was when I finally understood why Asuna jumped out of the bath. She intercepted Kizmel in a totally defenseless state and convinced her to go back so she could wear one of Asuna's hand-made swimsuits.

The Dark Elf followed Asuna into the tub and made her way over to me, sitting on the edge of the tub.

"So you are wearing your underwear…I mean, 'swemsoot' too, Kirito. Humankind certainly has some strange customs."

"Uh, I guess," I grunted.

A faint smile played over her lips. "But I seem to remember that in the camp's bathing tent, you were—"

"G-gosh, what a huge bath this is, though!" I shouted, cutting her off. I kept going, ignoring Asuna's suspicious glare. "If it's this big in the fourth-floor castle, I can only imagine how big the bathing chamber is in the queen's castle on the ninth floor!"

"But of course. It is located much higher up than this one, with a view of the entire ninth floor," Kizmel explained. Asuna's pointed stare melted into that of a dreaming young girl. Kizmel turned to her and looked apologetic.

"But I'm afraid that only the noble officials and the queen's sworn knights can use it. Sadly, it may not be possible for humankind to enter…"

"Oh, I see…But this bath is quite wonderful itself. I almost wish I could live in this castle forever," Asuna responded

The Dark Elf knight smiled again, then looked downward, her long eyelashes laid over her cheeks. She scooped up some of the water in her hand and shook her head. "I am happy that you like this castle…but it is best not to stay for too long."

"Huh…? Why?"

"As you've seen, Yofel Castle is an impenetrable fortress surrounded by lake water and cliffs on all sides. From time immemorial, it has never fallen to an attack by goblins, orcs, or even Forest Elves."

She paused for a moment. I lifted my face fully out of the water to ask, "Isn't that a good thing? We went to all that trouble to recover the Jade Key on the third floor, and now it's safe and sound in here, right?"

"Yes…but because of its safety, the troops stationed here are too lax. They've driven back Forest Elf attacks enough, but the Forest Elves have their fortress on land and have barely any ships. Winning every time through an easy advantage causes one's skills and heart to go soft."

The slight irritation I heard in her voice poked at something in the back of my mind, but I couldn't remember what it was.

Kizmel kicked at the surface of the water with her long, shapely leg, then murmured unhappily, "On top of that, the priests demand no metal armor within the castle grounds, as they find the noise unpleasant. With people like that around, it's no wonder that things around here are getting soft…"

"And that's why you've been in a dress this whole time," Asuna noted.

The knight grimaced and nodded. "It looks silly on me, doesn't it?"

"Not at all. But…it's best to wear what you like. I wonder if they would yell at us, too, if we had plate armor."

"Most likely. No need to test your theory."

"Good idea."

They giggled like sisters. Meanwhile, I was trying to pull that thorn out of my memory.

Long ago, how would the Forest Elves, with their lack of ships, have tried to send a great host of troops to seize the impenetrable

Yofel Castle? If they actually used the inner-tube fruit, I wouldn't mind seeing that.

However, this meant that if the Forest Elves did indeed acquire an adequate number of ships, the castle's defenses might not be prepared. But the Forest Elves probably had their own taboo about taking living wood, so they couldn't arrange for so many ships at once…

"*Oh!*"

At last, the thorn that blocked my thoughts fell out, and I exclaimed in shock. I stood up with a splash and pressed myself against the glass wall behind me, looking down at the lake surrounding the castle.

The lake, glowing white in the darkness thanks to the snow piling up on the ice, looked otherwise normal. But at this very moment, enough ships to support an army were under construction on the other side of the floor. In the Fallen Elves' hideout.

"Wh-what's wrong, Kirito?" Asuna said. I snapped around to face her.

"Asuna, today's the twenty-fourth, right?!"

"Obviously," she snapped, omitting the follow-up "*It's Christmas Eve.*"

I nodded vigorously. It was two days earlier that we'd overheard the conversation between General N'ltzahh and foreman Eddhu—the twenty-second. They'd said that the plan would go into motion in five days. That meant the twenty-seventh…three days from now.

Calculations complete, I turned to Kizmel, too locked in to bother drinking in the sight of her in the bikini.

"W-we've got trouble, Kizmel. I'm almost positive that the Forest Elves are going to attack this castle in three days with an entire army."

The Dark Elf knight's fine eyebrows tensed.

"I told you earlier, Kirito. The Forest Elves hardly have any ships, and they cannot bring others down through the spirit tree.

Even if they tried to swim to this shore, our ships would scatter them in moments."

"That's the thing…"

I stopped, unsure of how to explain, but Asuna filled the gap with a gasp.

"Oh…! Are you saying the Fallen aren't going to attack Rovia… but *here*?!"

"What? You've seen the Fallen on this floor?!" Kizmel demanded, rising from the edge of the tub. We both nodded, then took turns explaining everything that had led to this, starting with the suspicious ship we spotted in Rovia.

After a good ten minutes of explanation, the sound of the quest advancement notification sounded, and the log window opened to show that part three of the "Shipwright of Yore" quest had finished. Meaning that the "appropriate person" we were meant to alert was someone in the Dark Elf forces…in our case, Kizmel.

A considerable experience point bonus bumped me up to level 17 and Asuna to 16, but we didn't have time to celebrate. Kizmel stood up and said sharply, "We can't be relaxing here! You two, come with me!"

After a very rushed change of clothes, we were taken to the fifth floor of the castle, which I'd barely visited in the beta.

Two armed guards stood outside the large chamber door just to the right at the top of the stairs. With a determined glance from the elite knight, they both backed away quickly.

On the other side of the door was a very large office. But the windows were all covered with curtains, making the room unnaturally dark. We crossed the room, taking care not to trip on the much thicker rug here, then stopped before a heavy desk in the very back.

The ten-foot-wide desk was made of polished blackwood. As the elves could only fashion wood that had fallen naturally, this must be enormously valuable. With that in mind, I looked carefully at the figure seated on the other side.

A lamp on top of the desk cast flickering light on a half-written parchment and ink bottle, but for some reason, the light did not reach beyond the desk. I stared hard into the thick darkness enveloping the silhouette until a color cursor popped up bright against the black.

It read YOFILIS: DARK ELVEN VISCOUNT. What the heck was a viscount?

While I stood wondering, Kizmel performed the Dark Elf salute of right fist to left breast.

"Viscount Yofilis, pardon my interruption. I have an urgent matter that requires your attention."

After a pause, a voice returned from the darkness.

"Before I hear your report, may I ask why you have two humans with you, Kizmel?"

It was a flat voice that could be taken as young or brittle. But I couldn't tell if it was even male or female in the moment.

"Ah…"

Kizmel lowered her head to bow again, and I took a step forward and performed the same salute. The scroll with the details was in my belt pouch, so I produced it and ceremoniously handed it over the desk.

A slender hand extended from the darkness to take the scroll. With the trace of a finger, the seal evaporated, and the parchment fell open.

"…Ahh. I see, you are the ones who helped us recover the first key. I suppose it wouldn't do to feed you to the lake fish, then."

I couldn't tell if that last part was meant to be a joke or not. Viscount Yofilis put the scroll into a drawer on the other side of the desk.

You're not giving it back?! That's our identification inside the castle!

But my panic lasted only a moment. The viscount pulled something else out of the same drawer and held it out. I quickly put out my cupped hands and caught two rings. They were of delicate silver make, marked with the familiar sigil of horn and scimitar.

"Wear those, and you will not be harried by the soldiers of Lyusula. Assuming you do not betray our patronage, of course," the viscount warned. I bowed deeply and backed up next to Asuna.

The two rings were identical. I handed one to my partner and put the other on my left index finger. Despite my avatar having ten fingers, *SAO* only allowed one ring to be equipped on either hand. I already had a ring of +1 to strength on my right hand, a reward from a third-floor quest, so this used up all of my ring potential.

I resisted the urge to rudely check the properties of the brand-new ring and listened in on Yofilis and Kizmel's conversation.

"So, Kizmel. What is this report you have?"

"My lord, according to the human warriors Kirito and Asuna, our sworn foe, General N'ltzahh of the Fallen Elves is on this floor."

A moment later, the viscount's extended hand rapped the blackwood desk.

"...Ahh. This is indeed important tidings."

I figured that this conversation was all a preprogrammed part of the campaign questline, but I couldn't help but shiver as it felt like the temperature in the room dropped several degrees.

"What is that villain plotting this time?"

"Well...it seems that the Fallen have made a serious deal with the Forest Elves," Kizmel began, and summed up the important points of what we'd told her in the bath.

The great volume of ships being built in the Fallen Elves' hideout. The likelihood that the Forest Elves would use those ships to attack Yofel Castle in three days. Their target, the Jade Key being stored in the castle.

"I see...and do you know the number of ships the Fallen are building?" Yofilis asked Kizmel. She looked at me. I quickly snapped to attention and thought back to the image of the mountain of wooden boxes in the underground storeroom.

In all honesty, I had no idea how much lumber each box represented or how much was necessary to build a boat. But in that warehouse event, Asuna and I had managed to squeeze into a single box. That had to be a hint. In simple terms, one box would be required for a small two-seat boat. That would mean five boxes for the large ten-man ships moored outside the castle. And there were at least fifty boxes stacked into that storeroom, so...

"...I believe they are building at least ten ships capable of transporting ten soldiers each."

Yofilis's right hand rapped the surface of the desk again.

"Hmm. We have eight ten-man ships at the castle. And they will attack with more than that?"

"My lord, I do not doubt the mettle of the castle's troops...but should we not transport the first and second keys up to a higher floor?" Kizmel suggested. The viscount did not respond at first, but rapped on the desk more before speaking up.

"...There is merit to Kizmel's proposal. We cannot afford for the keys to be stolen again. But the duty of the people of Lyusula has always been to ensure the six keys are spread apart, so they might not be gathered. If we send the first and second keys to the next floor up, they will join the third. This is not a desirable outcome..."

Kizmel nodded. An uncomfortably heavy silence descended, only to be broken at last by Asuna.

"Er, my lord? What happens if the six keys are gathered together?" she asked bluntly. I stiffened up, but I wanted to know the answer, too. In the beta, I was too focused on finding and chasing down the keys, but the actual story behind them was never made clear.

Kizmel turned around first and hastily started, "Asuna, that's not—"

But the viscount's hand from the darkness cut her off.

"It is fine, Kizmel. I shall explain...but I cannot answer your question, human warrior. Even as the latest viscount of Yofilis, a line extending back before the Great Separation, I only know a small part of the legend surrounding the keys. The only person who knows the entire truth is our queen. No…"

The viscount trailed off and delivered such a heavy sigh that I almost couldn't believe this was still part of the campaign quest story event.

"It might be true that even Her Majesty does not know the real truth."

"But Viscount Yofilis," Kizmel started, her voice hard.

The viscount raised a hand in apology. "No, forgive me for saying that. Human warrior, this is all I can tell you. The people of Lyusula believe that if the six secret keys are gathered, allowing the door of the Sanctuary to be opened, terrible ruin will come to Aincrad. Meanwhile, our ancient enemies, the Forest Elves of Kales'Oh, have a different interpretation. They believe that opening the Sanctuary will return all the floors of Aincrad to their original locations on the surface and restore the great magic to the elves."

"Ah…!"

Both Asuna and I grunted in surprise.

Return Aincrad to the surface.

As Kirito the VRMMO gamer who lived in real life, I assumed that was completely impossible. The hundred floors of Aincrad, which were up to six miles across each, represented a tremendous amount of data. The idea that those hundred floors might be laid out side by side into an even larger map that held them all was preposterous. Now that we were trapped inside the game of death, the producers of the game, Argus, had no doubt gone out of business, the servers under the supervision of the police.

But did that mean the Forest Elf legend was false and the Dark Elf legend was true?

No, that was hard to imagine, too. I didn't know what "terrible ruin" meant in concrete terms, but if it actually meant the destruction of Aincrad and all the NPCs and players within it, that meant every player working the Forest Elf faction in the campaign was in danger of killing everyone here, including themselves. It was impossible to imagine that our GM, Akihiko Kayaba, wanted an end to his little game before we even reached the tenth floor—and based off of a misunderstanding, no less.

Besides, the "Elf War" questline had a separate conclusion for every player or party who initiated it. I couldn't see a single player who finished the campaign before everyone else being allowed to dictate the fate of all of Aincrad, and if the Forest and Dark Elf sides finished at the same time, the results would be self-contradictory.

Terms like *ruin* and *return* had to be no more than keywords meant to spice up the scenario and make it more exciting. No matter what happened in the quest, Aincrad wouldn't actually be affected.

After a brief moment to reach that conclusion, I was about to breathe and calm myself, when Asuna tugged on my sleeve.

"Hey, Kirito, didn't that Fallen Elf general say something about...opening the Sanctuary or whatever?"

"Eh? Actually...now that you mention it..."

I searched my memory frantically and succeeded in playing back General N'ltzahh's speech. I thought it might be important to relate to Kizmel and Yofilis, so I turned to the darkness across the desk and put on my stiff and proper tone of voice.

"Erm...my lord. General N'ltzahh said thus: When the Fallen Elves gain all of the keys and open the Sanctuary, the greatest magic of humankind would disappear..."

"...Magic of...humankind...?" Yofilis repeated skeptically. The hand atop the desk flipped over. "Kizmel. Do you know what this magic of humankind is?"

"Well...though they are far inferior to those of elvenkind, the humans still have a number of ancient charms available to them. The only ones that I am familiar with are the charm of Mystic Scribing, in which their arms and tools are placed within tiny paper scrolls, and the art of Farscribing, to send written messages to distant places in an instant..."

The former referred to our menu windows, and the latter was instant messages. As far as magic-like abilities that a player could make use of, those were about all I could think of.

"Ahh. They do sound useful, but..."

Yofilis seemed to have a habit of stopping to think. The fingers tapped on the surface of the desk yet again.

"I cannot imagine that N'ltzahh would go to the trouble of aligning with the Forest Elves just to take such paltry charms from humankind."

Such abilities might be "paltry" to a magic-wielding elf, but a player without their menu was in dire straits. On the other hand, that outcome was unimaginable. An RPG without its menu screen was like a bicycle without handlebars or pedals.

A few seconds later, Yofilis's voice returned, back to the steady cadence of a proper plot-centered conversation.

"But in any case, the Lapis Key sealed on this floor probably ought to be retrieved. But the castle guards must prepare for the Forest Elves' siege. Warriors of humankind, will you assist Kizmel in recovering the second key?"

A golden ! mark appeared in the midst of the darkness. This quest NPC marker was only visible to me and Asuna. For a moment, I wondered if that was another human charm. Asuna and I looked at each another and nodded.

"Yes, we will help."

The exclamation mark turned to a question mark. Thus, the campaign quest resumed on the fourth floor.

Kizmel bowed deeply to the viscount once more, then turned to us, beaming.

"It is a critical but dangerous duty, but I am overjoyed to fight alongside you again. Let us work together again, Asuna, Kirito."

"You bet!"

"Let's do it, Kizmel!"

No sooner were the cries out of our mouths than a third HP bar and name appeared in our party list to the upper left of my view.

The instant we were out of view of the guards outside of Yofilis's chamber, I raised my arms and stretched.

"Ooooh, that was nerve-racking..."

"I do not blame you. The viscount is one of the most elderly of even the Dark Elves. I was a bit nervous myself."

"You, too, Kizmel? By the way...how old are *you*?" I asked nonchalantly, but Asuna elbowed me roughly in the left side, and Kizmel cleared her throat uncomfortably.

"Kirito, I do not know your human customs well, but among elvenkind, it is considered rude to ask the age of another to her face."

"Oh, I didn't know. S-sorry."

"Let us just say that I am considerably younger than Viscount Yofilis."

"U-understood. I'm surprised that such a splendid castle master has soft warriors and arrogant priests working in his employ, though," I muttered as we descended the steps. Kizmel put on a worried look.

"Yes...but there is a reason. Viscount Yofilis suffers from a very challenging ailment. Because of that, he cannot be exposed to bright light. He has been in that chamber for so long, most of the soldiers here have never even seen his face..."

"He's sick? Even though he's an elf?"

"Elves are long-lived, but we are not immune to disease. The priests let their influence run unchecked because they are out of his sight. And yet they will be useless in a battle. It is a troubling state of affairs..."

Kizmel shook her head and stopped in front of her room on the fourth floor, but when she spoke again, she had recovered her normal manner.

"At any rate, I appreciate the crucial information that you two have brought with you. It is late already, so let us begin our duty in the morning. Get your rest—do not stay up all night."

"We promise."

"Good night, Kizmel."

The Dark Elf smiled and nodded, then retreated into her private room. The brand-new HP bar tinkled into nothing with a sad little noise, but she would rejoin the party when we met up in the morning.

Asuna and I walked ten yards down the corridor and into the suite room next door.

I opened my window and checked the time to see that it was somehow past ten o'clock at night already. The snow fell silently outside the window, and the trees in the front garden were already covered in white.

We stood in the middle of the living room, gazing out at the night view, when I remembered something and lifted my left hand. I tapped the silver ring with my other hand. The properties window told me that it was called the Sigil of Lyusula.

"Magic effects...ooh, agility plus one...and a small bonus to skill proficiency gain. That's pretty nice."

"Mmm," Asuna mumbled, looking at my hand. For some reason, she frowned, then looked down at her own hand, went bright red, and quickly touched her right hand with her left. Apparently she'd just changed the finger the ring was on, but I didn't know why she needed to rush to do that.

"...S-something the matter?"

"Nothing!" she stated flatly, so that was the end of that.

"Umm, well, I think I'll go to bed...oh, but before that, I was going to ask you something."

"...Wh-what?"

"It's about the castle master's name. What's a v...viss-count?" I asked curiously.

She gave me a weird look, then sighed a very long sigh.

"...It's pronounced *vigh-count*."

"Eh?"

"You don't pronounce the s. It's a noble rank. You heard Kizmel calling him 'my lord,' right?"

"Ohhh, s-so that's what it meant. Um, so…how high is a viscount…?"

"Normally, it goes duke, marquis, count, viscount, baron, from highest to lowest. I don't know how the Dark Elves order it, though."

"I see, I see. Thanks for the explanation. So, um…it's a bit early, but how about six in the morning tomorrow?"

She agreed without a word.

"Great. Well, then…good night…"

I was curious about why my partner would suddenly go so red and standoffish, but I figured she would be back to normal after a good night's sleep. But just as I opened the door to my bedroom, she spoke up.

"Kirito."

"Er…yes?"

I turned around to see that the fencer was still standing in the center of the room. She shrugged her shoulders a bit and looked up at me.

"Um…I said this before we went to the bath, but I mean it— thanks for today. It was more enjoyable and lovely than any Christmas Eve I had in the real world."

"…"

That took me by total surprise. I had no idea how to respond.

After a few seconds, I found myself asking what I thought was a harmless question in response.

"…What kind of Christmases did you have back there?"

"Hmm…"

She twirled the toe of her boot on the thick carpet and a little smile snuck across her face.

"There was one time we were supposed to stay home because there would be a family Christmas party, but my father and mother didn't come home until very late, and I had to eat the cake by myself…Actually, that was pretty much every year."

"Oh…I see…"

I felt ashamed that all I could do was offer simple murmurs in response, but I didn't have anything better to relate to her. For the last two years, I'd wrapped up my Christmas family celebrations early so I could log in and participate in online in-game holiday events.

"Well…I'm glad you had a good time. If only we could have gotten a cake prepared," I mumbled.

The wan smile on Asuna's face grew clearer. "Yeah. But…we can save that for next Christmas."

"…Yeah. Right."

"Well, I'm off to bed. Good night."

"Night."

I watched her go through the door on the other side of the room, then entered my own and shut the door. It was plenty spacious, though not as much as the common room. There was a double-size bed in the middle, a large chest that served as extra item storage beneath the window, and a dresser with a three-sided mirror, which served no use for me.

I took off my coat, boots, and protector before flopping back onto the bed.

"…Next Christmas, huh…?"

Asuna probably meant it in the most innocuous way possible, but the phrase carried a very heavy meaning. Today was the forty-eighth day of the game of death. We'd taken twenty-eight days to beat the first floor, ten for the second, and seven for the third. It took us three days to reach the midway point of this floor.

It was reassuring to see our pace picking up, but I didn't think we could go much faster. If we assumed that each floor would last around a week going forward, that put us on a pace to finish the remaining ninety-six floors in 672 days—about a year and ten months.

That basically ensured that we would still be stuck in Aincrad by next Christmas. Perhaps Asuna hadn't been thinking about that when she said it, but looking up at the ceiling and imagining all those floors above it made me feel like I was being crushed with the weight of it all.

We had an ample safety margin in terms of level, but there was no guaranteed safe zone in MMORPGs. Not if you suddenly got a whole bunch of powerful monsters linked up into a group. Not if you couldn't recover from a negative status effect quick enough. Not if you slipped and fell from a height of a few dozen feet. Those would be enough to knock my HP to zero, resulting in the NerveGear frying my real brain, wherever I was now. Just like that, Kirito and Kazuto Kirigaya would cease to be, disappearing from two worlds at once, like froth on a riverbed.

Of course, I had the option of staying put in the Town of Beginnings on the first floor. Instead, I leaped out of the city forty-eight days ago for the next town, driven by something. And before I split up with my very first partner—no, before I abandoned that poor *SAO* newbie—I left him with a piece of advice.

We have to get stronger and stronger in order to survive. MMORPGs are a battle over system resources. There's only so much gold, loot, and experience to go around, so the more you win, the stronger you get.

I knew that I was right. The reason I'd survived until this day was that I used my beater's knowledge and experience to skillfully and efficiently earn gold, levels, and rare loot. There were several occasions where I might have died if my level was just one lower or my gear one point weaker.

But that was because I chose to leave safety and conquer the deadly game on my own.

Why had I done that?

I played back what Asuna had said just after I met her in the first-floor town of Tolbana.

If I was going to just hide back in the first city and waste away, I'd rather be myself until the very last moment. Even if it means

dying at the hands of a monster...I don't want to let this game beat
me. I won't let it happen.

It was a very Asuna-esque motivation—dangerous, brave, and
admirable. But I didn't have the same thought within myself.

What about Lind of the Dragon Knights Brigade? Kibaou of
the Aincrad Liberation Squad? Diavel, the former beta tester who
perished in the battle against the very first floor boss? What reasons had tilted the scale toward actual death, driving them to
leave the safety of town into the dangers of the wild...?

I lay staring at the dark ceiling, unchecked thoughts spiraling
through my head, when I just barely heard the sound of the other
bedroom door opening out in the living room.

Probably just Asuna preparing to take another bath, I assumed.
But several minutes later, I hadn't heard the sound of another
door opening or closing. Asuna didn't go from the living room
into the bathroom or out into the hallway or even back into her
own bedroom.

"..."

After another ten seconds of listening, I snuck out of bed,
walked over the carpet in bare feet to the door, and carefully
turned the knob.

The lights in the living room were off. But the snowy illumina-
tion from the window cast the room in a monotone of light and
shadow.

I slowly panned around the room until I spotted a lonely,
rounded silhouette on the large sofa next to my wall, both legs
curled up into a ball.

After a moment of hesitation, I opened the door wide and
stepped into the common room. She should have noticed me by
now, but Asuna didn't budge from where she was.

I approached the sofa as silently as I could, though I didn't
know why.

"...Can't sleep?"

After a few moments, the little head nodded. A few more seconds
later, she mumbled, "The room and the bed are just too big..."

"...I know what you mean. When I used the big barracks room on the second floor to log out in the beta, we were packed into little bunk beds," I responded, sitting down on the other end of the sofa.

If only I had the skill to whip up a nice mug of hot milk. Sadly, I had no milk in my inventory, and the room didn't have a stove. Instead, I did something that I would never normally do: I spoke my own baseless conjecture aloud.

"Did you start thinking about next year?"

She went absolutely still where she sat, about five feet away, then nodded again, her forehead pressed against her knees. After a while, her quiet whisper trickled out into the room.

"Until now, I've been trying not to think about the distant future. I told myself that I would only focus on what needed to be done each day. But that's just the same as trying to run from the future. Not even just thinking about the number of floors left or how much time it would take...I was just trying to avoid facing the question of how much longer I could survive in this place. But then I was sitting in my room, looking out the window...and it all just sort of...bubbled up inside of me..."

The arms she held around her knees tensed and bulged.

"...I want to survive until next Christmas and see the snow falling in Aincrad again," she confessed, terribly painful but nearly soundless.

I knew that I needed to say something, but my lips felt as though they were glued shut. I couldn't speak.

I wanted to say, *"You won't die before next Christmas...or before the day we beat this game. You'll survive."* But what proof did I have of that?

Obviously, Asuna's battle skill was second to none in the front-line group, and the quality of her gear was guaranteed. But just as I'd told myself minutes ago, a single mistake here or an unlucky bounce could easily kill a player. If I couldn't reassure myself that I wouldn't die, I certainly couldn't offer that empty guarantee to someone else.

After a stretch of silence so long even I didn't know how much time had passed, I managed to croak something out of my avatar's throat.

"...I'm sorry. I can't say anything. I don't have the strength to offer you any advice right now..."

For the very first time, Asuna had revealed her fear of the game and hope for the future, and I was so pathetic that I couldn't come up with anything better to say back. I stood up, ready to retreat into my room.

But just as I passed by Asuna on the right end of the sofa, she extended a hand and caught the hem of my shirt. She pulled me down with surprising force until I was sitting next to her.

"Then get stronger."

I held my breath.

"Huh...?"

"Get stronger. Until one day...you can tell me, and other frightened people like me, that it'll be okay."

"..."

Once again, I was left speechless. I looked down at my hands.

How many levels would I need to gain to be able to say that to anyone? Another twenty or thirty wouldn't be nearly enough.

I felt plagued by a sense that the strength Asuna was speaking of was a very different kind—something I didn't usually find myself thinking about.

She tilted herself to the left and laid her little head on my right shoulder.

"You don't have to say anything now, as long as you sit there until I fall asleep."

"Um...uh, okay," I stammered. Asuna smiled and closed her eyes.

In less than a minute, I heard true sleep in her breathing. She said until she was asleep, so if I could roll her down onto the sofa and retreat to my bedroom, she couldn't complain, but given her difficulty in staying asleep, that seemed nearly impossible.

I was stuck where I was until she eventually woke up. I tried to relax my shoulders and leaned back against the back of the sofa.

Be stronger.

That was a command I gave myself when I was racing out of the Town of Beginnings—or fleeing, depending on how you looked at it. I rushed to gain levels, get new gear, and power myself up faster than anyone else, for some reason I couldn't really explain. I was driven by something I couldn't name.

Was it Asuna who gave me a reason? I had to be stronger so that the next time she or someone else revealed their weakness to me, I could be that reassuring presence who said, "No, you won't die, it'll be okay." Was it right for me to think that way...?

Suddenly, Asuna shivered as she leaned on me. She hadn't woken up—she must have felt a shiver in her sleep. The winter night seemed a bit chilly for just a sheer tunic.

If only I had some kind of player skill to whip up a nice warm blanket for her. Sadly there was nothing of the sort in my inventory—

"...Oh," I murmured and opened my window. Over in the storage tab, I selected a particular item and materialized it.

A thin, silvery fabric fell lightly into my hands—the Argyro's Sheet that came in so handy in the Fallen Elves' watery hideout. It was big enough to hide an entire gondola, so it would easily serve as a blanket. There was only a bit of durability remaining, but because we weren't on the water now, it wouldn't drain anyway.

I wrapped the blanket around us, and the chill that filled the room seemed to vanish at once, bringing a pleasant sleepiness into my head.

Before I closed my window, I set my alarm to go off at five thirty in the morning and closed my eyes.

December 25 and 26 passed in the blink of an eye as we spent them undertaking the "Lapis Key" quests for Viscount Yofilis.

They weren't easy quests by any means, but with the latest level-up for the both of us, plus the usual overpowering presence of Kizmel the elite knight, we never really struggled at any point.

The prelude quests on the first day had us running back and forth, but by the afternoon of the second day, we found the underwater dungeon that housed the key. We defeated a dullahan-type boss monster, its body covered in verdigris, to gain the second of the secret keys, this one a brilliant marine blue. There were no sneak attacks by masked Fallen this time, and we were back to Yofel Castle before dinner.

After reporting on the quests to the viscount and receiving our considerable rewards, the large window at the west end of the hallway showed a brilliant sunset. I stretched to my fullest in the red light.

"Mmmm...Well, we managed to get the second key right as planned. The viscount put it away in that little chamber behind his desk. I wonder if the first one's in there, too," I murmured to myself.

Kizmel answered that question, happy to be back in her familiar armor. "That's right. That means if the Forest Elves managed to reach the fifth floor of the castle, it's quite likely they might make off with the keys. Viscount Yofilis might be excellent with the rapier, but he cannot be forced to fight in his sickly state..."

"Don't worry, Kizmel. They won't even step onto the dock, much less reach the fifth floor," Asuna proclaimed confidently. She'd been quite energetic and spirited the last two days. She must have really enjoyed the chance to fight alongside Kizmel again. "Whether they come with ten or *twenty* ships, we'll sink them all!"

"Ha-ha, I am glad to hear it," Kizmel said, patting Asuna's back before she turned to me. "Kirito, Asuna, the fact that we have recovered the Lapis Key in just two days is a sign of not just your own strength, but that of your ship. And what makes me happiest of all is that you chose to give such a beautiful craft my sister's name..."

She trailed off and strode toward the nearby window. The north-facing window looked out upon the front garden and gate, as well as the long pier beyond that. To the sides of the pier were eight large gondolas painted black and one little white one—our *Tilnel*—bobbing in the waves.

"My sister loved to swim, ever since she was young. She and I often rode on a little pleasure boat in a city on the ninth floor. Looking at the *Tilnel* brings back old memories..."

Asuna quietly approached the reminiscing Kizmel from the right. I watched the setting sun sparkle in their hair and thought hard.

The possibility that a Dark Elf herbalist named Tilnel, who was Kizmel's twin sister, actually existed as an NPC in Aincrad was very low. *SAO*'s service period began only fifty days ago. In a sense, Kizmel's Dark Elves and their Forest Elf foes were born in that instant. Tilnel was nothing more than data created to serve as background for Kizmel.

But each time Kizmel spoke her memories of Tilnel, that data in the server got overwritten in a more detailed form. Even a woman who existed only as background information became truth through those memories...it seemed to me.

I cleared my throat at Kizmel's left and told her about something Asuna and I had discussed during the key quests.

"Um, Kizmel. We have a request."

"As long as I can help."

"Yes, well...our books of Mystic Scribing cannot hold large objects like ships, but we also cannot pick ours up and climb the Pillar of the Heavens with it. When we move up to the fifth floor, we will need to keep the *Tilnel* somewhere here on this floor."

As the Dark Elf listened patiently, Asuna spoke up next.

"You see, Kizmel, before we leave for the fifth floor, Kirito and I want to leave the *Tilnel* with you. Even if you just leave her here on the dock at Yofel Castle..."

Last night, the two of us had discussed whether this would be even possible. If the game system prohibited it, we were afraid that this might cause undue stress on Kizmel's AI.

Normally, it was not possible to pass items on to NPCs. When we found the Dark Elf knight's sigil in the third-floor cave and tried to give it to Kizmel, she claimed that we should pass it to the commander ourselves. And when Asuna gave Kizmel her purple bikini at the bath, Kizmel returned it before they left the changing room.

But there was no need to change ownership of the item if we were just leaving it moored at the dock. If Kizmel just accepted the *Tilnel* in spirit, and thought of her sister when she gazed upon it, that was all we could ask for. How to get from this castle to the labyrinth tower was a problem, but we had the inner tubes if it came to that.

As we waited on her answer with bated breath, the knight turned to the window, her armor clanking.

After a few moments, her voice emerged—quietly, but with emotion you would never hear from a NPC.

"...Of course. Of course you can. I will take responsibility for your precious boat. But promise me one thing."

"What is it, Kizmel?"

"Come back to this castle sometime, and give me a ride on her."

Then it was our turn to shout, "Of course!"

8

"FROM THE LEFT, KIRITO!" ASUNA SHOUTED.

I gritted my teeth and plunged the oar to the left. The *Tilnel* was maneuverable thanks to its small size, but it had its limits. The turning radius of the gondola at high speed was about twice the length of the boat, a full fifty feet, and required foresight at all times.

"Nuaaaah!"

I rowed with all of my strength. A large brown boat plunged into the corner of my vision. Though it was hidden behind the boat's spray, the prow was equipped with an enormous ram, and even with its excellent defensive ability thanks to our choice of fine materials, the *Tilnel* was not likely to emerge unscathed.

A Forest Elf soldier standing at the prow brandished a ten-foot spear.

"I've got him!" Kizmel shouted from the center of the boat, raising her saber. With a brilliant, speedy swing, she lopped the tip off of the spear as it plunged toward me.

It was worth trusting in Kizmel's assistance and staying the course, as it ensured the *Tilnel* just missed the ram and slipped past the large ship's port side.

The enemy ship began to turn, but once we were at their rear side, there was nothing they could do. Our foes' defenseless stern came into view as the two ships circled around each other.

204 Sword Art Online: Progressive 3

"Asuna, Kizmel, here we go!"

"All right!"

"Ready!"

They crouched and clutched the sides of the ship as we charged at full speed. The Fire-Bear's Horn affixed to the *Tilnel*'s prow crunched directly into the sturdy Forest Elven ship's sole weak point, its rear end. The red-hot ram split the thin wood and evaporated the water around it, causing an explosion that blew up the rear half of the ship.

Even as we used that backward pressure to reverse the *Tilnel*, the enemy ship began taking on water and sinking from the stern end. The eleven Forest Elves aboard the ship were thrown into the lake, screaming, and immediately began to swim away.

"Yes, that's two!" I crowed.

Meanwhile, Asuna shouted on lookout. "Enemy ship to the rear left! They're facing away from us, so this is our chance!"

"R-roger!"

I regripped the oar and plunged it to the right this time.

It was Tuesday, December 27. Just as the Fallen Elf General N'ltzahh had proclaimed, "five days later" was right on the money: A small fleet of boats carrying Forest Elves plunged into the lake around Yofel Castle just after noon.

We were ready for them, as our Dark Elf scouts warned us three hours in advance, but I couldn't prevent a chill from running down my back when the enemy ships appeared, horns blaring. They showed up sixteen strong, much more than my initial estimation of ten ships.

That was twice the number of ships for the Dark Elves at Yofel Castle. That meant that, assuming the ships on either side had the same battle power, our little *Tilnel* had to sink eight ships on her own.

I had never expected to experience a large-scale naval battle in Aincrad, but here we were, two lines of brown-and-black ships charging each other like ancient Greek fleets. Two Forest Elf ships and one of the Dark Elven boats took on holes and sank in the first clash. That left fourteen enemy ships against seven.

But as a roving wild card, the *Tilnel* had no obligation to line up properly. Instead, I utilized a tactic from the Battle of Salamis and surprised them on their flanks.

Of course, in a giant circular lake, there was no place to hide. But we did have the very useful Argyro's Sheet on our side. With Asuna's Tailoring skill and some patience, we even managed to repair some of its lost durability.

Safely hidden from sight at the east end of the battle area, we carefully timed our first strike for the exact moment both sides had stopped and sank the first boat with a perfect blow. After that, things got chaotic, but we had just sunk our second, which meant the Forest Elves *should* be down to twelve ships.

"Kizmel, count up the number of surviving ships!" I shouted as I rowed frantically. It took all of two seconds for her reply.

"Six on our sides, twelve for the enemy!"

"Ugh..."

The enemy number was right where I expected it to be, but we'd lost another ally.

As one might expect from ships hastily cobbled together from wood acquired from dismantled boxes, the Forest Elf ships had ugly, squarish prows and sterns. They were slower and less maneuverable than the Dark Elves' elegant gondolas, but much sturdier.

On top of that, as Kizmel had feared, the Dark Elf discipline and morale were lower than the enemy's. A few ships were lined up and locked in furious on-board combat, but more Dark Elves were falling to enemy blades and plunging into the water than the other way around.

"Valiant warriors of Kales'Oh!" bellowed a large knight who had the look of an enemy commander, at the center of a ship bearing a green flag with golden shield and sword. "Send these cowardly Dark Elves to sleep at the bottom of this lake! They have allied with humankind and built ships for the purpose of bringing down our castle! Fortunately, their plot was foiled, and we claimed their ships for ourselves! We must not miss this opportunity!!"

...*Whut?*

I puzzled over that one as I rowed with all my strength. Did the enemy commander just say that the Dark Elves were allied with the humans? Did that mean that the Dark Elves hired humans to build ships and the Forest Elves stole those ships? As far as I knew, that wasn't true. At the very least, I knew that the Fallen Elves had built those ships the Forest Elves were using now, at their behest...or so I thought.

"They've spotted us, Kirito!"

Asuna's shout brought me back to the scene unfolding before my eyes.

The oarsman of the Forest Elf ship we were aiming for was attempting to make a right turn as he stared at us. I pushed our boat left, then waited for the right moment to make a sudden right turn. Predicting the location the enemy ship would pass through ten seconds from now, I started rowing madly.

With two swift strikes faster than the eye could follow, Asuna disarmed two enemy spears, and in the next moment, the *Tilnel*'s ram burst through the enemy's rear starboard hull. Kizmel had to lean over and pull Asuna back before she fell over with the impact.

There was another blast of steam, and the enemy ship was destroyed. That made...

"Three!"

I ignored the enemy soldiers falling into the water and searched for our next target. On the north side of the lake where the main fight was taking place, the Dark Elves continued to fall behind. The six remaining ships were lining up to prevent entrance to the castle and engaging the enemy in hand-to-hand combat, but more Dark Elves were falling into the water than Forest Elves.

Meanwhile, the enemy still had eleven ships active, and three of them were spinning off the main fight to approach the castle dock from the west.

"That's not good," Kizmel murmured, just as the Dark Elf commander in the midst of their fleet raised a scimitar and bellowed at us.

"You there, the little boat! Stop wasting time and stop the enemy swing force!"

"H-how can he speak to us like that?" Asuna demanded, outraged. This was coming from the same commander who haughtily informed us that we wouldn't be a factor in the battle and to stay out of the official navy's way.

But in this case, we had no choice but to obey. There were only six guards left at the castle gate, and if the thirty Forest Elves on those three ships disembarked, they would easily break through those defenses.

"Damn! We just have to do it!" I growled, paddling furiously. I futilely wished that I had raised my strength a bit more, but even as it was, I had to be thankful that it wasn't real life, where my arms would be useless for all the lactic acid buildup by now.

The three swing-force ships in side-by-side formation were pointed away from us. We could sink one of them with a rear charge, but the problem was what came after that. For the battering ram to work properly, we had to be going at full speed, and the enemy wasn't going to sit there and wait for us to back up so we could charge again.

Kizmel could tell what I was worried about, so she turned back and shouted, "Don't worry, Kirito, just charge the center ship!"

"R-roger!" I had to respond. I set sights on the middle ship and adjusted our course. The spearmen at the rear of that ship had already noticed us, but they didn't seem inclined to stop their progress toward the castle.

"Gooooo!"

I plunged the oar one last time, roaring like every anime or movie hero making his last suicidal charge. Once again, Asuna defended against the enemy spears, and our burning ram broke right through the flat stern of the ship.

Our fourth target sank in moments, and the Forest Elf soldiers aboard swam away for safety. I watched them go and started to back the *Tilnel* up, but then the two remaining ships abruptly cut us off from both sides.

The *Tilnel*'s stamina gauge just below Kizmel's HP bar dropped about 5 percent. But the damage didn't stop there; it continued to fall bit by bit. The two oarsmen were rowing madly perpendicular toward our facing sides, trying to crush the boat between them.

On top of that, the spearmen on either side were jabbing their sharp weapons at me. I hurriedly drew my sword and knocked the points away, but it was only prolonging our decline.

Kizmel calmly suggested, "Kirito, Asuna, leap onto the right ship and strike down the oarsman! I will handle the left!"

"Whuh?!"

I was not expecting that command, but it was clearly the only way out of our pinch. Asuna and I made eye contact, then leaped recklessly over to the other ship.

"Filthy human rats!" an elven spearman spat, but those ten-foot-long spears were meant for naval battle, not close combat. I struck him directly with a Slant sword skill, not even bothering to feint. The elf flew overboard. On the left, Asuna overpowered another spearman with a two-part Parallel Sting, her special silk cape waving.

The fearsome Forest Elven Hallowed Knight we fought at the start of the third floor was quite memorable, but he was a high-level elite mob like Kizmel. But the Forest Elven spearmen and Forest Elven swordsman on board these ships were no different from the average fourth-floor monster in terms of power. This brief sparring reminded me that in a one-on-one fight, they posed nothing to worry about.

Still, there was no point getting careless. In a ship battle, the ship's hull absorbed the damage, but when fighting the sailors on board, our HP was at risk again. Even in the midst of this dramatic, climactic story event, it was imperative that we remember our lives were on the line in this cruel game of death.

Asuna pushed the spearman overboard with a knock back–heavy combo of attacks, and the swordsman behind him approached.

"No need to actually defeat him! Just use him as a wall to keep the guys in the back from getting closer!" I ordered my partner, stopping the blow of the swordsman attacking on my end. The oarsmen—officially named a Forest Elven rower—was on the other side of this fighter.

Though the Fallen Elf–built wooden crafts could hold ten in all, the deck only left room for two to stand abreast. If Asuna and I fought shoulder to shoulder, the rear enemies wouldn't be able to reach us. This kind of locational placement was a big part of playing a VR game, and we could use the enemies' bodies as blockades of their own in a tight space like this.

Asuna switched up to a defensive strategy, but in order to reach the rower, I needed to eliminate the swordsman in my way. There was a big gap in our power levels, so I could easily cut down his HP through sheer force. But suddenly I realized that I had an inner desire to avoid killing the Forest Elf soldiers. Thinking back on it, I had knocked all of the enemies I'd defeated so far into the water rather than wiping them out.

But this hesitation wasn't a product of just the last day or two. When I was tasked with stealing the top-secret orders from the Forest Elf camp on the third floor, I tried to sneak in and remove it with stealth, avoiding combat altogether. That feeling must have been on my mind then, too. I didn't want to invade their camp at night and slaughter them all, and I didn't want Asuna or Kizmel to do that, either.

The emotion itself was probably meaningless. Asuna and I started off the "Jade Key" quest that began this whole story line by killing a Forest Elf knight. Kizmel's beloved sister was killed by a Forest Elf falconer. Whether we killed the soldiers or not would have no effect on the progress of our quest. But...

"Cowardly humans!"

The elven warrior lunged at me, his skin and hair pale and his voice young—though he was probably far, far older than me. I stopped his blow with my Anneal Blade +8. My familiar blade, nearing the end of its usefulness now that it was fully upgraded, deflected back his attack with a pleasing weight and toughness. Staggered by my deflection, the elf lurched backward, and I kicked him in the side with a left roundhouse. The Martial Arts skill, Water Moon, left a trail of pale light streaming from my foot.

"Aaaah!"

I saw the elf fall into the lake screaming out of the right corner of my vision, but I was already moving forward. There was another enemy just to the left, but Asuna had his full attention and was focusing on parrying, so he wouldn't bother me.

Just ahead was the elven rower, his oar completely flat in an attempt to squash the *Tilnel* with the full force of the large ship.

"That's far enough!" I warned and split the oar in two with a swing of my sword, following it with a swift kick of the unarmed oarsman overboard. I didn't even wait to watch him knock over a few fellows on his flight—I was too busy turning around and knocking out the soldier attacking Asuna with a good Flash Blow punch.

"Let's go back!"

We both leaped onto the *Tilnel* again and found that Kizmel was returning at the same moment. I wondered what she had done with the enemy soldiers and was surprised to see not a single soul aboard the gondola on our left.

Kizmel noticed my stunned silence and said matter-of-factly, "I knocked them all into the lake and broke their oars."

A quick examination of the water around the ship showed a fair amount of splashing indeed, as the soldiers swam away for safety. Clearly, the soldiers knocked into the water were following an algorithm that told them to withdraw. After a while, they all began swimming away to the north.

There were still five or six enemies left on the right ship, but there was no way to move it anymore. I put my sword away and picked up the *Tilnel*'s oar, guiding it between the enemy ships and back to a point where we could see the main confrontation.

At this point, there were six ships standing for the Dark Elves, and eight in an active state for the Forest Elves. Not only were the overall numbers much closer, but with most of them engaged in shipboard combat now, there was little threat to the Dark Elf ships themselves.

"Good...Let's sink the enemy flagship before we get into another battering ram battle!" I urged Asuna and Kizmel, turning the *Tilnel* hard starboard.

About a hundred yards from the castle deck, where most of the naval combat was happening, the six remaining Dark Elf ships and an equal number of Forest Elf ships were lined up east to west, their sides pressed together so that fighters could engage in battle. The Dark Elves were clearly on the losing end, but they would hold up for a little while yet.

The two remaining Forest Elven ships were situated to the rear. At the head of the flagship stood the commander in glorious silver armor and flowing white cape, his arms crossed. He didn't seem concerned with us, despite the fact that we'd neutralized his three-ship swing force.

If he assumed that his forces were going to emerge triumphant, we could use his carelessness to ram the ship successfully.

"Asuna, Kizmel, let's do the usual," I suggested, and pulled the folded Argyro's Sheet from the rear of the boat. I didn't know if the same trick would work again, but there was no harm in being prepared. When the three of us spread the sheet over the *Tilnel*, it plunged the interior into darkness, but enough light got through the thin fabric to give us a view of the outside.

"...Gonna approach nice and slow," I whispered, moving the oar gently. I was afraid of the sheet being ripped off if we went too fast, so I sent us toward the flagship as quickly but carefully as I could manage.

Another twenty yards closer, and we'd take off the sheet and charge. We inched closer, closer...

But just when we were within five yards of the ambush point, the Forest Elf commander pulled his sword from his waist.

"Crap!"

"Did he spot us?!"

Asuna and I tensed up, and Kizmel carefully placed her hand on the hilt of her saber. But the commander's longsword was pointed not at the concealed *Tilnel*.

"Now! Ships one and two, begin the charge! Ships five and six, clear a path!!"

His voice echoed over the lake like thunder. Suddenly, out of the six Forest Elf ships engaged in combat, the two middle ones split to the sides.

That left two Dark Elf ships with their sides completely exposed, including the flagship.

"Oh no!" I exclaimed, quickly tearing the Argyro's Sheet off the boat and stuffing it into the space at the stern. Even as I did that, two Forest Elven ships were plunging toward the helpless Dark Elf boats.

"Stop that at once!" Asuna fumed as I rowed madly. The *Tilnel* sent up white wake in pursuit, but the Forest Elf flagship had at least a twenty-yard head start on us.

"We're not going to make it in time," Kizmel commented.

Two seconds later, the enemy flagship's crude ram crushed a hole in the Dark Elven flagship's beautiful hull in a deafening crash.

Just an instant later, the second enemy ship collided with the other Dark Elf boat. The two victimized ships took on water through the massive holes in their sides and began to sink.

"Damn youuuuuu!!"

The Dark Elf commander roared with sheer loathing as he fell into the water. Upon a second glance, the Dark Elves who had fallen into the water over the course of the battle were all treading water in place. Unlike the Forest Elves, they were not swimming toward a particular place, but it seemed to expose a similar rule: Once they had fallen into the water in this battle event, the system did not allow them to rejoin the fight.

Even after his perfectly timed maneuver had destroyed the Dark Elf flagship and its cohort, the Forest Elf commander did not rest. He raised his sword again.

"Ships one and two, forward! All soldiers, prepare for landfall!"

"Ugh," I grunted. I used all of my strength to row, but the two enemy ships were already proceeding through the new hole in the formation before the *Tilnel* could catch up. Nothing stood in their way to the castle pier now.

"Damn! We've got to make our way through that hole, too!" I announced, but the Forest Elf ships that had made way for their flagship to pass through were now returning to their positions in the line. The gap grew smaller by the moment, but it was too late for us to pull back now.

"Nuaaah!" I roared, using 120 percent of my strength to paddle. The tip of the *Tilnel* plunged into the tiny space remaining.

The keels of the enemy ships and the port and starboard sides of our boat made contact with an ugly scraping sound. In the upper left, the ship's durability gauge dropped from 80 percent to 70. But with its expensive materials that had cost Asuna and me our willpower and stamina to collect, and the best skills of old man Romolo, the *Tilnel* pried its way through the blockade of the much larger gondolas and pushed onward.

"We're through!"

"You can do it, Kirito!"

Asuna and Kizmel's encouragement gave me a second wind of energy that put a snap back into my rowing. Now that we were moving quickly again, the two ships ahead of us were a good fifty yards away. It wasn't clear that we'd be able to catch up to them in time.

Under a minute later, my fears were confirmed. The two ships made contact with the dock while we were still twenty yards behind.

Twenty soldiers, including the commander, leaped onto the dock with a roar. Ahead of the mass of Forest Elves was a group of just six Dark Elf guards at the castle gate. It seemed like they ought to be able to just lock the gates and stay inside, but even those sturdy-looking doors wouldn't last long in these circumstances.

"Can't the priests help, Kizmel?! Don't they have magic...er, charms they can cast?!" Asuna asked in a panic, but the Dark Elf only shook her head.

"I'm afraid the priests stationed in the castle are merely officials with no combat experience. They must be locked up in secret rooms underground, trembling with fear by now."

"No..."

Asuna bit her lip. I kept up my rowing at max power and asked a different question.

"What about the viscount and children?! Are they in hiding with the priests?!"

"...I do not know...After all, Yofel Castle has never fallen since ancient times. I cannot guess what decisions the viscount will make."

Though it was easy to forget, if Asuna and I were progressing through the "Elf War" questline properly, Kizmel shouldn't have been present. So unlike the other soldiers here, she wasn't given a specific role in the fight and could therefore act freely with us.

But what about Viscount Yofilis?

He was a master with the rapier, but couldn't be exposed to strong sunlight due to his illness, so he was stuck in his pitch-black office during the daytime. I had figured that piece of background was unrelated to this event, because it seemed apparent that the moment the Forest Elves touched down on the castle dock, we had failed the battle event.

But as a matter of fact, the battle wasn't over when the twenty elves reached the dock. The four remaining Dark Elf ships were fighting hard to prevent any further units from breaking through, and the six guards at the gate ahead were bravely brandishing their spears.

There had to be a way to find victory yet within these dire circumstances.

Though I had no proof, I couldn't help but feel that Yofilis *was* that key to victory. There were too many mysteries surrounding him. Enough that they could easily support a longer questline...

"Asuna, Kizmel!" I called to my companions. "We're going to cut the Forest Elves off!"

"All right!"

"It's in your hands!"

I sent the ship racing along the pier. We passed the ranks of advancing elven soldiers and put on the brakes once the *Tilnel* was just near the castle gate. I leaped onto the pier—no time to drop anchor.

The six ally spearmen were standing firm before the gate in a straight line that was as wide as the pier. The enemy had formed three similar lines of six, with the commander in the rear and a caped swordsman who appeared to be his aide. I stared at the ranks of marching soldiers with their longswords and shields, and a color cursor popped up.

The cursor that popped up was redder than those of the swordsmen and spearmen we'd fought until now. Their title was FOREST ELVEN LIGHT WARRIOR—a bit more imposing. It seemed the soldiers aboard the flagship and its companion vessel were a rank higher than the norm.

On the other hand, our castle guards were Dark Elven gate-keepers. I didn't know if that was higher or lower than a light warrior, but our inferiority in numbers was apparent. The three of us lined up certainly couldn't block the entire pier, and we couldn't prevent the guards from being overwhelmed by three times their number of Forest Elves. On top of that, the naval battle wouldn't hold out much longer. If the four remaining Dark Elf ships crumbled, the enemy would have reinforcements soon.

Did we trust that we could persevere and fight here?

Or follow my baseless instinct?

After an instant of indecision, I made up my mind.

"You two, hold out here for just five minutes!"

"What about you, Kirito?!" Asuna asked, looking worried. I wasted no time in reassuring her.

"Don't worry, I'm just going to call for backup. Don't push it, though. If you're in danger, run away for safety at once!"

I struck their shoulders bracingly and passed between them to run toward the back. As I approached the compact line of Dark Elf guards, I held the sparkling sigil ring high in the air.

"Let me through!"

The miracle power of the Sigil of Lyusula caused the guards to part down the center and the gate behind them to crack open just a bit. When rowing the gondola, I was using all of my strength stat, but now I let my agility number do the talking and raced through the castle gate and the front garden as the doors rumbled shut behind me.

Once I had pushed my way through the castle door, the interior was dead silent. Even the maids and nobles had gone into hiding.

If the viscount himself had evacuated for another location, this was all for nothing. But I could do nothing but trust that it would work out. I raced through the entrance hall to the great stairs and up to the top floor.

By the time I reached the fifth floor of the castle, one of the five minutes I had promised Asuna and Kizmel was gone. I took a hard right corner with my body tilted over and saw the great door at the end of the hall, but the guards were no longer there. I put on the brakes just in front of the door, a sinking feeling in my chest.

"My lord, I wish to enter!" I shouted. After several endless seconds, that odd voice sounded from behind the door.

"Come in."

I pushed the door open and stepped into the spacious office. As usual, the only light was the tiny lamp on the desk, and I couldn't see where I was stepping. But given that I had passed through here several times to turn in quests, I was familiar enough with it to quickly cross the room and stop before the desk.

I ran all the way to this spot on a hunch, but I had no idea what to say when the moment came. For one thing, the viscount was not an NPC with a high-functioning AI like Kizmel. He probably wouldn't even respond properly unless I used terms that matched his database…and yet, before I could even speak, his calm voice sounded from the darkness beyond the lamp.

"It seems the battle is going poorly."

I nodded and explained the situation. "Y-yes, my lord. Four of our ships have been sunk, including the flagship, and the enemy forces are on the castle pier."

"I see…Then it is only a matter of time until the enemy reaches this point."

"…At this rate, it could be twenty…no, fifteen minutes."

"Then I shall wait for them here. Warrior of humankind, your assistance is appreciated. Take your companions and leave this castle."

Two minutes had passed. If I was going to keep my promise to Asuna, I had to be out of this room and heading downstairs within another two minutes. I clenched my fists, trying to quell my rising panic.

"From the very start, the Dark Elven morale has been inferior to the Forest Elves'. I believe this stems from the lack of their true battle commander."

"Ahh. And who would their true commander be?"

"You, my lord."

I thought I detected a self-deprecating smile at my blunt answer, but that could have been my imagination.

His right hand extended from the darkness and tapped the blackwood desk twice.

"...I'm afraid that is not possible. It might be hard for a young human like you to understand, but if you fight eternally, defeat is guaranteed to arrive eventually. If Yofel Castle is fated to fall today, and I to the enemy's blades, then such is the guidance of the Holy Tree. The people of Lyusula must accept that fate."

There was such deep resignation in his sonorous voice that I could not believe it was a prewritten line of dialogue.

I unclenched my balled fists and stretched the fingers, then clenched them again with all of my strength.

"My lord, your soldiers are still fighting now! They must be waiting to hear the voice of their liege. Kizmel explained your illness to me. If you are going to wait for death in the darkness, why not venture outside so that you can deliver a final message to your guards?!"

I expected my plea would go in vain. I must have missed some kind of quest related to the viscount's illness. Maybe if I'd completed it, he could have overcome his aversion to powerful light and gloriously led the Dark Elven troops into battle, rather than leaving it to that haughty, useless commander...

As I expected, the castle's master had no response for quite some time. When the three-minute mark passed, I realized that my instincts were wrong and started to turn to leave the room.

But then—

"Young human. Answer just one question."

I turned to see that a golden ? mark was floating in the darkness. Some kind of quest had just begun. As I held my breath, I felt a clear, colorless gaze with a hidden strength pierce my soul.

"Why do you lend your aid to the people of Lyusula and not Kales'Oh?"

It was such a simple question that I had no immediate answer. Telling him that it was "because we were playing the Dark Elf faction of the campaign" wasn't a real answer.

When faced with the opening of the "Jade Key" quest on the third floor, Asuna and I chose the Dark Elf champion—Kizmel—without much debate. It was because I had done that in the beta. At the core, that's all it came down to.

"At first…I didn't have a real reason," I started to explain, no plan or certainty in mind. "But that's not true anymore. Both I and Asuna love Kizmel. So I want to help her protect her people and her nation."

Another long silence filled the darkness of the chamber.

Later—much, much later—I learned that the program that controlled the world of *Sword Art Online* was able to monitor the emotions and mental states of its players. In other words, if I'd lied to flatter Viscount Yofilis, the system would have seen that and possibly failed the quest.

When she heard that, Asuna beamed and said, "It's a good thing you answered honestly because you've always been a terrible liar."

Just before the timer hit four minutes, the golden quest marker disappeared without a sound. There was no little *bleep* to signal it had been completed; instead, the viscount spoke with a stronger tone than I'd heard yet.

"I shall take your words for truth. Therefore, I will answer you with truth. Young swordsman, the tale about my illness that you heard from Kizmel…"

The chair creaked as he rose. Faint footsteps circled around the desk and to my side. A scent of forest floated in the air, and a voice of merriment reached my ears.

"…is a lie."

"…Huh?!"

"Follow me."

The footsteps led away, and there was a thunking sound somewhere on the north wall. Midday sunlight pierced the darkness filling the room. Standing in the middle of the rectangle of pure white cut out of the wall was a slender silhouette, its long hair streaming in the wind.

It must have been a secret door along the wall. But this was the fifth floor of the castle. We had to be a good fifty feet above the ground. There was no way to jump down.

But the viscount's figure was suddenly gone. I raced to the opening in shock and looked down to see window frames jutting just two inches from the wall, forming a staircase that descended down to the first-floor entrance. The viscount was leaping nimbly down the series of ledges.

A chill shot up my back when I looked down, but there was less than a minute left. I could hear frantic clashing and the sound of sword skills coming from beyond the closed gate. The HP bars for Asuna and Kizmel had both lost over 20 percent since I left.

"…I can do this," I told myself, and stepped onto the ledge just below the opening. All I had to do was leap to each successive window ledge, five feet below the one above. That was a much smaller jump than the daredevil gondola jumping I'd attempted in Rovia.

When I reached the ground about ten seconds after the viscount, I let out a huge heave of relief.

Finally, I was able to take an accurate measure of Viscount Yofilis. His clothes were fittingly noble: a rococo-styled frock coat covered with moiré and buttons, a vest, pants that stopped below the knee and white tights. A white tie packed with frills sat on his chest, and his long black hair was tied behind him. At his waist was a fragile rapier, even thinner than the standard size.

The viscount raised a white-gloved hand and brushed the left side of his face, where I couldn't see. When he turned to face me and I saw his face in full, I forgot my panic about the situation for a moment and stared in shock.

An old vertical scar ran across his beautiful features, which looked just a bit older than Kizmel's. The scar ran from his hairline to his chin, clearly the result of a sharp blade.

Yofilis fixed me with a stare from his remaining green-gray eye, a sardonic twist in his cheek, which was rather light skinned for a "Dark" Elf.

"This scar is the greatest shame in a long life of regrets. I have hidden in the darkness for many years, hoping to spare my children from inheriting its disgrace...but it seems the time has come to expose it to humankind."

"Uh...s-sorry," I stammered, looking away. The viscount chuckled.

"No need to apologize. Perhaps I made a fool of myself by trying so hard to hide my shame. Let us go to where my soldiers and your friends are fighting."

His short boots clicked, and the viscount began striding quickly toward the closed gate. As he walked, he raised his hand and shouted, "Open!"

The giant doors began to rumble open, just as the sub-window I'd left open in the lower right corner of my vision hit five minutes.

Of the eighteen Forest Elf warriors on the pier (excluding the commander and his aide), only ten were left, but the defending Dark Elf spearmen had been halved from six to three. Asuna and Kizmel were fighting their hardest to make up the difference, but that rapier, a thrust-only weapon, had limited ability to hit multiple targets.

No sooner had that thought crossed my mind than one of the Forest Elves broke through the horizontal blockade. I drew my sword and intercepted him, overpowering the elf with our hilts clashing. Once I'd pushed my way up next to Asuna, I shouted an apology.

"Sorry, it took a little longer!"

"We're fine here! But the ships…"

I looked far ahead to the naval battle and saw that the four Dark Elf ships were still afloat, but the crew of each one was down to three or four. Once that line of defense was broken, we would have at least fifty fresh foes descending upon the dock.

"How'd it go with you, Kirito?!" she asked. For an instant, I wasn't sure of what to say. Ultimately, I didn't need to say anything.

A voice like a bracing wind blowing across the lake rang out behind our backs.

"I am knight of Lyusula and master of Castle Yofel, Leyshren Zed Yofilis!!"

Kizmel gasped from the other side of Asuna, but she kept fighting without turning around. The slick ringing of a blade was undoubtedly the sound of Yofilis drawing his blade. He shouted again.

"Warriors of Lyusula! I apologize for my long absence and beseech your strength! The future of our kingdom rests on this battle! For the sake of queen, friend, and family, stand strong and fight with me!"

For just a moment, the clashing and roaring of battle died out, and silence fell upon the lake. It was broken by a roar of such incredible volume that it seemed to be rising from the very depths of the fourth floor.

The soldiers on the dock, on the ships, and even floating in the water all raised their swords and fists as they bellowed. Ripples formed in the placid lake, melding together into larger waves that spread outward.

A bracing sound effect hit my ears, and I instinctively looked up to my left to a number of new icons above our HP bar readouts.

The upward arrow over the sword mark meant an increased attack buff. The arrow over a shield meant increased defense. The yellow explosion mark was an increased knock-back buff. The four-leaf clover was a bonus luck buff.

If these bonuses had been granted to every Dark Elf in the battle, then Viscount Yofilis's presence was worthy of worship, but we couldn't afford to waste a second of the precious boosts.

"Yeah!"

I cheered and swiped the flat sword skill Horizontal before me. The enemy Forest Elf was knocked clear into the lake by the increased knock-back effect. Asuna and Kizmel overpowered their foes likewise, and we pushed forward.

"Have no fear! The addition of one measly castle lord does not affect our advantage!" yelled the Forest Elf commander from the rear of his troop formation. He drew his large longsword and pointed it forward.

The remaining six enemies before us lined up in a row and raised their swords high in the exact same motion. The steel blades took on a faint blue glow. They were going to unleash the same sword skill all at the same time—probably the Vertical slash skill. Even a basic sword skill could be deadly if they were all swung at the same time.

Our only defense was countering with the same attack, but of the six of us, I had a longsword, Asuna had a rapier, Kizmel a saber, and then three spears for the guards. It would be nearly impossible to time up different weapon skills.

Suddenly, a command issued from the rear.

"Evade to the sides!"

My body moved without thinking. Me, Asuna, and one guard went to the right, while Kizmel and the other two guards went left, all standing at the very lip of the pier.

The enemy warriors ahead stomped the stone dock. Their six swords plunged downward with blue lines. I raised my sword valiantly to defend, but even if I blocked it, the force would knock me into the water.

But my fear did not come to pass.

A giant spear of blinding white light shot past us at phenomenal speed. It split our ranks like a comet and plunged into the six swordsmen mid-swing.

All six of them were thrown into the air with a powerful flash of light and a shock wave. They spun and flew, falling three each into the water on either side of the pier. When the light subsided, it left behind the figure of Viscount Yofilis, his body leaned far forward with rapier extended in pristine form, nearly forty feet from where he had been standing.

"Was that…a sword skill?!" Asuna breathed. All I could do was nod quickly.

I had never seen that move before in Aincrad, even in the beta. But I had seen a video of the effect and name on the official site just before the game launched. It was the greatest thrust attack in the rapier category: Flashing Penetrator.

We had barely any time to register the shock, however. The ultra-high-level attack had a considerable delay effect, leaving the viscount immobile as the enemy commander stared with rage.

"Let's go, Asuna!" I cried, leaping forward. I dashed past the kneeling viscount to intercept the white knight. Meanwhile, Asuna struck at his adjutant.

This had to be the final battle of the event.

"Out of my way, human!" the commander roared, swinging his longsword. I blocked it with my own, feeling the numbing shock of its force in my wrists.

It was too fast and heavy. Even with all of my buffs, it would be very hard to knock this foe into the water. The cursor identified him as a Forest Elven inferior knight. He was not an elite mob that boasted far better stats than other monsters of the same level, but it was clear from the bright red cursor that he would be tough enough in a one-on-one fight.

I couldn't turn back now or what I said to the viscount would become a lie.

"I cannot let you pass!" I replied, and swung for his right side, where the armor looked weakest. The white knight lithely pulled his sword back and effortlessly blocked the attack with his cross-shaped hilt.

The series of slashes he delivered next had to be parried or sidestepped, while his stout defense was enough to block my responses. At my right side, Asuna was having similar trouble getting through to the highly armored Forest Elven heavy warrior.

Despite this, Kizmel and Yofilis showed no sign of coming to our aid. Even in the naval battle, the soldiers on both sides had stopped fighting to watch the twin duels on the pier.

Even as I struggled in the fierce battle, a little part of my mind began to piece together the answer to a fundamental question I had about the Elf War campaign.

The Dark Elves claimed that when the six keys came together and the door to the Sanctuary opened, the floating castle Aincrad would come to ruin. Meanwhile, the Forest Elves believed that all the floors of Aincrad would return to the earth where they belonged. I didn't think that *either* case was actually going to come true.

So why had the production staff written this scenario and given the elves these background stories, made them believe these legends? In the beta test, the keys were just MacGuffins, simple props meant to be collected or stolen and nothing more. That was enough for the campaign story to function. So why had they included these obviously impossible and unrealistic concepts of "disaster" and "return" into the story for the retail release?

In fact, had the real-life staff actually written this scenario...?

Just as this bizarre and nonsensical question floated through my head, the enemy knight and I slashed at the same time, our hilts locked. I gritted and pushed back against the pressure, my blade creaking.

"Boy...Why does a human fight for the sake of the Dark Elves?" came the question from the knight's appropriately ornate helmet.

Just a few minutes ago, Yofilis had asked me the exact same question. But my answer about affection for Kizmel meant nothing here.

I had the feeling that this was being asked not of me personally, but of me as the representative for any and all players who chose this particular faction in the campaign quest.

Completing this campaign quest was not a requirement to beating and escaping the world of *SAO*. Sure, considerable experience, col, and items were available for doing it, but those things were also given for doing stand-alone quests, and strictly in terms of efficiency, it would be much more profitable to hunt at particularly active monster spots than get bogged down in time-consuming, story-heavy questlines. That was probably the main reason why the DKB and ALS had decided to put off the campaign for now.

But neither I nor Asuna had given any thought to casting the questline aside. We had our personal reason—our promise to Kizmel—but there was another motive, one a bit more nebulous.

A small cracking sound cut through the spark-inducing intersection of our swords. As though prompted by that faint sound, I shouted, "Because...I think the war between the elves is wrong!"

Even I didn't know why I said that. If I truly felt that way, it would be a contradiction to take one side and battle the other. But on the other hand, I knew that it was truly what I believed.

"Nonsense!" the knight barked in a voice like steel.

Maybe he was programmed to react that way no matter what answer I gave. But it felt like there was true, cognizant anger in his face.

"Since ancient times, the people of Kales'Oh have shed unending blood in our battle against the Dark Elves! All for the sake of releasing the lives trapped in this empty, meaningless prison! And our sacred duty will not be stopped by the likes of a foolish child such as you!"

A shock wave seemed to rip through the knight's tall body, and my Anneal Blade was suddenly knocked backward by the enemy's sword.

"*Nwuaaaah!*" the white knight bellowed. In my right ear, I

heard Asuna call my name. The four buff icons that the viscount granted us were now blinking.

"Gah..."

I gritted my teeth and tried to hold my ground. The enemy's longsword took on a clear silver glow high in the air. It was a sword skill: the three-part combo Sharp Nail.

It was too late to cancel out the attack with one of my own, and I wasn't in position to evade with a side step. All I could do was defend with my sword. But a normal block would result in my sword being knocked aside on the first blow, leaving me open for the second and third.

I had only one remaining option.

With my feet firmly planted, I held the Anneal Blade above my head. With my left hand, I supported the tip of the sword as it lay horizontal. This was a weapon defense technique called a "two-handed block," but its maximum defensive value came with its own risk.

The first Sharp Nail hit landed toward the end of the Anneal Blade, sending up a shower of sparks. The clash pierced my ears, but the vibration in my hands gave me the same creaking, cracking sensation that I'd felt earlier.

A two-handed block used the free hand to support the sword, which meant that any attack being defended naturally landed on the flat of the sword rather than the blade edge. That caused over twice the amount of damage to the weapon's durability than the normal way. On top of that, there was a small chance of the weapon being broken, regardless of its durability number.

Stay strong! I willed my beloved sword as I caught the knight's second swing. Once again, I got that nasty sensation in my palm.

The +8 points on my Anneal Blade went four to Sharpness, four to Durability. That meant its toughness against stress was now much higher than its initial value. I'd kept up on routine maintenance, of course, and I'd visited NPC blacksmiths for upkeep in both Rovia and Yofel Castle recently.

But it was true that I had put that sword through hell since earning it in my very first quest on the first floor. There was no data that suggested the length of use had any effect on the durability stat, but it certainly *felt* like the white knight's sword skills were terribly damaging to my weapon.

The idea popped into my head to catch the third blow with my arm, pull back, and leave the rest to Kizmel, as a means of saving my weapon. But instead, I summoned up all of my willpower and kept it held aloft.

Just before the naval battle began, this elven commander had announced that the Dark Elves were working with the humans to build ships and bring down the Forest Elf castle, but the plan had failed and the ships fell into the Forest Elves' hands.

That had to be a mistake. If the commander wasn't just lying to his subordinates, that would mean he was working on incorrect intelligence. But who fed it to him? The higher-ups among the elves or the Fallen.

In the case of the former, the Forest Elves and the Fallen Elves were working together, as we'd been thinking thus far. But in the latter case, that meant that both Dark and Forest Elves were being misled by the Fallen.

I had to see this through in order to find out the truth.

"*Haaah!*"

The third and final blow of the Sharp Nail attack descended. For the third time, I caught the blow on the flat of the Anneal Blade.

Kchiiing! A small chunk of the blade cracked loose, but the sword held. The message log in the bottom left of my view announced that my One-Handed Sword skill proficiency had reached 150.

An image of the sword skill details list flashed into my mind, so familiar from staring at it endlessly back since the start of the beta. I knew there were two moves that became available at skill level 150.

"Aaaah!"

The white knight fell into his postattack delay, and I took a heavy step forward.

My right arm moved of its own accord, holding my sword perfectly level. The four-part sword skill Horizontal Square.

The blade took on a deep, pure sky-blue glow. The sword, drawn back and to the right, turned into a streak of light that bit deep into the enemy's breastplate. The knight stumbled backward, overwhelmed by the bright flash and shock of impact.

My sword bounced back and held still at my left side for an instant. There was another flash, and the combination of system assistance and forward leap ripped the sword from left to right. It was another level strike, much shallower than the previous, clipping the target's gorget and left shoulder. Thanks to the help of my still-active buff, it knocked the knight farther back.

The force of the second blow sent my body spinning clockwise, the sword ending up at my left flank.

"Aaah!!"

I leaped hard off my right foot. The tip of the Anneal Blade sliced into the enemy's chest again, shattering the thick metal breastplate. It caught his flesh behind it, sending up a spray of little red particles meant to resemble blood.

"*Hrrg!*" the white knight grunted. He tried to hold up his sword for another attack.

But my skill wasn't done yet. The last swipe of Horizontal Square was a forehand from the right that completed a glowing square of light that expanded outward.

"*Raaaah!!*"

My blade and I danced, slicing through air that seemed to be thicker than usual with the acceleration of my senses. If this last shot hit his defenseless heart with a critical blow, that should eliminate his HP. But even as I roared, I altered my course slightly—for the kite shield in his left hand rather than his heart.

The flash of collision between sword and shield covered my vision in white. In the midst of that halation, the knight's silhouette grew rapidly smaller as his body flew away with the force of impact.

In a world of silence, I heard the sound once again.

A tiny little cracking sound. A voice of farewell.

About eight inches from the tip of the Anneal Blade +8, the metal splintered, shooting out fragile shards that melted into the air like ice.

When sound and color returned, the first things I heard were the harsh ringing of metal and an enormous splash. The Forest Elven inferior knight had plunged into the water over thirty feet away, his longsword the only part of him remaining on the pier.

I didn't know if he would remove himself from the battle once he'd fallen into the water, the way all the other elves did. But I didn't bother to follow the commander's status. I turned to my side.

In the rear, Asuna was still locked in combat with the heavily armed adjutant. Neither of their HP were even in the yellow zone yet.

I put the half-shattered Anneal Blade into my back sheath and called out, "Asuna, switch!!"

Instantly understanding my intent, the fencer smoothly pulled back and held her Chivalric Rapier +5 out before her.

"Yaah!!"

It was her signature Linear attack. It struck dead center of the enemy's shield. Though it was a basic move, the combination of Asuna's skill proficiency, weapon stats, force boost from her forward step, and the last few seconds of the viscount's buff effects all combined to blast the Forest Elven heavy warrior's considerable bulk backward.

Naturally, Asuna was put into a significant delay herself at having her sword skill successfully defended, but I was there to charge the adjutant and take advantage of the instant of standstill.

I was there to smash his defenseless side with Crescent Moon, a backflip kick attack. Lifted into the air by the skill, the heavy warrior bellowed with rage and consternation, plunging toward the water on the right side of the pier.

He splashed into the water with a splendid water spout. I blocked the spray with my arm and examined the lake surface.

The commander's aide sank face-first a foot or two, then released his broadsword and round shield and began to paddle up to the surface. He glared back at us ruefully, then turned and began to swim away. I was surprised that he could even swim with that plate armor on, but it was probably yet another elven charm at work.

Our buffs vanished at last, and I turned my empty-feeling view back to the dock. My partner recovered from her delay and walked over for a celebratory fist bump.

Though we had finally won the exhausting battle, Asuna didn't look very happy. I knew why, and I stroked the hilt of my sword to explain.

"It was about time for it to go…If anything, I'm glad it held out this long."

I lowered my hand and patted my partner's arm. We turned to look out beyond the end of the pier. The soldiers on the remaining Forest Elf ships were abandoning their posts and leaping into the lake. They swam over to join the commander and his aide and formed a long line swimming toward the canyon exit of the lake.

Meanwhile, the Dark Elves treading water climbed up onto the dock and assumed formation, while the soldiers on the four gondolas brought them back to their positions. While there was no way to know how many soldiers on both sides had died in the conflict, it was obvious that many of them had already been knocked out of the battle by falling into water.

Was this the best way for it to end? Given the possibility that the Forest Elves could attack again, perhaps we ought to have been more ruthless in seeking fatalities.

As the last line of the Forest Elves disappeared into the distant mist, a familiar voice called my name.

"That was brilliant fighting, Kirito."

I turned slowly and fixed the smiling knight Kizmel with a steady gaze.

"Do you think...this was the right choice?" I murmured, looking down. Kizmel strode right up before me and bracingly smacked my shoulder.

"Hold your head high. You were the one who warned us of a Forest Elf attack, helped even the scales, and defeated the enemy commander in one-on-one battle, Kirito. Most important of all, you safely protected the two keys in the castle. What more could we ask for?"

Given that this was coming from Kizmel, whose beloved sister was killed by Forest Elves, I could only nod silently.

As though it had been waiting for that gesture, my quest log popped up and announced that the quest had been completed—specifically, the "Laketop Fortress" quest that followed the "Shipwright of Yore." A huge amount of experience poured in.

I closed the window, unsure of how I really felt about it. Meanwhile, Asuna whispered, "I'm going to leave the lake for a bit and check for messages from Argo."

"Oh...thanks, do that."

Yofel Castle and its lake were an instanced map created for Asuna and me, which meant that, like dungeons, we couldn't send or receive instant messages here. We'd been spending most of our time out questing as we hung around the castle, so we'd been buying updates on the progress of the floor from Argo, but the Forest Elf attack had kept us busy and unable to receive the midday message.

Asuna hopped onto the *Tilnel* and handled the oar somewhat awkwardly, sending the little boat gliding across the now-quiet lake. As I watched her go, Viscount Yofilis approached.

"It is a shame, what happened to your sword."

I spun around and shook my head rapidly. "N-no, I put it through too much..."

The viscount's scarred but beautiful features crinkled into a grin.

"It is good that you do not blame your weapon. Within most of the blade remaining, the castle's blacksmith should be able to repair it."

"Mmm..." I shook my head. "No, I'll melt this one down and have it turned into a new weapon or piece of armor."

"I see. In that case..."

Yofilis raised his hand. Two soldiers trotted up from the gate, bearing an enormous chest at least six feet wide. They lowered the heavy-looking chest next to their master and bowed before running back to resume their places among the troop formation.

"What's this?" I asked, curious. Yofilis pulled a golden key from his pocket—not one of the six secret keys, of course—and unlocked the chest, pulling it open. A shine several times brighter than the afternoon sun filled my eyes.

The enormous chest was absolutely stuffed with weapons, armor, and accessories that had been buffed to a mirror shine. As I stared with shock, a dialog window appeared offering a choice of quest rewards.

Yofilis stood and smiled. "These are the treasured heirlooms of the Yofilis family. Human warrior, please accept any one of them as a personal gift from me and another as a reward for your valor in combat."

"Huh? Er, but—"

The viscount's stunning generosity completely obliterated the leftover gloom shrouding my mind after I hadn't been able to finish off the Forest Elf knight.

"T...two? Are you sure?"

"Of course."

"For me and my partner? Two each?"

"Naturally."

"Th...thank you, my lord!"

I excitedly gave a Dark Elf salute, to which Kizmel smiled and rolled her eyes. But I couldn't be blamed for my reaction. Countless times I'd been greeted with quest reward options and thought, *If only I could pick two!* It was a credit to my phenomenal self-control that I hadn't thrust my fists into the air and screamed with triumph.

"W-well, if you say so," I finished, tapping each of the items in the lengthy rewards list in turn to check out their properties— the greatest pleasure to be found in Aincrad.

Five minutes later: *If only I could pick three!*

I was still agonizing over which to pick when I heard a loud splash next to me. It was Asuna dropping the anchor of the *Tilnel* as she returned. I looked up from the list and beckoned my partner over.

"Hey, Asuna, check it out! We get two this time—*two!*"

Her face was grave as she leaped onto the pier and raced over. I couldn't blame her—two items was serious news.

"And not two between the both of us, I mean two *each!*"

"Enough about tutus, Kirito!" she yelled, sparks flying from her boots with the impact of her sliding stop. She grabbed my shoulder and sucked in a deep breath. "This is important! They just left already!"

"Who did?"

"Who do you think?! The floor boss raid!!"

"...Wha...?"

Whaaaaat?! Kizmel and Yofilis blinked in surprise at my scream.

"B-but...this morning's info said that the boss battle would be tomorrow afternoon at the earliest..."

"That's right, but they found the boss chamber earlier than expected this morning, and they scouted it already. So they took a break at the nearby village to resupply and decided that they should just 'git on with the battle already' this very afternoon!"

"...You don't have to elaborate on who said *that* one," I groaned, summoning a mental image of the fourth-floor map. Yofel Castle was in the lower right of the circular map—the southeast. The Forest Elves' castle was on the plateau to the southwest. And the labyrinth tower was just between the two, at the very southern tip of the floor.

The nearest village to the tower was barely a few hundred yards away, as I remembered it. And the layout of the labyrinth was quite simple on this floor. If they already had the route to the boss chamber mapped out it would take two...no, one and a half hours to get there from town.

"Do you know the exact time the raid left?!" I demanded.

Asuna looked back at her message. "Fifty-five minutes ago!"

"Then they're already in the tower now...Hmmm, I guess we have no choice but to leave it to them this time..."

"Yeah...maybe you're right..."

With the quick pace the DKB and ALS were making, I was sure they could defeat the floor boss at first glance without suffering any casualties. I just had to swallow my concerns in this case. Meanwhile, Kizmel approached the two of us.

"Kirito, Asuna, will you be challenging the guardian of the Pillar of the Heavens?"

"Uh...yeah, but it seems that our other companions have already begun climbing the tower..."

A faint shadow fell over her face.

"I see. If you trust them, then there is no reason to worry...but from what I understand, the beast of this floor..."

She trailed off, and the viscount filled in for her.

"We only know based on the legend, but it is said that the guardian beast who lurks in the tower of this floor wields some eerie power."

"Eerie power...?" I wondered.

The floor boss we fought in the beta was known as a hippogriff—half eagle, half horse. Its beak was powerful, but in an internal chamber with a ceiling, all its wings could do was cause wind. I didn't remember much challenge or any kind of special "eerie" power.

But in the next moment, I was reminded that my knowledge of the beta meant nothing anymore.

"The guardian beast of this floor is called a hippocampus—

a cross between horse and fish. It causes water to spring from even the driest earth and can flood one's feet from beneath him," Yofilis announced, then added, "Any who fight the beast will need a charm to float in water, it is said."

"...!"

Asuna and I held our breaths.

If we interpreted his words directly, the hippogriff-turned-hippocampus had the ability to fill the entire boss chamber with water. Therefore, we needed the means to float. But there was no way Kibaou and Lind would have their men hauling gondolas by hand up that tower. The system wouldn't even allow us to do that.

What struck me as even worse was the possibility that in order for the room to fill with water, there must be no leaks—meaning that they might force the exits shut. If an inescapable boss chamber filled with water, the entire raid would be wiped out.

"W-we need to send them a message!" Asuna shouted, racing for the *Tilnel*. I quickly stopped her.

"No, the message won't reach the players inside the labyrinth!"

"What should we do, then?!"

"We have to go ourselves. If we're lucky, at least half of the raid members will still have their inner-tube fruit from the trip to the main city. As long as they can hold out with those, we'll have time to reach the chamber and open the door from outside!"

I chose not to mention what would happen if we *couldn't* open the door from the outside. It was too disastrous a possibility, and I didn't want to believe that they'd set up such a lethal trap so close to the beginning of the game.

Asuna's reaction was quick. She nodded with conviction and turned to Kizmel.

"I'm sorry, Kizmel—we need to go. But we'll be back, I swear!"

But the Dark Elf knight's shoulders simply shrugged, her expression one of affront.

"What do you humans call this? 'Being distant'? I will join you, of course."

"Wha—?" both Asuna and I uttered simultaneously. But that surprise was nothing compared to the shock that came two seconds after.

"And so shall I," pronounced His Lordship Viscount Yofilis, master of Yofel Castle, as though it were perfectly ordinary. Asuna and I stared at him.

"Whaaaaaaat?!"

To fill in for my broken Anneal Blade +8, I called upon the services of the longsword the Forest Elf commander left on the pier. Asuna and I headed out into the lake in the large Dark Elven gondola, not the *Tilnel*, leaving the selection of quest rewards as a treat for afterward. And with the viscount, Kizmel, and two other stout guards, we had a full party of six.

With the soldiers managing the oars, the gondola raced through the empty lake and plunged into the canyon. A single terrific blow from its battering ram was enough to take care of any aquatic monsters in our way, and when we reached a branch in the river, we headed south.

Every time I looked at one of the labyrinth towers that stretched up to the floor above, I was overwhelmed by the scale, but as a representative of humanity in the presence of impassive Kizmel and Yofilis, I couldn't afford to show fear. We raced up the brief path from the end of the canyon to the foot of the tower.

Argo was there at the entrance, ready with the map data. While her face went pale when she saw the cursors of the Dark Elves, she valiantly announced that she would join us.

We never stopped running, even inside the tower. The raid party ahead of us had cleared out nearly all the monsters on the way, and the few we saw were dispatched instantly by the viscount.

Sadly, unlike Kizmel, Viscount Yofilis never actually officially joined our party. If he had, then I could have learned what his level was—but perhaps that was something I didn't really want to know. After all, depending on our choices in the campaign, the possibility was there that we might have fought *him* instead.

After a mad rush, we reached the entrance to the boss chamber just forty-five minutes after leaving the lake. That meant we were just ten minutes behind the raid.

The thick granite doors were shut tight. And through the narrow gap where the doors met trickled a tiny stream of water.

"...Kirito!" Asuna cried. I nodded and we leaped to the doors. I forced the Dark Elves behind us, then gripped the rusty handle with both hands, braced my feet, and pulled with all my strength.

But ultimately, there was no need to have pulled with much force. The giant doors were just barely holding put against enormous pressure from inside, and they burst open the instant I pulled.

"Whoaaa?!"

The shout came not from me or Asuna, or the four Dark Elves, or even Argo.

Along with a wave of water rushing through the doors came a large, shaven-headed man with an ax—Agil. He slid into the corridor on his belly and looked up at me, trying to get a smile across his lips.

"Hey, you showed up."

"S-so you *did* get flooded!"

I pushed against the current and helped him up. More and more players washed out after Agil, but they were being caught by a fence surrounding the circular hall before the boss chamber. The water passed through the fence and drained down the stairs in a waterfall.

"Yeah. I told 'em it might be trouble, since the boss looked different than what the strategy guide said," Agil grumbled. On the other side of the room, Asuna was clinging to the fence.

"Agil, are there victims?!"

"Don't worry, no one's died. Someone greedy picked all the little floaty-tube fruits they could back at the staircase…so thanks to those, nobody's drowned, at the very least. We've just been trying to avoid the boss's attacks and get this door open, but it was made so that it couldn't be opened from inside."

"Y-yeah, I see…"

Meanwhile, all of the water that had filled the boss chamber had drained away. Nearly forty players wearing inner tubes were piled up in the front hall, groaning and moaning.

I peered around the door into the chamber, still holding onto the door ring.

It was very spacious. The rectangular room was at least fifty yards deep. There were no windows, and the floor and walls were gray granite. The only light was the blue tips of an eerie series of pillars.

In the center of the soggy floor was an enormous silhouette.

Just as Yofilis had told us, its front half was a horse, and its back half was a fish. But instead of hooves on its front legs, the beast had clawed flippers, and its mane was a mass of wriggling tentacles. The color cursor told me its name was WYTHEGE THE HIPPOCAMPUS.

The six-part HP bar of the wetly snickering boss was almost at the end of its first bar. So even as they dealt with the unexpected flooding, the raid party had managed to keep up some offense on the beast.

Just as I began wondering how to start tackling the boss, a loud, crude voice erupted from the mass of players behind me.

"Well, if you were gonna show up, ya might as well have done it on time!"

Next came a pained voice at the bottom of the pile. "Get these people off of me, Kibaou! Everyone off the pile, start taking potions!"

"Y-you don't mean ta keep goin', Lind!"

"Of course I do! We know its attack patterns, and we've already taken down one gauge; no use wasting that hard work!"

"Don't act like yer in charge! If it weren't for my inner-tube fruit, y'all would be drowned by now!"

"You were simply hogging community resources for yourself! Don't act like you were being generous!"

Either way, if you don't make up your mind now, we'll lose the boss's aggro and his HP will recover, I thought.

I was about to speak up and try to get the guild leaders on the same page, but—perhaps fortunately—I didn't need to. The moment they saw Kizmel and Yofilis walk up, the entire raid party went silent, not just Kibaou and Lind.

To them, the Dark Elf viscount's cursor must have gone beyond black into the color of pure darkness. The nobleman spun around to view the group as a whole.

"Warriors of humankind, if you intend to fight, then stand at once. If not, be quiet. In either case, through my pact with Kirito and Asuna, I will dispatch the summon beast."

And Yofilis drew his rapier and held it forward, the metal ringing.

"In my name, Yofilis, knight of Lyusula, I command all who can stand to follow my lead!"

A conical aura emerged from the tip of his weapon, and upon touching it, the four buff icons blinked into existence above my HP bar again.

It wasn't long until all the raid members were on their feet, raising their weapons and roaring mightily.

At 2:32 PM on Tuesday, December 27, 2022, Wythege the Hippocampus was defeated by a seven-party, forty-man raid, plus one extra party.

The boss's special ability, Water Inflow, deluged the entire chamber with water, but the means of counteracting it was quite simple. The boss's power caused the door of the chamber to shut, making it impossible to open from within, but if it was pulled from the outside when a certain level of water pressure was pushing

against it, the door would swing open like a charm. We had Argo wait outside with simple instructions to open the door if water started trickling out through the crack. That essentially nullified the special ability.

Then again, Viscount Yofilis might not have needed such a specialized strategy to begin with. Through his magical charm, he was able to run about on the surface of the water and continue to attack the boss, even when the room was flooded.

9

"SO, I WAS THINKING," ASUNA BEGAN TO MUMBLE AS we climbed the spiral staircase to the fifth floor, "Kizmel and the viscount took that black gondola back to the castle, right? And we left the *Tilnel* moored at the castle pier. So how will we return to the castle?"

"Hmmm..."

I considered several options. "Once we activate the fifth-floor teleport gate, we can use that to return to Rovia and then travel to Yofel Castle again...I guess..."

"But we don't have a boat in town. Are you suggesting we swim with the inner tubes all the way there?"

"No, we can make another one. It'll be a snap, as long as we don't focus on high-quality materials this time."

"Well, sure...but you're naming the next one."

Whatever I was going to say got stuck in my throat. I was well aware of my own inability to come up with a good name.

I hemmed and hawed as I trotted up the steps, my arms crossed. Meanwhile, Asuna spoke up again.

"...So, are you just going to keep using that sword?"

"Eh? Uh, no..."

I undid my arms and brushed the hilt extending over my right shoulder. Its leather grip was well used, it stayed true during the battle with the floor boss, and its stats were not far off from my

Anneal Blade +8, but it was still someone else's sword. Some other NPC's sword.

Perhaps I might one day again fight that Forest Elven inferior knight. It wasn't impossible, but I couldn't escape the thought.

"When we get back to Yofel Castle, I'll take a one-handed sword with my quest rewards and use that for my next main weapon. You should think hard about what you'll pick, Asuna. We get two, remember."

"Were you *that* excited about getting two items?" she asked, groaning. "That lord was a very strange person, wasn't he? Spending years of his life locked into a pitch-black room, even pretending that he was sick..."

"Yeah, it's odd. I wonder if Kizmel will tell us how he got that scar, if we ask..."

"No, don't go prying into that."

"H-hey, you were the one who started wondering about him."

We kept climbing the dim stairway, chattering all the while.

Upon further reflection, this was the third time I'd climbed these stairs from the boss chamber to the next floor with Asuna—fourth, if you counted the first time when she was just a few minutes behind. Each time, we were the first up because the two guilds were busy squabbling over their rewards after beating the boss and demanded that we do the busy work of activating the gate. It couldn't be easy to make everyone satisfied with their share between so many people.

Technically, Asuna and I had the right to participate in their dice-rolling tournament, but we'd refused every time. For one, it was a long, boring slog. For another...

"No matter how he got his scar, the viscount is a very nice person," Asuna muttered, reading my thoughts perfectly.

"Of course he is. He helped us beat the boss."

"Not just that. I think he eased up on his final attack so that you could get the Last Attack bonus, Kirito."

"...M-maybe he did," I mumbled, coughing uncomfortably.

I looked up to see that beyond the gloom, the double doors that were at the end of our climb were in sight. But would the relief carved into them be the same scene from the beta or different?

Suddenly I realized the footsteps to the right and behind me had stopped. I turned around and saw the hooded fencer looking up at me like she had something to say.

"...Wh-what? Did you want the LA bonus that bad?"

"No!"

She puffed her cheeks out for a moment, then took on a serious, hesitant look. The question she eventually came out with had to do with the future she'd been trying so hard not to think about, in a way.

"...Hey. How long are you planning to work with me?"

"..."

I stared back into the unblinking, hazel-brown eyes.

"Until you're strong enough that you don't need me."

"...Hmm," Asuna muttered, putting on a smile as brief and fragile as tiny bubbles rising from deep water. She hopped up to the next step.

I quickly turned, looking up at the doors leading to the fifth floor of Aincrad, and resumed racing up the steps.

AFTERWORD

It's been a full year, but thanks for reading the third volume of *Sword Art Online Progressive*! Well, I'm relieved that we at least climbed one floor this year. If I can just keep this pace up next year...Okay, I'll admit, I hope to pick up the game's pace...

Now, then. The subtitle of this book is "Barcarolle of Froth," which I ought to explain, since it didn't come up in the text. A *barcarolle* is a type of classical piece that translates to "boat song." The reason I put it in the title is because Kirito and Asuna ride in boats on the fourth floor...simple as that!

I've always wanted to write a story about traveling across the map on a boat. It's a classic vehicle in RPGs (though there are very few MMORPGs in which players can own boats), and I like boats in real life. But the only kind I've rode in recently are car ferries. A few years ago there was a big boom in fishing interest, and I bought an inflatable rubber boat, which was quite fun to ride down the Arakawa River. But it was quite a pain to set up and store, so I got tired of it quickly...and on the other hand, a proper pleasure boat is dangerously expensive, not to mention the marina docking fees and fuel costs. If I ever get the time, I'd like to earn a boating license, though.

Excuse me, I got off topic. Anyway, the theme of the third volume is boats...or should I say, the scenery of Aincrad. Until this point, I've spent very little time on describing the scenery, but I tried to put more effort into that this time. I hope that you were able to imagine the sights of Rovia, the city of water, and the looming Yofel Castle on the lake. Of course, because of that, I had to provide an extremely brief and abridged version of the boss fight again...

But if there's not going to be great danger in the boss fight, there's not much to write about, and I'm not sure I really want for every floor to be like the second, where everyone was nearly wiped out. Up next is the fifth floor, a nice milestone number, so I feel a tougher boss coming up!

As for my usual acknowledgments, I feel that this time is less out of thanks than personal apology...To abec for her even more wonderful illustrations despite the boundary-pushing schedule, and to my always courteous and helpful editor, Mr. Miki, I'm sorry and thank you! And to all of my readers, I hope to see you again next year!

Reki Kawahara—November 2014

Sect.001
THE BITER
REKI KAWAHARA
ILLUSTRATION BY SHIMEJI
THE ISOLATOR
REALIZATION OF
ABSOLUTE SOLITUDE